C000176509

Durpey-Allen Publishing Ltd

This edition 2015
1

Pauline Devaney and Edwin Apps © 2015

The Authors assert the moral right
to be identified as the authors of this work

A catalogue record of this book
is available from the British Library

ISBN 978-1-910317-02-0

All the stories in this book are fictitious. The names, characters and incidents portrayed in them, other than those clearly in the public domain, are the work of the author's imagination. Any resemblance to real persons, living or dead, is purely coincidental.

—

All rights reserved. No part of this publication may be reproduced, stored in a retrieval system, or transmitted, in any form or by any means, electronic, mechanical, photocopying, recording or otherwise, without the prior permissions of the publishers.

—

Find out more about Durpey-Allen Publishing Ltd

www.durpey-allen.co.uk

Printed and bound in EU
by bookpress.eu

Pauline Devaney
Edwin Apps

All Gas and Gaiters

The Lost Episodes

I

DURPEY-ALLEN

2015

Edwin Apps's other publications:

L'abbaye de Maillezais
Geste Editions, 2002

Maillezais
the story of a French abbey
Geste Editions, 2002

•

Pursued by Bishops,
the Memoirs of Edwin Apps
Durand-Peyroles, 2013

Anyone wishing to give an amateur performance of any of the scripts contained in this book should apply to the Publishers by letter or email, who will forward the enquiry to the Authors. No performance, either amateur or professional, may be given unless written permission has first been obtained from the Authors.

Contact at:
http://www.durpey-allen.co.uk/crbst_1.html

In affectionate memory of
Robertson Hare, William Mervyn, Derek Nimmo,
John Barron and Ernest Clark

The authors discussing a script near their home
on Blackheath in 1969. Press photo.

Contents

—

Robertson Hare, John Barron, Derek Nimmo and William Mervyn
in *The Bishop Rides Again*, 1966.

Prologue 9

SERIES ONE
Only Three Can Play – 7 January 1967 19

SERIES TWO
The Dean Goes Primitive – 24 November 1967 58
The Bishop Goes To Town – 15 December 1967 93

SERIES THREE
The Bishop Learns the Facts – 8 January 1969 131
The Bishop is Hospitable – 22 January 1969 169
The Bishop Takes a Holiday – 5 February 1969 216
The Affair at Cookham Lock – 12 February 1969 257

SERIES FOUR
The Bishop Gives a Shove – 15 April 1970 298

Epilogue 339

GLOSSARY OF TERMS

Close-up (CU)
The subject fills the screen.

Credits
Text on screen – composed of a list of technical personnel, cast, and director.

Cue
A signal or sign to an actor or the technical crew.

Cut
The splicing of two shots together. Between sequences the cut marks a rapid transition between one time and space and another.

Fade up/down
A punctuation device. The image brightens to full strength in fade up, and the opposite in fade down.

Film
Indicates where film is inserted as opposed to action in the Studio (qv) in front of the live audience.

Framing
The way in which images are framed within a shot to produce a specific effect.

Mix
A transition between two sequences or scenes. A first image gradually dissolves or fades out and is replaced by a second which appears over it.

Pan
(Abbreviation of panorama).
Movement of the camera from left to right or right to left of the subject.

Pull back
A tracking shot or zoom that moves back from the subject to reveal the context of the scene.

Scene
Complete unit of narration. A series of shots that take place in a single location.

Shot
Defined in terms of camera distance with respect to the object within the shot. The most commonly used are:
       close-up
       medium shot
       medium long shot
       long shot

Studio
Those scenes that are performed live in a TV studio. General direction is given as in day, night, interior, and exterior.

OOV
Out of Vision

AUTHORS' NOTE

The scripts for *All Gas and Gaiters* were typed on an old Underwood typewriter long before computer searches and spellchecks became available at the click of a mouse. In preparing the scripts for publication, we have therefore taken the opportunity to make minor corrections and amendments where desirable.

PROLOGUE

Edwin:

In 1972, shortly after *All Gas and Gaiters* was repeated on BBC One, someone in the organisation ordered that the tapes on which the entire collection of all five series were recorded must be wiped, and that other sets in Australia and elsewhere must be returned to suffer the same fate.

We were not the only people whose work was destroyed in this way; several other successful series were also wiped.

Neither we, the authors, nor the actors who starred in the series were told this was happening, so we had no opportunity to have the tapes copied, and all our expectations of residuals from repeats and overseas sales disappeared at a stroke.

Such a high-handed act was possible because the Corporation considered the series to be its property to do what it liked with. This was, of course, in part true: the contract stated that the series was BBC property, but it went on to say that the Corporation might not show the work or use it in any way without the express written permission of the writers and actors – which would suggest that we had a stake in the property and that our permission should have been sought before the series was destroyed.

No explication as to why the series was wiped has ever been forthcoming from the Corporation. It had spent many thousands of pounds making it, there were thirty-three viable episodes that, according to the BBC's Audience Research data, had been watched by 19.3% of the population of the United Kingdom, and the series had been equally successful abroad. It had been nominated for the Comedy of the Year Award in 1967, the appreciation figures had been excellent and the press enthusiastic right to the end.

I have no doubt that today the BBC is embarrassed by the gap in its archives and the considerable amount of revenue it has lost, for it reaps rich rewards from repeats, overseas sales, cassettes and DVDs of *Steptoe and Son* and *Dad's Army,* neither of which, as contemporary viewing and appreciation figures show, was more successful than *All Gas and Gaiters.*

Then in the late 1990s, when nostalgic programmes about successful comedy series of the 1960s began to appear, *All Gas and Gaiters* was never mentioned. Apparently, as far as the BBC was concerned, it had never existed.

However, in May last year (2013) my autobiography, *Pursued by Bishops*, was published, and, when the press asked questions about the fate of the series, I mentioned we still had the scripts in cardboard boxes in Pauline's attic. This seemed to intrigue the journalists, and someone suggested we might think about publishing them. So, in spite of it being nearly fifty years since we wrote *All Gas and Gaiters* and our paths having separated and both of us independently having turned to painting rather than writing or acting, our curiosity was aroused. Accordingly, and with a certain amount of scepticism, Pauline went up to her attic, dug the boxes out from a dark corner and, removing all the dust and cobwebs, brought them into the light.

As Pauline lives in Sussex and I live in the West of France, she gave a set to our son to bring to me when he was next here with his family. So in March this year (2014), I watched him take a large cardboard box out of the boot of his car, carry it up to my bedroom and dump it on the floor. And there it remained for several weeks until—

10 May 2014

The telephone rings.

Edwin: Oui, allô?
Pauline: It's me.
Edwin: Oh, hullo.
Pauline: What's the weather like in France?
Edwin: Very warm and sunny. What's it like in Sussex?
Pauline: Tipping down. I'm ringing to ask if you've read the scripts?
Edwin: No. The box is still on the floor.
Pauline: But you've had it for over a month.
Edwin: What about you? Have you read them yet?
Pauline: What's the point? They must be terribly dated.
Edwin: That's what I'm afraid of.
Pauline: Let's forget the whole thing. I can't really afford the time anyway: I've got an exhibition in August.
Edwin: It seems a bit feeble not even to look at them.
Pauline: Tell you what then: if you open your box, I'll open mine.
Edwin: And, if they are no good, we'll forget the whole thing and have a bonfire.

Pauline: Done. Speak to you later.

Replaces phone.

The same day, some hours later. The telephone rings.

Pauline: What did you think?

Edwin: I couldn't stop laughing! They came as a complete surprise – I kept wondering what would happen.

Pauline: Me, too. But that doesn't mean we have to publish them.

Edwin: Why not?

Pauline: Why would anyone want to read a lot of old television scripts?

Edwin: If they made us laugh, they might make other people laugh as well – and the story of how they came about and what happened to them, that's interesting.

Pauline: Then why don't we both write what we remember about it all and e-mail each other from time to time to see if what we are saying is relevant?

Edwin: That should work. It's more or less how we wrote them in the first place – except we were sitting opposite each other at a table.

Pauline: Shall we begin by writing about how *All Gas and Gaiters* started?

Edwin: Seems as good a place as any. I'll do something about Stuart. But first I must get lunch. Bye.

Pauline: I'm glad you've got your priories right. *Bon appétit!*

Replaces telephone.

E-mail Edwin 12 May 2014, 10.49

I've written something about Stuart:

Stuart Allen, the first director of *All Gas and Gaiters*, was an old friend of mine. We had met in the RAF during our National Service, he had trained at the Royal Academy of Dramatic Art (RADA) and we had worked together, notably in a company touring Shakespeare. But he had given up acting because of a growing family and was working as a floor manager for the BBC in their studios in Manchester. Early in 1965 he was put on a director's course. At the end of these courses, the students had to find and direct a short piece to show whether or not they had potential as directors. Stuart suggested we write something for him and act in it as well.

E-mail Pauline 14 May 2014, 15.34

I've written something about Stuart, too:

Edwin and I were reasonably successful as actors, working mainly in television and the theatre, but still spent a certain amount of time 'resting' between jobs and, in the days before mobile phones, that meant having to be stuck at home all day close to the telephone in case our agent rang. So to combat the frustration of the situation, we began to write. By the time Stuart asked us to do something for him, we had adapted several old stage farces for television, several of which had been produced by the BBC.

Incidentally, isn't it your birthday today?

E-mail Edwin 15 May 2014, 18.03

Yes, it was.

A writer Pauline and I admired was N.F. Simpson, whose plays *One Way Pendulum* and *A Resounding Tinkle* broke new ground in comedy and were later to inspire the Monty Python team – still at that time impressionable undergraduates.

A Resounding Tinkle is about an ordinary suburban couple, Middie and Bro Paradoc, to whom extraordinary things happen. We decided to adapt it for Stuart's test piece, and it worked very well.

Afterwards the three of us had dinner in a Greek Cypriot restaurant in Soho and over the hummus and retsina Stuart said what he needed, as a fledgling director, was a script he could present to the BBC as a pilot for a possible series and had we any ideas?

We said no we hadn't – but had he?

"Well," he said, "I've been wondering if there is anything in the old joke 'As the actress said to the bishop…' Perhaps something about a bishop whose niece is a stripper?"

Then he turned to me and said, "You know about bishops!"

This was because I had been to school at St Edmund's, Canterbury, the school for the orphaned sons of Church of England Clergy. In fact I was not an orphan, nor was my father a parson, but my great uncle played golf with the headmaster – perhaps as good a reason as any for choosing a school.

St Edmund's had the Archbishop of Canterbury as its president and an array of archdeacons, deans and bishops on its governing body (not to mention on the platform on Speech Day), so I had seen a good deal of the upper echelons of the C. of E. in my formative years. We decided to go away and think about Stuart's idea.

E-mail Pauline 16 May 2014, 11.06

However, we soon discovered that, although the actress said to the bishop may be a good joke, it is a very limited one, so we chucked out the actress but hung on to the bishop. This was because our experience of adapting farces had shown us that they were becoming almost impossible to write, as they depend on transgressing rules – and rules, in the early sixties, with its Permissive Society, were going out of fashion. But the Church, we realised, was the one remaining institution where rules were still in place, and indeed the very clothes our characters would wear would be a constant visual reminder of that.

E-mail Edwin 18 May 2014, 01.05

I like your piece about the reason we chose the Church. It underlines the fact that we were not writing about religion, but about the Church as an institution. It was something people seemed to have difficulty understanding – at least the critics did.

So we wrote a script about the Cathedral being left a bequest on condition the Bishop reinstates a medieval custom, which involves his having to ride around the diocese, dressed as a monk on a white horse and give forty pairs of white stockings to forty virgins: "To thee, fair maid, I these white hose do give, in honour of the state in which you live." In 1965 virgins were beginning to be in short supply.

With the title *The Bequest* (later changed to *The Bishop Rides Again*), we posted it to the Light Entertainment department of the BBC under the pen-name John Wraith, because we didn't want to confuse casting directors and directors who knew us as actors.

E-mail Pauline 19 May 2014, 14.56

We heard nothing for six weeks, then Frank Muir, who was the Head of Comedy, rang to say that he had asked N.F. Simpson to see Stuart's test piece, that he had liked both it and our performances as Middie and Bro, and so he had commissioned him to write four scripts for us to do on BBC Two, which Stuart would direct. He went on to say that our cover had been blown, he knew we were John Wraith, that everyone had read the script of *The Bequest* and liked that as well and it was to be produced for Comedy Playhouse with Stuart as its director. So, for us, Christmas 1965 came early.

E-mail Pauline 22 May 2014, 11.00

How many scripts are we going to publish?

E-mail Edwin 23 May 2014, 12.15

Sorry, I couldn't get back to you yesterday; some people came to see the studio and bought a big canvas. I rang the publisher about the scripts and he thinks we should do four books of eight episodes each. That way they will be easier to handle than one monster book with all the episodes in it. So we have got to choose eight to start with.

E-mail Pauline 23 May 2014, 17.30

Then we must write an introduction to each of them. Glad about the big canvas!

E-mail Edwin 24 May 2014, 12.00

He says it doesn't matter if they are not the most successful, as long as they show the whole range of the series. Incidentally, I've written something about the casting. Here it is:

Once the BBC had bought the script of *The Bishop Rides Again* and decided to do it for Comedy Playhouse, we began to think about the actors we wanted to play the parts. After several suggestions, such as Alastair Sim, Robert Morley and Wilfred Hyde-White, William Mervyn's name was mentioned. He was well known to television audiences at the time as he was in a long-running series for Granada. Moreover, he had a Church of England background, having been a choirboy and his wife was the daughter of a canon of Windsor.

Then Stuart suggested Robertson Hare for the Archdeacon. Robertson Hare, or 'Bunny' as everyone called him, had been part of the Aldwych Farces team, with Tom Walls, Ralph Lynn and Mary Brough, which had been famous throughout the 1920s and 1930s, and as the small, bald, respectable figure who was the butt of all the others he was a household name.

We had written the part of Noote for me, but Frank Muir said it would be taking on too much, so I suggested Derek Nimmo, who was a rival (we had often been up for the same part), but whose work I admired.

The one actor Pauline and I both agreed we wanted for the Dean was John Barron. We had seen him as a manic headmaster in a play in the West End and knew he would be perfect casting.

Once the actors were assembled for the first reading, there was no question that we had the right cast.

E-mail Pauline 26 May 2014, 14.35

Got your piece on casting. I think people in the business will be surprised that we were able to choose the actors, as from what I hear, writers are no longer even consulted about casting.

E-mail Edwin 26 May 2014, 19.15

I've looked up the press-cutting books and found these (the success of *The Bishop Rides Again* was almost unanimous and there was universal praise for Bunny):

James Thomas in *The Daily Express*, under the banner headline GREAT TRIUMPH ON TV FOR ROBERTSON HARE:

"The first play in the 1966 *Comedy Playhouse* series was remarkable for the emergence of Mr Robertson Hare, at 70-plus, in his first real attempt at Television comedy. In fact Mr Hare found himself a contributor to one of the richest comedy trios TV has uncovered for some time. It was for him a complete and personal triumph."

Mary Crozier in *The Guardian*:

"Who ever he may be, John Wraith is fertile in invention and gave us a constant explosion of comic situations. The English preoccupation with funny clerics was indulged with a marvellous quartet: The Bishop by William Mervyn, the Chaplain by Derek Nimmo, the Dean by John Barron, all complemented Robertson Hare's mischievous and plummy Archdeacon. His simplest phrases such as "Oh, thank you" are still pronounced inimitably. One might indeed echo "Oh, thank you" for this proof that television can produce farce with such style and vigour."

Peter Black in the *Daily Mail*:

"Expanded into 90 minutes, this joke could make a farce good enough to fill a theatre for a year. For Edwin Apps and Pauline Devaney, who wrote it under the pen-name of John Wraith, there is the consolation of having sold the idea as a series on the merits of this single script."

E-mail Pauline 27 May 2014, 10.00

This is my piece on how we wrote them. What do you think?

We wrote the five series of *All Gas and Gaiters* in a coal cellar. I don't mean it had water seeping through the walls or a nest of rats in the corner, and we had had the coal removed some time before, so to be strictly truthful it was a former coal cellar, which we had painted white. But it was tiny, with just enough room for a table and two chairs, and the only natural light came from the miniscule window which was high up under the ceiling, looking out on to the side passage which led to the front door of our basement flat in a big Victorian house in Blackheath, in south-east London.

So there we were, in our cellar, surrounded by copies of the *Church Times*, the Bible and *Cruden's Concordance*, fortified by endless cups of strong black coffee and nicotine, trying to make each other laugh.

We had both been in situation comedies on television when the script was frequently altered during the short six-day rehearsal period, nearly always to the detriment of the final performance. After all, it is unwise to start tinkering with the ingredients when the cake has to be ready by teatime. So before we began work on the first episode of what we would always refer to as AGAG, we made the decision that we would write properly constructed scripts with a beginning, a middle and an end, and not allow them out of our hands until we were certain they worked. This paid dividends at rehearsals because no time was wasted.

One of the most successful ways we had of developing a story was to ask ourselves, given the characters we had created and their relationships with each other, what would really happen? The answers to this question would nearly always suggest a plot, which we would hammer out, usually trudging in all weathers round and round Greenwich Park before returning to our cellar to improvise possible dialogue. In this, as in everything else to do with AGAG, the fact that we were both actors was invaluable. Comedy is like music: the words, like notes, have all got to be in precisely the right place, and the rhythm of the lines exact. Throughout the day I would write everything down in longhand; and in the evenings, while I got the supper, Edwin would decipher my misspelled scrawl and type it up.

The next morning we would read it, hoping we had found something that had the potential to be funny and that could be shaped into precisely twenty-nine minutes and would avoid the 'Shit Point'. The 'Shit Point' is a technical term we learned from an endearing old Hollywood screenwriter we met. It refers to the moment in a comedy about five minutes into the setting up of the plot, which if it is too complex or not entertaining enough, the viewer, sitting expectantly on his or her sofa, says "Oh shit!" and switches to another channel.

As the deadline got nearer we would lengthen the hours we spent writing, occasionally even working through the night, only too aware that there was an army of set designers, wardrobe people, publicity people and technicians, not to mention the actors and director, all waiting for the information they needed to make the show happen.

We found writing AGAG extremely stressful and would often wake in the middle of the night with the nagging doubt that what we were writing wouldn't work and wasn't funny – and the fact we thought it was, simply an indication that we had lost touch with reality.

But there were compensations. The improvement in our bank balance (which after many years of never being sure if we would be able to pay bills was very satisfying), and those magic occasions during the recording of the show – its first public outing – when we would hear the studio audience's reaction and know, for the first time, that yes, it does work, yes they do like it, and yes, they do find it funny!

E-mail Edwin 27 May 2014, 18.09
You should perhaps mention that it was in *Cruden's Concordance* we discovered that AGAG was a person in the Bible:
1 Sam.15. 9: "The people spared Agag."
1 Sam.15. 33: "Samuel hewed Agag in pieces."

And explain that *Cruden's* is the life's work of a clergyman: an index which indicates where every word in the Bible is to be found.

E-mail Pauline 27 May 2014, 18.27
No comment!

E-mail Edwin 27 May 2014, 18.42
Forgot to mention I've written my introduction to the first script.

Only Three Can Play

Edwin:

All Gas and Gaiters was 'situation comedy', a new form of writing that had emerged with the need for a comic half-hour format on television.

The earliest version had come from the music-hall: a comedian and his 'feed' in a sketch extended to fill the half-hour slot. Over time the sketches had become more complex and other actors had been introduced, but the basic form was the same. As 'straight' actors, Pauline and I were familiar with the three-act play formula, so when we came to write situation comedy the three-act play was our model.

We kept an 'Ideas Book' in which we wrote down ideas for story-lines, so before beginning a new series, we would go through it and choose the most promising one to start working on. But, invariably, once we began to examine it, we found that it was only half a storyline, which needed another whole plot to weave into it to make it work. This search for a second plot – or sub-plot – was always a torment.

From the time of signing the contract, we always had six months before the first rehearsal, giving us, in theory, a month to write each episode, but finding a sub-plot for the first script always took longer, and it was sometimes two or more months before the first script was finished.

The second script, too, invariably overran the time schedule for the same reason, and panic would begin to set in – followed by gloom and depression – out of which a third script miraculously emerged, then a fourth – but the first rehearsal would be approaching fast and there were two scripts to write and we were down to a few weeks.

Then the miracle would happen. Suddenly, all the remaining ideas, the original ones in the book, and the ones that we had thought of and rejected as sub-plots fitted together, and the last two scripts would be written quickly – sometimes in days.

Only Three Can Play is a good example of this: clergymen seem always to have been fascinated by trains and railway timetables, and we had the idea of their inventing a game like Monopoly based on Bradshaw – the classic railway guide. It was our most promising idea and we began work on it right at the outset, but nothing seemed to go with it, and it was only in the last weeks, when an elderly neighbour told us, with stars in his eyes, that he had seen *The Sound of Music* seven times, that we suddenly saw the way ahead.

Pauline:

This episode was the last of the first series, and one of the few scripts where we managed to get some women into the plot. Admittedly they were not very large parts, but at least there were three of them, and they played an important role in the development of the story.

Getting women into the scripts was a constant problem for us, and one that as an actress I felt keenly, but having decided to set the comedy in the Church of England, which in the sixties was almost as exclusively male as the Light Entertainment department of the BBC, it was always a problem. We did give the Bishop a housekeeper, Mrs Loosemore, and the Archdeacon had his Mrs Banner, but alas, although both were spoken of on many occasions, they remained stuck somewhere in limbo behind the scenery, forever waiting and ready, but never receiving the call. Dear Ladies, I tried very hard for seven years to bring you both to life, but failed. I apologise.

The reason why clergymen are obsessed by railways is unknown, but the author of *Thomas the Tank Engine,* the Reverend Wilbert Awdry, when asked why, replied "The Church of England and steam engines are both the best way of getting you to your final destination."

Only Three Can Play

Series One
First transmitted on BBC One, 7 January 1967

Scene 1
Film / Evening

The Cathedral Close.

Through the entrance arch comes an elderly tourer. It is not a vintage car, but is old-fashioned enough to have a dicky or rumble. At the wheel is an attractive young girl in her twenties, **Christine***.*

Cut to:

The **Dean***, as he walks in the Close, sees the car.*

Cut to:

The car pulling up outside the front door of a house. **Christine** *gets out of the car and, as she does so, looks up and waves across the road, smiling.*

Pan across the road and up to the first floor of the Palace.

Noote *stands framed in a first floor window. He registers embarrassment.*

Scene 2
Studio / Interior / Day

The study of the Palace.

On a table covered by a green baize cloth is a large home-made games board. It is not unlike a Monopoly board, except that the course is a railway track. The spaces between the sleepers are numbered and contain directions to the player who lands on them. Three model engines, steam, diesel and electric, act as counters, and in the middle of the board are two home-made packs of cards, a dice box and a single dice. A pile of railway timetables lies beside the board. At the table, sit the **Bishop** *and the* **Archdeacon***.* **Noote** *stands at the window.*

Bishop
Your turn, Noote. Come on.

Noote *confused*
What? Coming, my lord.

Scene 3
Film

*Christine enters house. The **Dean** comes into shot, he takes out a tape measure and begins to measure the distance between the car and a fire hydrant on the pavement.*

Scene 4
Studio / Interior / Day

The study.

Noote has joined the others at the table. He is shaking the dice and tips it out.

Noote
A four. *(He moves engine forward four spaces.)*

Bishop *looking eagerly*
What is it?

Noote *reading*
"Stations."

Archdeacon *delighted*
Here we go! *(Rubs his hands.)*

Noote picks up a card from the first pack.

Bishop
What is it?

Noote
King's Lynn.

Bishop
Norfolk. Where are you going to?

Noote *picking up a card from the second pack and reading*
Welshpool, Montgomeryshire. *(He picks up dice and begins to shake it.)*

Archdeacon
Right across the country! That's a bit stiff.

Noote *shaking dice*
I hope I don't get a one!

Bishop *doubtfully*
You might just manage it in four.

Noote *throwing dice*
A six! My luck's in. Let me see, from King's Lynn to Welshpool with six changes. *(Considering)* Via Birmingham, and I suppose— Shrewsbury.

Archdeacon *encouragingly*
Well done, Noote.

Noote
Right, here we go: King's Lynn to Cambridge. *(Thoughtfully)* Hm, better make an early start.

Bishop
You'd better, or you'll never do it in a day.

Noote
The 7.31 from King's Lynn to Cambridge arrives at 8.40.

Bishop *joyfully*
Wrong!

Noote
Sorry, 8.41.

Bishop
You nearly went off the rails there.

Noote *thinking hard*
Six changes, six changes......

Archdeacon
You've got one.

Noote
Bedford! No, that's no good— Banbury.

Archdeacon
Splendid, you are doing well. That's two.

Noote
The 11.18 from Cambridge to Banbury, arriving 3.17.

Bishop *unimpressed*
That's a two and a half hour wait at Cambridge. You can't afford many like that.

Noote *concentrating hard*
Banbury to Birmingham. Of course! *(Excitedly)* The 3.31 arrives at 4.26.

Bishop *trying to catch him out*
Which station?

Noote
Snow Hill, my lord.

Archdeacon *nostalgically*
One of my favourites. You're in terrific form. That is three.

Noote *coolly*
Three to go. Now I've got to improvise. Via Stafford! Yes, that's it, then Stafford to Shrewsbury. *(Decisively)* Right. I want something from Stafford to Shrewsbury.

Bishop *craftily*
From Snow Hill?

Noote
Certainly not, my lord. From New Street. The 4.50 from New Street, arriving at Stafford at 5.45.

Archdeacon *beside himself*
Oh, colossal! That's five changes, only one to go!

Noote
Now, it is 5.45 and I am at Stafford.

Bishop
Let's hope the buffet is open.

Archdeacon *to Bishop*
Sh!

Noote
I know! The 6.56 to Shrewsbury arriving at 9 p.m.

Bishop *triumphantly*
That's done it! You'll never get a train from Shrewsbury to Welshpool at that time of night— I warned you you couldn't afford to hang about!

Archdeacon
Pipped at the post, bad luck.

Bishop
You miss a turn Noote, bad luck. Now *(Expansively)* it's me…

Noote *suddenly*
What about the 9.42?

Bishop
What about it?

Noote
There's a 9.42 from Shrewsbury to Welshpool.

Bishop
I don't believe it.

Noote *confidently*
Would you care to challenge me, my lord?

Noote picks up the timetable and hands it to the **Bishop**.

Bishop *undecided*
Well—

Archdeacon
You miss a turn if he's right, Bishop.

Bishop *ungraciously*
Well, I suppose it's possible—

Noote
It leaves Paddington at 4.10 and arrives at Shrewsbury at 9.40.

Bishop *scornfully*
Oh, that one! That doesn't stop at Welshpool.

Noote *excitedly*
It does, it does— "To set down only".

Bishop *crestfallen*
Oh, oh, yes, so it does. *(Remembers)* But you have to give notice to the guard at Shrewsbury.

Noote *on his dignity*
I fully intend to do so!

Bishop
Oh, do you? Well shake up and let's get on.

Noote shakes and throws the dice.

Noote
Three. *(He moves his engine on and reads the board.)* "You have missed your connection. Spend the night in the Waiting Room and miss a turn." How rotten!

Bishop
I must say we've really got this game right now. It works splendidly. *(Shakes dice.)* Three. *(He moves his engine on and reads the board.)* "You have caught the Pullman Express, move on six squares." See what I mean? *(He moves his engine on.)* I can't see what it says, Henry, can you?

Archdeacon *reading*
"You have had lunch at Crewe. Food poisoning: miss two turns." *(He holds out his hand for the dice.)* My turn, Bishop.

Bishop *losing interest*
So it is. Before you go on— *(to **Noote**)* Just see if there's any more coffee, Noote.

Noote *peering into jug*
We appear to have finished it, my lord.

Bishop
Oh dear, sorry about that, Henry.

Archdeacon
That's all right. May I? *(Holds out his hand for the dice.)*

Bishop *ignoring him*
Shall we make some more, Noote?

Noote
Well, we could, my lord.

*The **Archdeacon** holds out his hand again.*

Bishop
Just a moment, Henry. *(To **Noote**)* Do we have enough milk?

Noote
Possibly not, my lord.

Archdeacon
Er, Bishop—

Bishop
Oh, sorry, Henry. Of course, it's your turn. Here you are. *(Handing dice to the **Archdeacon**, who takes it eagerly.)*

Archdeacon
Oh, thank you, thank you— now! *(He shakes the dice furiously.)*

Bishop
Would you like a sherry?

*The **Archdeacon** stops in mid-shake and puts the dice box down.*

Archdeacon *torn by indecision*
Oh, Bishop— er, are you?

Bishop
Noote !

***Noote** rises, goes to the sherry table and pours a glass of sherry.*

Bishop
I must say I enjoy these Thursday evenings, Henry.

Archdeacon *warmly*
Oh, so do I, Bishop. *(Leaning back in his chair)* "Behold how good and pleasant it is for brethren to dwell together in unity". Eh, Noote?

Noote *arriving at his elbow and handing glass*
Oh, yes, Archdeacon: "It is like the precious ointment upon the head that ran down upon the beard, even Aaron's beard."

Bishop *cutting in quickly*
Yes, yes, psalm one hundred and thirty-three. Now, come on, Henry. For goodness' sake don't hold us up any longer, we haven't got all night.

Archdeacon *surprised*
Me? Oh, my word, yes. (*Picks up dice box, shakes it and throws dice.*)

Sound of doorbell.

Bishop *crossly*
Who can that be? Are you expecting anyone, Noote?

Noote
No, my lord.

Bishop
Our one free evening, interrupting the game like this.

Noote
Shall I see who it is?

Bishop
I suppose you'd better.

Noote *rises and exits.*

Bishop *turning to the* **Archdeacon**
What have you got?

Archdeacon
A one.

Bishop
Oh, well, come on, move it.

The **Archdeacon** *moves his engine forward and reads eagerly.*

Bishop
What's it say?

Archdeacon
"You have been caught travelling in a first-class carriage with a second-class ticket. You are disqualified."

The **Archdeacon** *puts the dice in the dice box with an air of finality and drinks sherry.*

Noote *enters followed by the* **Dean**.

Noote
The Dean, my lord.

Dean
Good evening, my lord.

Bishop
Oh, Dean.

Archdeacon
Good evening, Dean

Dean *severely*
Drinking and gambling, Archdeacon?

Bishop
Gambling? Certainly not! We are playing an innocent game of our own devising.

Dean *scornfully*
A game of chance, I suppose.

Bishop *nettled*
On the contrary, a game of skill.

Archdeacon
It has taken us three years to perfect, Dean. Noote thought of it.

Noote
You see the essence is that you take a card from each pack and they each have the name of a station on them. Then you have to work out a journey between the stations with a certain number of changes.

Bishop
You have to know the times of all the trains in the British Isles.

Archdeacon
By heart— both summer and winter services.

Dean *interested*
How do you decide on the number of changes required?

Noote
You throw a dice.

Dean
As I said, a game of chance.

Bishop
May I ask to what we owe the pleasure of this visit? Our Thursday evenings are sacrosanct.

Dean
I am aware of that, my lord. However, when I tell you that lawlessness is stalking the Close, I think you will welcome my intrusion.

Bishop
Lawlessness?

Dean
I have just witnessed five cases of lawbreaking.

Bishop *impressed*
Dean!

Archdeacon
Is it an inside job?

Dean
It is, Archdeacon, and you are one of the culprits.

Archdeacon
Me?

Bishop
Henry? You can't be serious!

Noote
The Archdeacon?

Bishop
What has he done?

Dean
His offence is vehicular.

*The **Bishop** and **Archdeacon** look blank.*

Bishop *suddenly worried*
Henry, how could you?

Archdeacon *indignantly*
I didn't, Bishop!

Dean
It relates to his vehicle. In the course of my evening stroll, I have observed no less than five motors, each one parked within four feet of a fire hydrant, and in such a manner as to obscure it from view, in direct contravention of the local byelaws, Section 402, Subsection 89c.

Bishop
And you've come to warn Henry?

Dean
No. I have come to tell him to move his motor immediately. Now I have to see the young woman whose mother has taken Canon Prosser's house. She too is a culprit. However, I am in some difficulty as I am not acquainted with the young lady.

Bishop
What's that got to do with it?

Dean
I should not like to be thought officious.

Archdeacon
Perish the thought!

Dean
I was wondering, my lord, whether you, as her neighbour, would care to point out the infringement?

Bishop
Me? Go to our new neighbour who I have not even met and… Certainly not!

Dean
Then perhaps Noote?

Bishop
Noote? Oh, that's different. Noote, you'll slip across the road and tell her she's upset the Dean, won't you?

Dean *correcting him sternly*
Tell her she has contravened a byelaw.

Bishop
Yes, yes, that's what I meant. It is just that as Bishop, I can't very well—

Noote *alarmed*
Oh, my lord, I can't, don't ask me.

Bishop *surprised*
Why not?

Noote
I haven't been introduced.

Bishop
Well introduce yourself.

Noote
Oh, I couldn't, my lord.

Bishop *annoyed*
Noote, do as I say at once.

Noote
But, my lord—

Bishop
Do as I say!

Noote *unhappily*
Very well, my lord. You are sure you want me to?

Bishop *exasperated*
Haven't I just said—

Noote *solemnly*
You have, my lord— and I just hope you won't live to regret it.

*Exit **Noote.***

Bishop

What an extraordinary thing to say! *(Turning to **Dean**)* Dean, let me show you out.

Dean

One moment, my lord—

Bishop

Yes?

Dean

This game—

Bishop

What about it?

Dean

It interests me.

Bishop

That doesn't surprise me. It is a most original game, really excellent. Now, let me show you out—

*The **Bishop** rises and makes for the door.*

Dean

I should like to stay and watch you play.

Bishop *horrified*

Oh, er, well— I'm afraid that's impossible.

Dean

Why?

Bishop *searching desperately*

Well, because, er— Tell him, Henry.

Archdeacon

We can't play without Noote.

Dean

Oh, well, in that case—

Bishop *quickly*

Did you have a coat?

Dean
I shall wait till he returns.

Bishop *nonplussed*
Oh, will you?

Dean *sitting in* **Noote**'s *chair*
Yes.

The **Bishop**, *undecided, sits too. There is a pause.*

Bishop
I wonder how long he will be.

Mix to:

Scene 5
Studio / Exterior / Night

The front door of Canon Prosser's house.
Noote *stands at the door. It is opened by* **Christine**.

Chris
Oh, it's you. Hullo.

Noote *very embarrassed*
H-h-h-ullo. I— er—

Chris
Yes?

Noote
Er— the Bishop— er, I'm—

Chris
Yes, I know. You're the Bishop's chaplain, aren't you?

Noote
Er— the Dean— er, the Dean—

Chris
No, I'm afraid I don't know the Dean.

Noote
Er, your car, er— your car, your car—

Chris
Do you like it?

Noote *suddenly finding his voice*
Yes, tell me, is it the 1922 or the 1923 model?

Chris
1923. It is my Grandmother's. Look, why don't you come in?

Noote
May I? Thanks most awfully. *(Exits to house.)*

Cut to:

Scene 6
Studio / Interior / Day

The study.

*The **Bishop**, **Archdeacon** and **Dean** sit at the table. A pause.*

Dean
I have an idea.

Bishop *wearily*
Oh yes?

Dean
Why don't you teach me the rules of the game? Then when Noote returns I shall be able to take a more active part.

*The **Bishop** and **Archdeacon** exchange a look of horror.*

Bishop
But I thought you only wanted to watch?

Dean
I have never relished the role of spectator.

Bishop *discouragingly*
It's rather a complicated game, you know.

Dean *firmly*
Nevertheless I wish to play.

Bishop
I'm afraid that's impossible.

Archdeacon *firmly*
Quite impossible.

Dean *bridling*
Indeed, and why is it impossible?

Bishop
Because— Henry, tell the Dean why it's impossible.

Archdeacon
Because only three can play.

Bishop
Yes, that's it, only three can play. Thank you, Henry.

Archdeacon
A pleasure, Bishop. (*Lifts glass cheerfully, but sees the* **Dean** *looking at him and lowers it again.*)

Sound of a car starting.

Bishop *rising*
Ah, good. It sounds as though Noote has been successful. She's moving the car.

Archdeacon *rising and going to window*
He'll soon be back now.

Bishop
Your troubles will soon be over, Dean.

The **Bishop** *and* **Dean** *join the* **Archdeacon** *at the window.*

Scene 7
Film / Exterior / Night

Noote and Christine in the car. They look up at the Palace window and wave.

Pan to:

Palace window. The **Bishop**, **Archdeacon** *and* **Dean** *framed.*

Scene 8
Studio / Interior / Night

The study.

The **Bishop, Archdeacon** *and* **Dean** *at the window. They turn back into the room.*

Bishop *angrily*
What on earth does he think he's doing?

Archdeacon
Rather messed us up.

Bishop
Messed us up? He's ruined our whole evening!

Dean
Not entirely, my lord.

Bishop *crossly*
What do you mean? How can we play without Noote?

Archdeacon *to* **Dean**
You see, Dean, you can't play with only two.

Dean
Precisely, gentlemen, but we are three!

Fade on **Bishop**'s *and* **Archdeacon**'s *reaction.*

Scene 9
Studio / Interior / Night

The hall of the Palace.

The **Bishop** *in pyjamas and dressing gown enters from the study and exits to kitchen.*

Sound of a key in the lock. The front door opens cautiously. **Noote** *enters and crosses to the stairs on tiptoe.*

Bishop *entering from the kitchen, holding a hot-water bottle and seeing* **Noote**
Noote!

Noote
Oh, my lord.

Bishop
Where have you been?

Noote
Er— out, my lord.

Bishop
How dare you? I send you out on a simple errand— and the next thing I see, you are driving about— quite irresponsibly— with a young woman— and then you come creeping in at this time. Do you realise it is midnight?

Noote
No, is it really? Hasn't the time passed quickly?

Bishop *outraged*
Quickly? It may have done for you. The Archdeacon and I were left here to play the game with the Dean!

Noote
Oh dear. I suppose he wasn't very good at it.

Bishop
On the contrary, he won all four games.

Noote *surprised*
Surely he doesn't know the times of all the trains in the British Isles?

Bishop
Of course not— But he managed to change the rules so much that it hardly mattered. Really, Noote, your behaviour is unforgivable. Where have you been?

Noote *dreamily*
Well, Christine and I—

Bishop
Who?

Noote
Er, Miss Buckley. We went to the cinema. She took me in her car. Do you know, it belonged to her grandmother—

Bishop
I am not interested in who it belonged to!

Noote
She was a suffragette.

Bishop *surprised*
Miss Buckley?

Noote
No, her grandmother. We saw *The Sound of Music*. It was wonderful. You should see it. It's all about Miss Julie Andrews, she's a nun and she sits on a hill and sings about her favourite things, kitten's whiskers, brown-paper parcels and having snow on her eyebrows— And there are all these nuns—

Bishop *unimpressed*
Huh, it's an R.C. film, is it?

Noote *ecstatic*
Oh, my lord, it's lovely, really lovely!

Bishop *coldly*
Is it? Well, I'm going to bed. You go into the study and check tomorrow's engagements.

Noote *dreamily*
Engagements!

Bishop *sharply*
Noote!

Noote
Yes, my lord?

Bishop
Did you understand what I said?

Noote
Of course, my lord— engagements!

Bishop
Very well, then, good night.

Noote
Goodnight, my lord.

Noote exits to the study.

Scene 10
Studio / Interior / Night

The study.

Noote enters, switches on the light, closes door carefully and crosses to window, singing "Raindrops on roses". He opens the window.

Noote *calling*
Coo— ee.

Scene 11
Film / Exterior / Night

The exterior of Canon Prosser's house.

Christine comes to bedroom window and waves.

Scene 12
Studio / Interior / Night

The study.

Noote at the window, blows a kiss. The Bishop puts his head round the door.

Bishop
Noote!

Noote turns in consternation and hurriedly shuts the window.

Fade.

Scene 13
Studio / Interior / Night

The study.

The Bishop and the Archdeacon are setting out the game.

Archdeacon *holding engines*
I've got the Steam and the Electric. Have you got the Diesel?

Bishop *handing engine*
Here it is, Henry. Have you shuffled?

Archdeacon
Noote usually does that.

Bishop
Oh, don't mention that man!

Archdeacon
Isn't he any better?

Bishop
Better? Christine Buckley and *The Sound of Music*— that's all I hear!

Archdeacon
They say it's a very good film. My Mrs Banner's been twice.

Bishop
That's nothing. Noote has been every night this week. It's turned his brain. I asked him to type my address to the Ordinands, and when I got up to read it I heard myself saying "Let us never forget the things the blessed Saint Augustine held most dear; raindrops on roses and whiskers on kittens..."

Archdeacon
He's not going to see it tonight, is he?

Bishop
And miss the game? I think you can take it, Henry, that even Noote is not completely abandoned.

Scene 14
Studio / Interior / Night

The hall.

Noote *comes down the stairs wearing a sports coat, grey flannel trousers and a flowered tie. He is singing* "The hills are alive with the sound of music".

He crosses the hall and exits to study.

Scene 15
Studio / Interior / Night

The study.

Noote enters.

Noote *gaily*
Just off, my lord.

Bishop
Off where?

Noote
To meet Christine. I'm taking her to the *Sound of Music.*

Bishop
You're what? Do you know what day it is?

Noote *casually*
Yes, Thursday, my lord. *(Enthusiastically)* It's awfully good. Have you seen it, Archdeacon?

Archdeacon
No, but Mrs Banner's been twice.

Bishop
But what about the game? We can't play without you.

Noote
I'm sorry, my lord. *(Turns to go.)*

Bishop *beside himself*
I've never seen such selfishness!

Archdeacon *pleading*
I say, old chap, don't desert us!

Noote
But Archdeacon, I've promised Christine.

Bishop
This has gone far enough. *(He moves to block the doorway.)* Noote, I forbid you— *(He stops suddenly.)* What have you got round your neck?

Noote
It's a flowered tie, actually— isn't it pretty?

Bishop
Pretty? It's grotesque. Take it off at once!

Noote
But, my lord— Christine made it for me.

Bishop
It looks like the outside of a seed packet.

Noote
That does it! I'm going, I'm going this minute— Excuse me! *(Pushes past the Bishop.)*

Bishop
Stop, I won't allow you—

Noote
You won't stop me— *(Exits to hall.)*

*The **Bishop** and **Archdeacon** look at each other in disbelief.*

Scene 16
Studio / Interior / Night

The hall.

Noote enters from study and strides to the front door.

Bishop *entering from the study*
Come back, come back, I say!

Archdeacon *entering from study*
I say, look here chaps—

Bishop
If you go now, you needn't trouble to come back!

Noote *with dignity as he opens the front door*
Then goodbye, my lord. I am sorry it has to end like this. *(Exits.)*

Bishop *shouting after him*
All right, go! Go to your Delilah!

Archdeacon
Aren't you going to stop him, Bishop?

Bishop
No, Henry, I'm not. He's not worth it— wretched, feeble man.

Archdeacon
She's an attractive little thing.

Bishop
Attractive? She's not my idea of a woman, Henry.

Archdeacon
Isn't she?

Bishop
In trousers? No, no. If ever this heart has felt a flutter — and there have been moments, I confess it — it has been on account of a real woman, some little feminine person; warm, loving and well versed in all the domestic skills. Don't you agree?

Archdeacon
Me? I like a woman of spirit. I always admired Amy Johnson, the way she flew solo to Australia!

Sound of the doorbell.

Bishop
If that's Noote, don't let him in.

Archdeacon
But if he's repented?

Bishop
I don't care. I won't have him back. Tell him to go away, tell him I've made other arrangements.

Archdeacon *shaking his head*
I think you are making a mistake. Still, if that's what you want— *(Goes to door.)*

Bishop
I do, Henry, I do!

Archdeacon *reluctantly*
Very well then— *(He opens front door and shuts it immediately.)*
It's the Dean!

Bishop
The Dean? What does he want on a Thursday evening?

Archdeacon
He must have come to play the game.

Bishop *horrified*
Oh no! We can't have another evening like last week.

Archdeacon
There's only one way to stop him.

Bishop
What's that?

Archdeacon
Get Noote back!

Bishop
No, Henry, No!

Archdeacon
Please, Bishop, please— Couldn't you go and ask him?

Bishop
Out of the question! My pride, Henry. A bishop must have some pride.

Archdeacon
In spite of last week?

Sound of doorbell.

Bishop
Well, I suppose pride is a sin. But what shall I say to him? How shall I get him back?

Archdeacon
Easy, Bishop. Remember what David did.

Bishop
Ah, you mean when he fetched Mephibosheth out of the house of Machir?

Archdeacon
Two Samuel, nine, verse five—

Bishop *thoughtfully*
Fetching Noote out of the house of Miss Christine Buckley could be a bit more complicated. Still— *(Nods thoughtfully.)* All right, you hold the fort. I'll slip out the back way. *(Exits to kitchen.)*

Sound of doorbell ringing urgently. The **Archdeacon** *opens the door gingerly. The* **Dean** *stands there. He carries a briefcase.*

Dean *accusingly*
Archdeacon.

Archdeacon *feigning surprise*
Oh, Dean. Is it you?

Dean
May I ask why you shut the door in my face?

Archdeacon
So sorry, I didn't recognise you.

Dean
Didn't recognise me? Really, Archdeacon! Who did you think I was?

Archdeacon *indicating the briefcase*
The man from the Pru.

Dean
Hm. Well, you will be pleased to know that I enjoyed myself so much last week I have decided to come and play with you again.

Archdeacon *gloomily*
How jolly.

Dean
Where is the Bishop?

Archdeacon
Oh, er— He's gone to fetch Mephibosheth out of the house of Miss Christine Buckley.

On the **Dean**'*s reaction, mix to:*

Scene 17
Studio / Exterior / Night

The front door of Canon Prosser's House.

The **Bishop** *is waiting. The door is opened by* **Mrs Buckley**. *She is a feminine little person and carries a sock on a mushroom with needle etc.*

Mrs B.
Good evening? *(Recognising the* **Bishop***)* Oh, it isn't really, is it? You're not, are you?

Bishop *grandly*
I am the Bishop of St Ogg's.

Mrs B.
Oh, how lovely! Do come in, won't you?

Bishop *undecided*
Well, I— er— *(Puzzled)* Are you Miss Christine Buckley?

Mrs B.
No, I'm her mother.

Bishop *gallantly*
Really? Well, well. If I may say so, you hardly look old enough.

Mrs B.
Oh, Bishop! You flatterer— do come in at once.

Bishop
Well, Madam—

Mrs B.
Come in, come in— *(Takes the* **Bishop**'s *arm and draws him into the house.)*

Scene 18
Studio / Interior / Night

The hall of Canon Prosser's house.

Bishop
Madam, I have come to retrieve my chaplain.

Mrs B.
Dear Mervyn? I was just mending one of his socks.

Bishop
So I see. *(Impressed)* What a beautiful darn!

Mrs B.
I love doing little things for him. He's such a sweet boy.

Bishop
Sweet?

Mrs B.
Christine is so fond of him. He's taking her to see *The Sound of Music* again this evening. Do you know, he's quite dotty about that film.

Bishop
So I have observed.

Mrs B.
I hear it's very good. Have you seen it?

Bishop
No, Madam, I have not and as a matter of fact—

Mrs B. *interrupting*
You want to? So do I. They've asked me to go with them, but between ourselves, I felt I couldn't. I didn't want to play 'gooseberry'. Do go into the sitting room.

Mrs Buckley ushers the Bishop into the sitting room.

Scene 19
Studio / Interior / Night

The sitting room at Canon Prosser's house.

Noote and Christine are sitting side by side. The Bishop enters. Noote leaps to his feet.

Noote
Oh, my lord—

Bishop *sternly*
Surprised to see me, Noote?

Noote
Er, well, yes— very.

Bishop
Do you know why I have come?

Noote
Er, no, my lord—

Bishop *sententiously*
I have come, Noote, because—

Mrs B *breaking in*
The Bishop has been telling me how much he wants to see *The Sound of Music*.

Bishop *surprised*
Madam— I—

*Christine rises and runs to the **Bishop**.*

Chris
Oh, smashing. What a super idea. You can bring Mummy, she's been dying to see it.

Noote
Yes, why don't you, my lord? It would make a change from the game.

Mrs B *smiling happily*
Oh, Bishop, would you?

Bishop
Madame, I should be delighted, however there is one small problem—

Noote
What problem is that, my lord?

Bishop
A small bald problem.

Cut to:

Scene 20
Studio / Interior / Night

The study.

*The **Archdeacon** sits huddled in his chair opposite the **Dean**, who sits bolt upright clutching his briefcase.*

Dean
They surely cannot be much longer.

Archdeacon *staunchly*
They'll be back. Never fear!

There is a pause.

Dean
I have given this game some thought during the week.

Archdeacon
Oh dear! *(Hastily)* I mean, oh, have you?

Dean
And as a result, I have written a new rule book.

He takes a large black book from his briefcase.

Archdeacon
But Dean—

Dean *his eyes gleaming*
I have introduced many stricter penalties, which will make it more fun. Of course the track will have to be altered—

Archdeacon *protesting*
But it has taken us three years—

Dean *sternly*
There is always room for improvement, Archdeacon.

Sound of a car starting.

Archdeacon
What was that?

Dean
Only a car starting.

Archdeacon *rising*
Shouldn't we see who it is?

Dean
Stay where you are, Archdeacon. *(He goes to window and looks out.)*
Strange.

Archdeacon
What's strange?

Dean
You seem to be misinformed. The Bishop and his chaplain will not be back.

Archdeacon
Of course they will. They wouldn't leave me with— I mean, without them.

Dean
Then why have they just driven off in a car with women?

Archdeacon
Women? Let me see— *(Hurries to window.)*

Dean *pointing*
There— going through the Pilgrim's Gate.

Archdeacon
But they can't— they wouldn't— it's not cricket!

Dean
Never mind, Archdeacon. You and I can play without them.

Archdeacon *horrified*
Oh, no, no, no, we can't, we can't possibly— eh— remember, only three can
play!

Dean
Only three could play, Archdeacon. That is another of my improvements.

*On **Archdeacon's** reaction, fade down and fade up on the same scene some while
later. The **Archdeacon** and the **Dean** are playing.*

Dean *sternly*
No, Archdeacon, no! You can't do that.

Archdeacon
Surely I'm allowed a move sometimes?

Dean
Not until I tell you.

Archdeacon
But we've been playing for twenty minutes and you've had all the turns.

Dean
That is because I threw a six. You failed to do so. Naturally you are penalised.

Archdeacon
I don't seem to be able to do anything right.

Dean
And whose fault is that?

*Sound of a car arriving. The **Archdeacon** jumps up.*

Archdeacon
What was that?

Dean *sternly*
Stop fidgeting!

Archdeacon
I thought I heard a car.

Dean
Really, Archdeacon, you have thought you heard at least a dozen cars.

Archdeacon *going to window*
But I'm sure I did. *(He looks out of window.)*

Scene 21
Film / Exterior / Night

In the street in front of Canon Prosser's house the car has drawn up. The four occupants are waving furiously.

Cut to:

*The **Archdeacon** framed in the window of the Palace.*

Cut to:

*The **Bishop** indicates the fire hydrant.*

Cut to:

*The **Archdeacon** smiling and nodding.*

Scene 22
Studio / Interior / Night

The study.

*The **Dean** seated at the table, the **Archdeacon** at the window.*

Dean
Was it a car?

Archdeacon
No, no. I was mistaken.

Dean
Then come and sit down and let us get on with the game!

Archdeacon
Of course, of course. *(Returning to his seat.)*

*There is a pause. The **Dean** is deep in the game and busy consulting his rule book.*

Archdeacon *coughing politely*
Er, Dean—

Dean
Yes, Archdeacon?

Archdeacon
I've suddenly remembered.

Dean
What?

Archdeacon
I've parked my car in front of a fire hydrant.

Dean *his mind on the game*
Have you?

Archdeacon *rising*
I must go and move it at once.

Dean
But you can't leave the game!

Archdeacon
I'm afraid I must.

Dean *looking up*
Why must you?

Archdeacon
Because I am contravening Section 402, Subsection 89c of the local byelaws.

Exit the **Archdeacon**.

Scene 23
Film / Exterior / Night

The **Bishop**, **Mrs Buckley**, **Christine** *and* **Noote** *are waiting anxiously in the car.*

Chris
Do you think he understood, my lord?

Bishop
There's every hope, he gave us the thumbs up. *(Seeing the* **Archdeacon***)* Here he is!

The **Archdeacon** *enters shot.*

Archdeacon
Oh, Bishop, am I glad to see you! He has rewritten the rule book.

Noote
But he can't!

Bishop
Never mind that, Henry. You're coming with us. We are going to see *The Sound of Music*. Now, do you know Mrs Buckley and her daughter?

Archdeacon
How do you do? *(Shakes hands.)*

Bishop
Right, let's go!

Archdeacon
But I can't.

Noote
Why not, Archdeacon?

Archdeacon
I can't play 'gooseberry'!

Bishop
Don't worry, Henry, you won't have to.

Chris
No, Archdeacon. May I introduce my Grandmother?

*The camera pulls back to reveal a **smart old lady** sitting in the rumble.*

Bishop
We've been to fetch her for you.

G'mother
How do you do, Archdeacon. I hear you are taking me to the cinema.

Archdeacon
Delighted, Madam, delighted. My word, I haven't been to the cinema since they showed the life of Amy Johnson!

G'mother
Amy Johnson? Did you know her?

Archdeacon
No, but I admired her. *(Remembering)* The first woman to fly all alone to Australia!

G'mother
She was my greatest friend.

Archdeacon *amazed and delighted*
She wasn't!

G'mother
Indeed she was— I taught her to fly. Come on, jump in.

The credits roll.

*The **Archdeacon** climbs into the rumble. The camera pans to the window of the Palace where the **Dean** is framed.*

*The car drives off as they all wave to the **Dean**.*

* * *

E-mail Edwin 29 May 2014, 17.50
Pauline, I've been looking through the cuttings books and I see we have the BBC Internal Report on how *Only Three Can Play* was received by the public with a 'Reaction Index'. It's a bit quaint, but it would give the reader an idea of how the show was seen at the time. I've done it as a 'postscript'. What do you think?

Postscript:
Only Three Can Play was broadcast on 7 March 1967, and the *BBC Listening and Viewing Survey*, which has survived, estimated that its audience was 19.3% of the population of the United Kingdom, adding that *"Programmes on BBC 2 and ITV at the time were seen by 0.1% and 24.% (average)."*

This 'Reaction Index' was based on questionnaires completed by a sample audience of 372 (15% of the BBC One viewing panel), who saw all or most of the broadcast. The reactions of this sample of the audience gave a Reaction Index of 76 and quoted the following comments:

"It was for me the best script we have yet had in this series, and I should like to thank the scriptwriters and all concerned for the most delightful half-hour's viewing I have had for a long time..." (Housewife)

"This innocent, clean humour appeals to me greatly, and the four characters – so different yet falling together so well – are a joy to watch." (Manager holiday business)

"Excellent entertainment – it's so refreshing to have an amusing programme which does not rely on foul language – one of the few I could leave my children to watch unchaperoned without a qualm. That is praise indeed!" (Medical social worker)

"Extremely good clean funny scripts. I enjoyed every one." (Railwayman)

"This is one of the most enjoyable of programmes. I love the gentle humour. One of the few times I bothered to look to find the authors..." (Housewife)

The *Survey* continues: *"There was an enthusiastic response from the major-ity of viewers reporting, for whom this was evidently an extremely amusing and entertaining episode of* All Gas and Gaiters. *Indeed, according to many it was "the best yet". "I laughed and laughed" "a riot from start to finish" "the funni-est of the series" were some of the many remarks in the same vein. The game of railways, the vintage car and the* Sound of Music *game, seem to have appealed enormously... The introduction of women was thought by some to have made it even more human and appealing... A Housewife summed up a general feeling when she wrote "I am very sorry this series has ended, and would like to see it back in the near future with the same cast."*

E-mail Pauline 30 May 2014, 10.37

You're not wrong, the BBC's Internal Report certainly is quaint! Especially the bit about being able to leave the children "unchaperoned"!

The Dean Goes Primitive

Pauline:

Rehearsals started on a Monday morning and continued until Friday afternoon, with the actors squeezing in time for costume fittings or publicity interviews whenever they could. We would go to the first reading and the technical run-through on Friday morning. We had devised a routine for these occasions. If I spotted something that might help Bill's performance, I'd ask Edwin to mention it to him pretending that it was his idea, because Bill did not like to be given notes by a young woman. And I would deal with Derek in the same way, because he would never accept any suggestions from Edwin, always saying "You might play it like that, but I have my own ideas." This routine worked well provided that we remembered which one of them we had spoken to first, so that we could reverse the situation next time we saw them, in order not to ruffle feathers. During rehearsals, the director, as well as working with the actors, had to design his camera script; so that by Friday morning all the shots (about 280 of them), plus the sound and lighting effects needed, would be ready to give to the technicians when they came to see a run-through for the first time. Friday afternoon was spent sorting out any problems that had arisen during their visit, and Saturday was a day off in preparation for studio day on Sunday. Studio day began early for the technicians, who had to prepare everything before the actors arrived at ten o'clock, when a slow technical run-through began which frequently continued until the early afternoon. This would be followed by another run-through, mercifully quicker than the previous one, followed by a dress rehearsal, after which last-minute problems would be sorted out. The recording took place in front of the studio audience at 7.30 in the evening, which meant that, when the actors came to give their performances, they had been standing on the set under the powerful lights for many hours. Even for young actors it was tiring, but for older actors like Bunny it was exhausting.

Although transistor radios were developed in the fifties, they only became fashionable around nineteen sixty seven when we wrote this script, and were owned exclusively by young people, so anyone over twenty-five seen with a wire in their ear was assumed to be wearing a deaf aid.

The two programmes the Archdeacon listens to are *Three Way Family*

Favourites, a very popular record request programme broadcast specifically for service personnel stationed in Cyprus and Germany, and later on, in scene two, *Round the Horne*, a comedy show which can still be heard on BBC radio four.

The way these two programmes were presented is an illustration of what oddly schizophrenic times the sixties were. For, while the BBC stipulated that because *Three Way Family Favourites* was transmitted at twelve thirty on a Sunday "there was to be no banter, or noisy jazz played." no such censorship was imposed two hours later when it broadcast *Round the Horne*, a comedy show specialising in banter of an overtly sexual nature, and starring the flamboyantly camp Kenneth Williams (perhaps their material was allowed because they didn't play noisy jazz?)

Meanwhile, to add to the confusion, Dr John Robinson, the Bishop of Woolwich, whom the Archdeacon mentions later and who was in fact the only bishop we ever met, was busy setting the cat among the pigeons by saying things like "Heaven is the greatest obstacle to an intelligent faith" and challenging the theology of the Anglican Church with his book *Honest to God*, which caused the traditionally minded a great deal of trouble, but furnished us with many opportunities for comedy.

Edwin:

The circumstances surrounding the writing of the second series were not auspicious. Frank Muir, who, as Head of Comedy, had been a friend and mentor, left the BBC to become Head of Entertainment at London Weekend Television, a move seen by the BBC executives as disloyal, and word had gone out that his name was no longer to be mentioned – the "clear your desk and leave the building immediately" syndrome.

His successor, Michael Mills, no doubt wishing to sweep with a new broom, had announced that AGAG would be phased out and the decision Frank had taken that it should be filmed in colour cancelled – which worried us all because it would prejudice overseas sales in the future. On top of this bad news, John Barron was in a West End play that was transferring to Broadway and would not be available to play the Dean. Altogether things looked about as black as they could. But, however uncomfortable things had become, we were contracted to write the series.

We had the idea for this script after a visit to Norwich Cathedral where we saw that the Bishop's throne, formerly out of sight, had been moved to a prominent position in full view of the congregation as a first step in trying to recapture the spirit of the early Church.

As we had always wanted to get our characters out of the Palace and into their Cathedral, we saw the possibility of a conflict sparked by the Dean who, in the middle of preaching a long and tedious sermon, spots that the Bishop, hidden from the congregation by the heavy curtains around his throne, is fast asleep, and decides to take the first step towards realising his ambition of returning to the austerity of the primitive Church, by proposing that the curtains be taken down and the throne exposed to the congregation, thus preventing the Bishop from ever being able to nod off again.

This entailed scenes in the Cathedral, a prospect that threatened to explode the budget. However, Stuart, with the aid of the designer, Peter Kindred, built a convincing St Ogg's at Denham Studios for £1,000. Ernest Clark replaced John Barron as the Dean, and the second series was launched.

The Stage newspaper recorded that the new series "opened with 10 million viewers".

The Dean Goes Primitive

Series Two
First transmitted on BBC One, 24 November 1967

Film / Day

*The choir of the Cathedral, a service is in progress. **The Dean** is preaching.*

Dean
And so we see throughout the history of the Primitive Church, according not only to the testimony of Eusebius of Caesarea and, to some extent, Socrates Scholasticus but also from the writings of such popular authors as Hermias, Sozomenus, Theodoret— not to mention Lactantius...

The camera pans down the north side of the choir. The choristers and choirboys look bored stiff.

Dean *(OOV)*
Epiphanus, Hieronymus, Theodoret of Cyrus, Philostorgius, Nicephorus, Callistius...

*At the west end of the choir are the canons' stalls. In the first sits an **Elderly Canon** with his hand cupped behind his ear. He strains forward attentively.*
*Beside him sits a **Second Elderly Canon** with a hearing aid. He takes out the earpiece, looks at it and puts it back, then takes out the set and retunes it.*
*In the third stall sits the **Archdeacon**, also wearing a hearing aid. He takes out the earpiece, and a few bars of the "Family Favourites" signature tune is heard. He replaces earpiece and takes set from pocket. It is unmistakably a transistor radio. The **Second Elderly Canon** looks at the **Archdeacon**. The **Archdeacon** beams at him and settles back in his stall.*

Dean *(OOV)*
Lector, Evragius, Paul Warnfried and the Venerable Bede. In all these authors we find the same emphases on simplicity. Stark, joyous simplicity. It was both the keynote and the watchword of the Primitive Church. And even in modern times, as recently as the year eleven hundred and seventy when our founder, the blessed Bishop Ogg, built this Cathedral, it, too, was characterised by this same simplicity: stark, joyous simplicity...

*The camera pans down the south side of the choir, past more bored choristers and comes to rest on the **Bishop**'s throne. This is a vast gothic structure opposite the pulpit, heavily curtained and surmounted by a carved mitre. Beside it, on a mean seat, **Noote** listens eagerly.*

Dean *(CU)*
But where is this simplicity now? *(His attention is caught by something that annoys him.)* Alas, we find little evidence of it in this Cathedral today. *(He looks increasingly annoyed.)*

*Cut to the **Bishop**, visible only to the **Dean**. He lolls back on the cushions, his mitre slightly awry, he is dozing.*

Dean *with distaste*
Everywhere, comfort, luxury and opulence abound!

*The **Bishop** stirs and, seeing the **Dean** looking, nods benevolent approval.*

Dean *firmly*
We must renounce it. We must return to simplicity. The stark, joyous simplicity of the Primitive Church.

*The **Bishop**, not understanding a word, gives a warm smile and settles back again.*

Dean *registering this*
To the stark, joyous simplicity that characterised the writings of Eusebius of Caesarea, of Socrates Scholasticus, and to some extent Hermias, not to mention, Sozomenus, Theodoret, Lactantius, Theodoret of Cyrus, Philostorgius, Nicephorus…

*The **Bishop** sleeps.*

Scene 1
Studio / Interior / Day

The hall of the Palace.

Cue sound: The key in the front door lock.

*The **Bishop** enters followed by the **Archdeacon**, they are no longer in vestments.*

Bishop *sniffing happily*
Smell that, Henry?

Archdeacon
My word, yes!

Bishop *enthusiastically*
Know what it is?

Archdeacon *doubtfully*
Your drains again?

Bishop
Drains? Really, Henry, can't you forget you're Archdeacon for five minutes? That is the smell of a beautiful twelve-pound salmon roasting. *(Proudly)* I caught it myself, yesterday.

Archdeacon
We thought you'd gone to the House of Lords.

Bishop
That's what Noote believes. Between ourselves, I decided to do something useful instead. *(Looking round)* By the way, where is Noote?

Archdeacon
He was just behind us when we left the Cathedral.

Bishop
Henry, that reminds me: the sermon. Can you tell me what it was about?

Archdeacon *warmly*
Certainly, Bishop, "Sex Before Marriage". It was instructive. I learned a lot.

Bishop *shattered.*
The Dean preached on "Sex Before Marriage"? I don't believe it!

Archdeacon
Not the Dean, the Bishop of Woolwich.

Bishop
Henry, I may have failed to grasp the content of the sermon, but not the identity of the preacher— and it certainly wasn't the Bishop of Woolwich.

Archdeacon
It was at St Paul's. The reception was excellent *(produces transistor)*, I heard every word.

Bishop
What's that?

Archdeacon
My new transistor: my aunt gave it to me for my birthday.

Bishop
Your aunt gave you a thing like that?

Archdeacon
Last year, she gave me a new hairbrush. I shall always be a boy to her. Care to listen?

Bishop *coldly*
No, thank you.

Archdeacon
I expect it will still be "Three-Way Family Favourites". *(Puts earpiece in his ear and listens intently.)*

Bishop
You mean you were playing with that thing instead of listening to the Dean? You know I always rely on you to tell me what he says.

*(The **Archdeacon**, not having heard, nods enthusiastically.)*

Archdeacon
The sun is shining in Düsseldorf— but they're expecting a storm.

Bishop
They're not the only ones. What shall I do if he asks me what I thought of it?

Archdeacon
Can't you get Noote to tell you?

Bishop *doubtfully*
I don't like to: he's new to the Church, young, impressionable, easily shocked. After all, Henry, I'm his first Bishop. What would you have thought if you'd discovered your first Bishop had gone to sleep in a sermon?

Archdeacon
He usually did. Can't you ask him tactfully?

Bishop
Looks as if I shall have to. *(Brightening)* Come on, let's go and have lunch.

*The **Bishop** puts his arm round the **Archdeacon's** shoulders.*

Archdeacon *reluctantly*
Er— you mean— now? This minute?

Bishop
Yes. Why, is something wrong?

Archdeacon
No, Bishop, no. It's just that I rather wanted to— *(Breaks off embarrassed.)*

Bishop *suddenly releasing him*
Of course! How thoughtless of me. I'm so sorry, Henry. You know where it is, don't you?

Archdeacon *beaming*
Yes thank you, Bishop.

Exits to study.

Bishop *going after him*
Hey, not through there!

Cut to:

Scene 2
Studio / Interior / Day

The study.

*The **Archdeacon** enters and goes purposefully to the sherry. He pours himself a glass.*

Bishop *entering and seeing him*
I thought you wanted to wash!

Archdeacon
No thank you, I'm quite clean. *(Raises glass.)* Cheers Bishop!

Bishop *expostulating*
Really, Henry— where are your manners?

Archdeacon *contrite*
Oh, Bishop, I am sorry. Can I pour you one?

Bishop *haughtily*
No thank you. I still find it possible to eat my midday meal without the aid of alcoholic stimulants.

***Noote** enters hurriedly*
Noote! At last— where have you been?

Noote
So sorry, my lord. I just had to congratulate the Dean on his wonderful sermon.

Bishop
Did you? Good. Then you can tell me what it was about. *(Remembering)* Er, I mean, I was unfortunately prevented, by the thick curtains round my throne, from hearing quite all that the Dean said in his discourse this morning.

Noote *coolly*
I know my Lord. You went to sleep.

Bishop *shattered*
But how—? You can't see me from where you sit. How could you possibly know?

Noote
The Dean told me.

Bishop *appalled*
The Dean?

Noote
He said your mouth was hanging open.

Bishop
Did he?

Noote
He also said—

Bishop *interrupting*
I can guess what he also said!

Noote
He took the attitude that—

Bishop *interrupting*
I don't want to know his attitude, thank you.

Noote *earnestly*
I think you should know it, my lord.

Bishop
Thank you, Noote— that the Dean saw me is sufficiently serious—
*(The **Archdeacon** laughs heartily.)*
Henry what are you laughing at?

Archdeacon *removing earpiece*
"Round the Horne", Bishop. *(Admiringly)* I don't know how they get away with
it!

Replaces earpiece.

Bishop *crossly*
Really Henry! *(Shouts)* Henry!

*The **Archdeacon** laughs heartily, then sees the **Bishop** is speaking and takes out
earpiece.*

Archdeacon
Did you speak, Bishop?

Bishop
Oh never mind, you'll just have to tell me what the Dean said over lunch,
Noote, and if I meet him I'll brazen it out. Come on, let's go and discuss this
salmon.

Noote *excitedly*
Oh, of course it's salmon. Do you know, Archdeacon, on his way back from the
House of Lords yesterday, the Bishop met a nice man on the train who gave
him the most lovely salmon. Didn't you, my lord?

Bishop *quickly*
Never mind all that, let's go and eat it.
*(Puts arms round their shoulders. **Noote** holds back.)*

Noote
Oh. Er— now?

Bishop *tetchily*
What do you mean, "now"? Of course I mean now! Why, is something the
matter?

Noote *hastily*
No, my lord, no. It's just that I rather wanted to—

Breaks off in confusion.

Bishop
Not you too?

Noote *very embarrassed*
I'm so sorry, my lord.

Bishop *sternly*
I must tell you frankly, Noote, I don't expect this sort of thing from my chaplains. It's one thing for the Archdeacon at his age but—

Noote *surprised*
But, my lord—

Bishop *continuing*
It is very self-indulgent of you— and it will hold up lunch— Can't you manage without?

Noote
I'm sorry if it's inconvenient—

Bishop
It is, most.

Noote *unusually firm*
I'm afraid I must insist, my lord.

Bishop *crossly*
Well, if you must, you must, I suppose. But I can tell you, Noote, that is not the path to Ecclesiastical preferment—

Noote *with dignity*
I never imagined it was, my lord.
(He walks solemnly to the door and exits.)

Bishop *shattered*
I thought he wanted a drink!
*The **Archdeacon** looks up and takes the plug out of his ear.*

Archdeacon
A drink? Thank you, Bishop.

Goes to decanter and pours sherry.

Bishop
Really, Henry—

Doorbell.

Bishop
What can that be? People really are most inconsiderate. Fancy calling at lunch-time!

Archdeacon *decanter in hand*
Don't worry— I'll get rid of them.

Moves to door.

Bishop *seeing decanter*
Henry, is it wise to open the front door with a decanter in your hand?

Archdeacon
Oh. *(Turns, retraces his steps and replaces the decanter.) (Then, apologetically)* That wouldn't do, would it? *(Chuckles.)* Never get rid of them if they see that!

Bishop *picks up decanter, hesitates, goes to replace it, then changes his mind and pours himself a glass. He begins to drink as the* **Archdeacon** *enters hurriedly.*

Archdeacon *loudly*
Bishop!

Bishop *hastily putting down glass*
Purely medicinal. *(Sees the* **Archdeacon***.)* What's the matter?

Archdeacon
It's the Dean!

Bishop
Oh, Henry! What shall I do? He knows I slept through his sermon.

Archdeacon
Don't let him in.

Bishop *shocked*
What *are* you saying?

Archdeacon
Keep quiet and he'll think you're not at home.

Bishop
Are you suggesting that I, your Bishop, should practise a miserable, petty deception just because— *(Doorbell.)* Quick, where shall we hide?

Archdeacon *whispers*
No need. Wait here and he'll go away.

Bishop *whispers*
Shall I shut the door?

Archdeacon *whispers*
No, he might hear.

Bishop nods.

There is a pause.

Doorbell.

Further pause.

Bishop
He must have gone. I'll go and look *(Tiptoes to door.)* *(A heavy knock on door.)*
He's breaking in, Henry— he's breaking in!

Archdeacon *calmly*
It's only the knocker, Bishop. A last resort—

Bishop
I hope you're right. *(A distant lavatory flushes.)* What's that?

Archdeacon and Bishop look at each other.

Archdeacon and **Bishop** *together*
NOOTE!

Bishop
Let's hope the Dean didn't hear!
(Heavy footsteps above.)
Listen to him! Great flat-footed— chaplain, *(Goes to door)* I'll have to tell him
to keep quiet.

Archdeacon
Take care, Bishop!

Scene 3
Studio / Interior / Day

The hall.

Noote comes hurriedly down the stairs. The study door opens and the Bishop and Archdeacon's faces appear.

Bishop
Noote, Noote!

Noote *cheerfully*
Coming, my lord.

Bishop
Noote, will you please—

Noote
All right, my lord.

Bishop
Noote, for goodness' sake!

Noote *haughtily*
I'm going as fast as I can, my lord.
(He goes to front door and opens it. The Bishop reacts.)
Oh, Dean, do come in.
(Calling) My lord, it's the Dean.

Bishop *entering with Archdeacon*
Oh, what a surprise. *(Scowling)* Thank you, Noote.

Dean *enters, carrying a briefcase*
I had begun to think you were not at home, my lord.

Bishop *feigning surprise*
Really? Why was that?

Dean
I have been ringing the bell for several minutes.

Archdeacon
Out of order, I expect.

Noote
Oh, no, Archdeacon, I heard it clearly upstairs.

Bishop
Thank you, Noote— again.

Noote
That's all right, my lord.

Dean
I trust I'm not interrupting anything important, my lord.

Bishop *brightening*
Well, Dean, since you mention it, we were just about to have lunch.

Dean
Good. Nothing important.

(He stalks past them into study. **Noote** *begins to follow, but the* **Bishop** *catches his arm and drags him back.)*

Bishop
Henry, go in and talk to him.

Archdeacon *alarmed*
Me, Bishop, talk to the Dean— alone? What shall I say to him?

Bishop
Job— chapter thirty-four— "Speak what thou knowest"!

Archdeacon *doubtfully*
I'll try, Bishop *(Goes to door)*, but when I'm with the Dean I never seem to knowest anything.

Exits to study.

Bishop
Quick, Noote, what was the sermon about?

Noote
But he knows you went to sleep, my lord.

Bishop
Nevertheless, please tell me what the sermon was about!

Noote
Mayn't I tell you what he said about your being asleep?

Bishop
If you don't tell me what the sermon was about, he'll do that himself. Quickly, what did he say?

Noote
Er— well, I shall have to think.

*On **Bishop**'s face, mix to:*

Scene 4
Studio / Interior / Day

The study.

*The **Dean** is sitting bolt upright in a chair. The **Archdeacon** hovers beside him anxiously, looking round for help. None is forthcoming. He clears his throat.*

Archdeacon
Er— Dean.

Dean
Yes, Archdeacon?

Archdeacon
Did you know the sun is shining in Düsseldorf?

Dean
Indeed?

Archdeacon
Yes. Mark you, they're expecting a storm.

*The **Bishop** enters smiling. **Noote** follows looking exhausted.*

Dean
At last, my lord.

Bishop
So sorry Dean. Just had to have a word with my chaplain on a pressing matter. (**Noote** *sags into a chair.*) However, I am now able to tell you how much I enjoyed your sermon on (*With relish*) the Primitive Church. I listened avidly.

Dean
You surprise me, my lord. I thought you were asleep.

Bishop *blandly*
Ah, I wondered if you would think that. Appearances are so deceptive. No, no, Dean, I merely lowered my eyelids as an aid to concentration.

Dean *continuing blandly*
I told your chaplain that in your position I, too, might have done the same.

Bishop
Just try asking me a few questions and you'll soon— *(Realises)* What? What was that? Noote, why didn't you tell me this?

Noote
I tried to, but you said you only wanted to know about the sermon so you could pretend you'd heard it and—

Bishop *hastily*
Yes, yes. We don't want to go into all that, do we? *(Graciously to **Dean**)* My dear Dean, you overwhelm me. In all my years toiling in the vineyard, never have I met a finer example of true Christian humility.

Noote
My lord, you don't understand—

Bishop
Of course I understand. The Dean has just admitted that if he had to listen to himself preaching, even he would go to sleep.

Dean *rising furiously.*
I said nothing of the kind.

Bishop *startled*
You did. I heard you!

Dean
I said, my lord, were I in your position, *(Speaking deliberately)* your physical position: lolling among silken cushions on a throne more suited to an Eastern Potentate than an Anglican Divine— I, too, might find it difficult to concentrate.

Bishop *disappointed*
Oh, I see. *(Brightening)* Well, Dean, this is all very interesting— but if you've nothing else to say, we were just on our way into lunch, so—

Dean *interrupting*
I have brought this to show you, my lord. *(Produces drawing from his briefcase and hands it proudly to the **Bishop**. **Noote** peers over the **Bishop**'s shoulder.)*

Bishop *mystified*
Is it a new sort of table mat?

Dean
It is my wife's freehand drawing of the Cathedral interior.

Bishop
She's certainly had a free hand. Where are all the chairs?

Dean
They have been removed.

Bishop
Removed ? Then what does the congregation sit on?

Dean
The congregation stands.

Bishop *with rising horror*
But where are the carpets? The memorial plaques? What's happened to the painting of old Bishop Hawkins?

Dean *smiling*
Banished! All part of my plan to return to the stark, joyous simplicity of the Primitive Church.

Noote *enthusiastically*
Doesn't it look nice, my lord?

Bishop
Nice? It looks as though we've had the bailiffs in! And when, may I ask, do you propose to perpetrate this desecration?

Dean
Unfortunately it will take several years to clear away all the accumulated rubbish.

Bishop
That's some comfort, I suppose.

Dean
But Stage One will be executed tomorrow morning.

Bishop
Stage One?

Dean
The removal of the screen behind the altar.

Bishop *outraged*
Oh, there you go too far! The screen behind the altar? That screen was put there for a purpose.

Dean
Indeed? For what purpose, my lord?

Bishop *floundering*
Well, I don't know— but there must have been a purpose. It was probably put there to cover something up. What's behind it?

Dean
A stone.

Bishop
A stone?

Dean
Hewn from the living rock. *(Indicating drawing.)*

Bishop
It looks like a tea chest.

Dean
It is the stone on which your great predecessor, the blessed Bishop Ogg, sat when the Cathedral was first built.

Bishop
You mean he sat on a bare stone?

Dean
Yes.

Bishop
Without even a cushion?

Dean
Certainly.

Bishop
Poor man. You'd think they'd have found him something better than that.

Dean *sharply*
No doubt he found it good for his concentration, my lord.

Bishop
I can think of something it can't have been good for. He must have been extremely uncomfortable.

Dean *coldly*
Comfort was not then the desideratum it has, unhappily, become.

Bishop
Possibly not. However, Dean, I still think you are making a mistake to remove that screen.

Dean *officiously*
As Dean of the Cathedral I am empowered…

Bishop *interrupting*
Oh, I know you're within your rights. I would not dream of interfering.

Dean
I am glad to hear that, my lord.

Bishop
And now, if you will excuse us, we are rather late for lunch. *(Confidentially)* It is salmon and you know how easily it is spoiled by overcooking.

Dean *haughtily*
Salmon? At the Deanery, Mrs Pugh-Critchley and I are not familiar with such luxurious viands.

Noote
Oh, we didn't buy it, Dean. The Bishop was given it by this nice man on the train…

Bishop
Noote, will you please show the Dean out?

Noote
Oh, of course, my lord.
*(Goes to door followed by the **Dean**.)*

Dean *turning*
By the way, my lord—

Bishop
Oh, what is it now?

Dean
I should perhaps have added that when the altar screen is removed tomorrow morning, I have ordered the curtains and cushions to be removed from you throne at the same time.

Bishop
You've what? You can't do that!

Dean
On the contrary, my lord, as you just remarked, I am within my rights. Good morning, my lord.

*Exit **Dean**.*

Noote
Oh, isn't that a good idea, my lord. It will really help you to concentrate, won't it?

Bishop *wrathfully*
Noote!

Noote *hastily*
Just a moment, my lord. I must show the Dean out.

*Exit **Noote**.*

Bishop
Of all the— This is too much. I shall fight this, Henry, I shall take this to the very top. I tell you Henry. *(Notices the **Archdeacon**.)* Henry!

Archdeacon *removing earplug*
Yes, Bishop?

Bishop
Did you hear what the Dean just said?

Archdeacon *chuckling*
No, Bishop, but I heard what Kenneth Williams just said.

Bishop *grimly*
Henry, please will you get me that pair of scissors from the desk?

Archdeacon
Of course, Bishop. Anything to be useful. *(Gets scissors and returns to **Bishop**.)*
May one ask what you want them for?

Bishop *taking scissors*
You may. This!

Bishop cuts transistor wire. On the Archdeacon's reaction, mix to:

Scene 5
Studio / Interior / Night

The library.

Noote and the Archdeacon sit reading at a table piled high with bound copies of the Cathedral records. The Bishop paces up and down. Noote puts down a book and sighs.

Bishop
Don't waste time sighing, Noote.

Noote
Mayn't I have a little rest, my lord? I've been reading solidly for five hours. It is after midnight.

Bishop *sternly*
We have got to find out why that screen was put up and stop the Dean taking it down.

Noote
But I still say that won't stop him taking away your curtains and cushions, my lord.

Bishop
And I say it will! It will discourage him. Remember the first principle of a resistance movement is to harass the enemy, undermine his morale— break his spirit— eh, Henry? *(The Archdeacon does not reply.)* Henry!

Archdeacon *looking up*
Er, what's that, Bishop?

Bishop
I was just saying— *(Stops.)* You've been reading that book for hours.

Archdeacon *embarrassed*
Have I?

Bishop
What is it?

Archdeacon
Oh, just a book.

Bishop *picking it up and reading the title*
"Pagan Fertility Rites".

Archdeacon *defensively*
It happened to catch my eye.

Bishop
Really, Henry! We are here to search the Cathedral Records.

Archdeacon
But they are so boring.

Bishop
Nonsense, Henry. They are most interesting.

Archdeacon
Then why don't you read some of them.

Noote
Yes, my lord, why don't you?

Bishop
I have already explained that reading dusty books brings on my hay fever.

Noote *putting down book*
Anyway, that's the last, my lord. There's nothing in any of them.

Archdeacon *cheerfully*
That's that, then. *(Picks up book and begins to read.)*

Bishop
That is not that, Henry! There are plenty of books you haven't looked at. *(Points to top shelf.)* What about those up there?

Noote *looking up*
Aren't they rather high, my lord?

Bishop
Oh, the Anglo-Catholic shelf, is it?

Noote
No, I mean they're out of reach.

Bishop
Well then— *(He indicates the library ladder.)*

Noote
Oh no, I couldn't. Don't ask me, my lord. I've no head for heights.

Bishop
Don't be silly. We'll hold the bottom, won't we, Henry? Henry!

Archdeacon *looking up from book*
Did you speak?

Bishop
I want you to come and hold the ladder. Can't you put that book down for a moment?

Archdeacon
Of course. That is— *(Picks up book and marks place carefully. Still holding book, he goes to **Bishop**.)*

Bishop
I don't know what's got into you today.

Archdeacon
Sorry, Bishop. It's just that I've always wondered what "unspeakable practices" were.

*Archdeacon holds ladder on opposite side from the **Bishop**.*

Bishop
Right, Noote, up you go!

Noote
Must I?

Bishop
Of course!

Noote
Right, my lord. *(Stands on first rung of ladder.)* I don't think I can go any higher.

Bishop
Of course you can!
Noote climbs another rung.

Noote
I'm not enjoying this.

Bishop *kindly*
Look, Noote. It's no good going up one rung at a time, that would frighten anybody. Wouldn't it, Henry?

Archdeacon
Definitely.

Bishop
Just run up— and you'll be there before you know what's happened.

Noote *doubtfully*
Are you sure?

Bishop
Certain. I'll count up to three and on the "three"— up you go!

Noote *unenthusiastically*
If you insist, my lord.

Bishop
Splendid. Ready? *(Counts.)* One, two, three!

Noote runs to top of ladder.

Bishop
There, what did I tell you? You're up there!

Noote
So I am! Oh, isn't it the most— *(He looks down and yelps.)* Agh!

Noote rushes down ladder.

Bishop *crossly*
What did you do that for?

Noote
I looked down.

Bishop
Well don't. Now, up you go!

Noote
Oh, don't make me, my lord.

Bishop *impatiently*
Noote, do as you are told!

Noote
Of course, my lord. If you say so. Er— *(He runs halfway up ladder and clasps it to him.)*

Bishop
Higher, man, higher!

Noote
I can't, I can't!

Bishop
Of course you can !

Bishop shakes ladder.

Noote
Don't shake it, don't shake it!

Bishop
Then go on up.

Noote
But how shall I get down?

Bishop
We'll cross that bridge when we come to it.

Noote climbs up gingerly.

Bishop
Don't look down and you'll be all right. What can you see?

Noote
I'm not sure, but it looks like Bishop Potter's Remains.

Archdeacon *surprised*
Impossible, we buried him in the crypt.

Noote
Not his physical remains, Archdeacon, his literary remains.

Bishop
What else is up there?

Noote *(reading)*
"Kalisch on Leviticus", "Cudworth on the Intellectual System". *(Stretches to book and pulls it out towards him.)* "Bishop Bonner on—" *(Drops book.)* I couldn't see what that one was on.

Bishop
My head, Noote!

Noote
Sorry, my lord. *(Suddenly interested)* I say! Here's Canon Hackett's "History of St Ogg's".

Bishop
Good, see if there is anything in it.

Noote
What, up here?

Bishop
Of course.

Noote *anxiously*
You will hold the ladder?

Bishop
Stop fussing, Noote!

Noote
Sorry, my lord.

***Noote** gingerly takes out book and begins to read. Cut to **Archdeacon** reading.*

Bishop
Henry, you're not still reading that book?

Archdeacon
It is very interesting, Bishop.

Bishop *coldly*
So it would seem.

Archdeacon
There's a lot about St Ogg's. Did you know the Cathedral was built on the site of a pagan temple?

Bishop
Of course, Henry. Most cathedrals were. *(To **Noote**)* Any luck, Noote?

Noote
Not yet, my lord.

Archdeacon
Look, there's a picture. *(Hands book to **Bishop**.)*

Bishop *taking it*
"A typical pagan ceremony". *(Scandalised)* Good gracious!

Archdeacon
Rather different from confirmation, eh, Bishop?

Bishop
Extraordinary. And they appear to be doing it on the altar.

Archdeacon
Looks like a tea chest.

Bishop
A tea chest? Wait a moment! *(Reads)* "The ceremony is being performed on the stone altar that was hewn out of the living rock. This altar was later incorporated in the building of St Ogg's Cathedral, where it was used not as an altar but as the Bishop's seat to prevent the congregation from remembering it's lurid past." *(He breaks off.)* Henry, I've had an idea—

Archdeacon
What's that, Bishop?

Bishop
We must see the Dean at once.

Archdeacon
What, now? He'll be asleep.

Bishop
Don't worry, this will wake him up! Come on.

*The **Bishop** grabs the **Archdeacon**'s arm. Exeunt. Camera cuts to **Noote** on ladder reading.*

Noote
There doesn't seem to be much here, my lord. *(Pause.)* My lord? *(Looks down and realising he is alone, panics.)* My lord, my lord, Help! help! help!

Mix to:

Scene 6
Studio / Exterior / Night

*Front door of the Deanery. The **Archdeacon** and the **Bishop** are talking to the **Dean**, who is in pyjamas and dressing gown. He is not pleased.*

Bishop
And so, in the light of this information, I feel sure you will agree the altar screen must have been erected to hide the stone from the congregation, to prevent them thinking about its lurid past.

Archdeacon
All those unspeakable practices!

Bishop
Precisely. And so to remove it would be most unwise. As unwise as it would be to tamper with anything else— such as curtains or cushions.

Dean *angrily*
Am I to understand, my lord, that you have roused me from my slumbers in order merely to communicate this balderdash?

Bishop *taken aback*
Balderdash?

Dean *firmly*
It is past credence.

Bishop
Surely you admit the screen was put there for a purpose?

Dean *wearily*
My lord, I am extremely tired. I should be grateful if I might be permitted to return to bed.

Bishop
I'm sorry, Dean, but as spiritual head of the diocese, I must insist on your guarantee that you will not expose our people to the contaminating sight of this pagan stone.

Dean
Do I understand, my lord, that your objection to my moving the screen is based solely on your wish that this stone should not be revealed, and that, were I to find some alternative method of concealing it, you would be satisfied?

Bishop
Er, yes— I suppose so.

Dean
Then I am pleased to tell you that I see a solution.

Archdeacon
May we have a peep?

Bishop
What is it, Dean?

Dean
That, my lord, you will see when next you attend service in the Cathedral. Goodnight, gentlemen.

Dean exits, closing front door.

On the faces of the Bishop and Archdeacon, mix to:

Scene 7
Film / Day

The choir of the Cathedral, a service is in progress. The Dean is preaching.

Dean
And so, as we move step by step nearer to the simplicity of the Primitive Church, we are reminded of the testimony of those early authors, Eusebius

of Caesarea, Socrates Scholasticus, the writings of Hermias, Solomenus. *(The* **Dean** *continues OOV)* Not to mention Lactantius, Epiphanus, Theodoret, Hieronymus...

The **Canons** *are seen with their hearing aids, as before. The* **Archdeacon** *with transistor, which has a conspicuous repair in the wire.*

Dean *(OOV)*
Philosorgius, Theodoret of Cyrus...

The camera pans to the south side of the choir. **Noote** *sits on his mean seat.*

Dean *(OOV)*
Not that the path back to this simplicity has been smooth. Problems there have been. One in particular—

The camera explores the throne. Stripped of cushions and curtains it stands empty.

Dean *in vision*
—a problem that threatened to wreck our entire project. Happily even this problem has been solved. Solved, moreover in a manner satisfactory to all parties and in a manner especially in keeping with the simplicity of the Primitive Church.

The camera pans to the **Bishop** *seated on the stone. He looks uncomfortable and dejected.*

Dean *(OOV)*
The stark joyous simplicity of the Primitive Church.
(The **Bishop** *scowls.)*
That simplicity that characterises the writings of Eusebius of Caesarea, of Socrates Scholasticus— also of Hermes—

Fade and mix to:

Scene 8
Studio / Interior / Day

Hospital Ward.

The **Bishop** *sits up in bed. His head on one side and bandages round his throat. A nurse is straightening the bedclothes.*

Nurse
Will you see your visitors now, my lord?

Bishop
Yes, show them in, Nurse.

Nurse *goes to door.*
You may come in now.

*Noote enters followed by the **Archdeacon**.*

Noote
Brought you a few grapes, my lord.

Bishop
Thank you, Noote. How kind.

Archdeacon
I thought you might like to borrow this, Bishop. *(He offers his transistor.)*

Bishop
Henry, I call that generous.

Archdeacon
Not at all, you're bound to be out before Sunday.

Noote
How is your neck, my lord?

Bishop
Well, it is still very painful. The doctor says it is the second most severe case he has ever seen.

Noote
I am sorry, my lord.

Bishop
Thank you, Noote.

Archdeacon
So am I, Bishop.

Bishop
Thank you, Henry.

Noote
Er, my lord—

Bishop
Yes, Noote?

Noote
Well, the Archdeacon and I have been wondering, haven't we, Archdeacon?

Archdeacon
Definitely

Bishop
What about?

Noote
Well, my lord, we don't see how sitting on a stone—

Archdeacon *correcting him*
A bare stone.

Noote
A bare stone— could affect you in quite this— er— er— er…

Archdeacon
Area?

Noote
Yes, area. We thought you'd have felt it in a different— I mean— a more— lower-down area.

Archdeacon
Fundamental.

Noote
Yes.

Bishop
This is nothing to do with sitting on the stone, uncomfortable as that was. No, I've got a severe spasm of the neck muscles caused by a howling draught that blows across from the Lady Chapel.

Archdeacon
Because the Dean took the screen down?

Bishop
I always said it was put there for a purpose.

Noote
Then you'll be glad to hear the news, my lord. Eh, Archdeacon?

Archdeacon
My word yes!

Noote
Will you tell him?

Archdeacon
Rather! No one has seen the Dean for a week!

Noote
Not that, Archdeacon, I mean about the screen.

Archdeacon
Oh yes, he's put it back.

Noote *excitedly*
And all your cushions and curtains.

Bishop
I know. The Dean told me.

Archdeacon
The Dean? But nobody has seen him—

Bishop
The Dean and I have been working together on the problem and, I'm glad to say, he has come round to my way of thinking.

Archdeacon
You mean he is not going to go primitive after all?

Bishop
Far from it. He plans to make the Cathedral rather more comfortable than it is at present.

Noote
It must be seeing you like this, my lord. Your case has softened his heart.

Bishop
I think he has been more affected by the other case.

Noote
Golly! You mean someone else caught it too?

Bishop
I'm afraid so. A very severe case.

Noote
Mr Parry-Jones, the organist?

Bishop
Not Mr Parry-Jones. *(To the **Nurse**)* Nurse, will you?

Nurse
Certainly, my lord.

*The **nurse** wheels away the screen that has formed the back of the scene and reveals the **Dean** in the adjoining bed. His head is on one side and his neck swathed in bandages. He waves wanly at **Noote** and the **Archdeacon**.*

On their faces, the credits roll.

The Bishop Goes to Town

Pauline:

This episode needed outside filming. We always tried to keep filming to the minimum, as it was expensive, time-consuming, and could lead to unpredictable situations.

On one occasion we were filming in Deptford Broadway, in south-east London, and Stuart, who wanted to take a quick establishing shot of the shops opposite, asked a man who was leaning against a wall watching what was going on if he would mind walking across the road to break the shot up a bit. "Right sir," said the man. "Yes, you leave it to me sir, I'll do that, no trouble at all, thank you very much." So the cameraman lined up the shot, Stuart shouted 'Action!' and the man crossed the road yelling "Fucking television, fucking television, fucking television!" at the top of his voice, accompanied by violent gestures. So Stuart stopped the filming and said "That was very helpful, but I wonder if you could possibly do it again, only this time don't say anything. Just walk across the road towards the shops when I shout 'Action!'. Do you think you could do that?" And the man replied, "I'll do that for you, sir, no trouble at all, you leave it to me. It will be a pleasure." So Stuart shouted 'Action!' and the man did precisely the same thing again. Stuart stopped the filming once more, and said to the man "Well, we've got what we wanted. You've been a great help, thank you." and the man replied "No, no. Thank you, sir. Think nothing of it. It's been a pleasure, and good luck to you, sir." and, shaking Stuart's hand, went back to leaning against the wall.

Edwin:

Outside filming also created problems during recording, because, unlike now when everything is done electronically, it involved stopping the tape during the performance to cut in the scenes on film, which interrupted the flow of the action. It also meant that the studio audience had to be entertained during these delays and reminded, before the recording started again, where we had got to in the story, and, if, as often happened, we had to start the scene earlier than where we had left off, we had to just hope people would laugh again as they had before. There were other editing problems connected with cutting the tape, as well. Once when Stuart asked an editor if he could cut out a moment in the action where one of the actors had fluffed his lines, he was told very severely that "It is not my job to improve the quality of your programme."

Pauline:

This was yet another episode where we failed to get any women into the plot, although there is a slight flurry of them towards the end, as well a few shots of trendy ones on film, but we did manage to get the Bishop, Noote and the Dean out of the usual setting of the Bishop's study and on to an express train to London with a dining car.

Dining cars were a much loved part of trains in those days, but were axed when the railways were privatised in 1994. Their demise continues to be a great loss not only to the public but also to writers of fiction (just think of all those vintage films, great chunks of which are set in the dining cars of trains). In this particular scenario, however, although the dining car is featured, the plot relies on the time-consuming complexity of the London Underground system, of getting from Victoria to Bond Street, before the Victoria and Jubilee lines were built, in less than forty-five minutes.

The Bishop Goes to Town

Series Two
First transmitted on BBC One, 15 December 1967

Scene 1
Studio / Interior / Day

The dining room.

*Noote at breakfast, reading paper. The clock chimes eight. The **Bishop** enters.*

Noote
Good morning, my lord.

Bishop
Morning, Noote. Anything in the papers?

Noote
There's been a revolution in South America.

Bishop *surprised*
Another? They had one last week.

Noote
Did they? This one's in Sant'Antonino.

Bishop *surprised*
But that's where the last one was! Extraordinary!
(Excitedly) Well, where's the local paper?

Noote
By your place, my lord.

Bishop
Oh, yes. *(Looks at it eagerly.)* Ah! *(Reads.)* Here it is! "Prize Giving at the Choir School Yesterday". Oh, really! How irresponsible.

Noote
What?

Bishop
They've put a photograph of the Dean on the front page.

Noote *interested*
May I see?

Bishop *holds up paper with large photo of the* **Dean**.

Noote
Oh, doesn't he look distinguished?

Bishop
Distinguished? Not really, it's just a rather flattering photograph.

Noote
Oh, look— There's Mrs Pugh-Critchley— What a smart hat! And the Wing Commander. Oh! *(Puzzled)* Who's that stout man at the back?

Bishop
Where?

Noote *points*
There. Is it Mr James, the butcher?

Bishop *indignantly*
James, the butcher?— That's me.

Noote
Oh, sorry, my lord.

Bishop
Really, the standard of photography in these provincial papers is appalling. Where's my speech? *(He begins to search paper.)* Dreadful thing about old Bishop Bromley.

Noote *surprised*
Do you think so? I'm sure he deserved it.

Bishop
Deserved it?

Noote *earnestly*
Well you must admit he'll be useful up there, my lord.

Bishop *drily*
Possibly, but at sixty-five he might still have been quite useful down here.

Noote *indicates paper*
It says here they should make more Life Peers like him.

Bishop
Who's talking about him being made a Life Peer?

Noote
I thought you were.

Bishop
No. I'm talking about him being knocked down by a bus.

Noote *surprised*
I'd no idea. How dreadful. It's not in my paper.

Bishop *surprised*
Isn't it? This one's full of it. *(Suddenly)* Oh! Really, this it too much, they've reported the Dean's whole speech. I suppose that means mine has been stuck on the back page.

There is a pause.

Noote
I see Lord Brackley's divorced, my lord.

Bishop *nodding*
Yes. *(Considers.)* Divorced? You mean married— don't you?

Noote *firmly*
No, divorced.

Bishop *puzzled*
But there's a picture of him getting married here. *(Reads)* "Lord Brackley married at Caxton Hall yesterday."

Noote *knowingly*
Ah! Yesterday. That wouldn't be in here, would it? *(Indicates paper.)*

Bishop *mystified*
Wouldn't it?

Noote
No. This is the Sunday paper.

Bishop
But it's Wednesday today.

Noote
I know. It always takes me three days to read the Sunday paper.

Bishop *amused*
Three days? Really, Noote. *(Looks at newspaper and explodes.)* This is too much!

Noote *mildly*
Oh, do you think so? I like to read it thoroughly, you see.

Bishop *crossly*
Not that, this *(Indicates paper)*— They haven't reported my speech!

Noote *aghast*
But they must have said something—

Bishop *grimly*
"The bishop also spoke"— Oh, wait a moment— *(Reads)* "See Editorial"—
Ah, I didn't think the Editor would ignore me.

Noote *earnestly*
I should hope he wouldn't. Especially after you gave him that nice box of cigars.

Bishop *sternly*
Noote, I gave him a box of cigars because I like and respect him. He is a most
intelligent and worthy man, who does a very difficult job— *(Interrupting himself, excitedly)* Ah, here it is! It's headed "Memorable Churchman".

Noote
Oh, do read it, my lord.

Bishop
What— out loud?

Noote
Yes, please—

Bishop *modestly*
Well, if you insist. *(Reads)* "Few Church dignitaries in recent years have made
such an impact on the life of our city as— *(His voice changes)* the present Dean"!

Noote
It's a misprint. They must mean the present Bishop.

Bishop
"Tall and upright, with the lissom figure of youth—"

Noote
It's not a misprint—

Bishop *continuing*
"Dr Pugh-Critchley already has an assured place in the history of the Cathedral." *(Crossly)* Really, the Editor of this paper is a complete ass. I can't think why we take it. Give me some coffee.

Noote
Coffee? Oh, I'm afraid it's tea this morning, my lord.

Bishop
It would be! Huh— "an assured place in the history of the Cathedral"— Huh.

A pause.

Noote
Golly, did you see this, my lord?

Bishop
If you intend to read me the Test score, Noote— don't bother. There's been another innings since Sunday.

Noote
No, my lord, it's this advertisement. Look, it's something I think you should buy.

Bishop
Where?

Noote
There! *(Points.)*

Bishop *reading*
"Get back your appearance with an Adonis Body Belt? *(Sternly)* Noote, if this is some sort of a joke, I consider it in very poor taste—

Noote *appalled*
Oh, no, my lord! I didn't mean that advertisement.

Bishop
I should hope you did not!

Noote
It's the advertisement for Christerby's, the auction rooms in Bond Street. They are selling the Brice-Parkinson collection today and there's a book of sixteenth-century sermons.

Bishop *mystified*
Sixteenth-century sermons? Why should I buy them? They'd be out of date.

Noote *amused*
Not to preach, my lord— as a relic— they're Bishop Gurdon's sermons.

Bishop
Bishop who?

Noote
Bishop Gurdon, my lord. He's one of ours.

Bishop
Is he?

Noote *encouragingly*
Yes. You know, he's in the nave. At least, most of him is.

Bishop *puzzled*
Most of him?

Noote
He was beheaded by Queen Mary in 1556.

Bishop
Oh, the tomb on the left by the radiator?

Noote
That's right. It has some Early Flamboyant moulding round the base.

Bishop
I know. I caught my shins on them the other day.

Noote *excitedly*
Well— don't you think something should be done about it?

Bishop
No need, the swelling's practically gone.

Noote *earnestly*

But don't you think you should go to London and buy the book? After all, my lord, they were very important sermons and he did preach them in our Cathedral. You could put it in a glass case beside the tomb. I'm sure people would welcome it.

Bishop

What as? Something else to bark their shins on? Besides, have you forgotten what I have to do today?

Noote

Oh, the questionnaire to the clergy and churchwardens—

Bishop *solemnly*

Precisely, two hundred clergy and four hundred churchwardens— making, in all, six hundred envelopes to be addressed, stamped and tucked in. Not to mention a delegation from the St Ogg's Ladies Guild coming for their annual day at the Palace— and what I'm going to do with them— I can't imagine—

Noote

Oh— and your contribution to the *Diocesan Newsletter*. You promised two hundred words on Fellowship—

Bishop

There you are! And you, Noote— you, my domestic chaplain, the man above all others who knows the burden I carry, sit there calmly proposing that I should abandon my responsibilities and rush up to London to buy a second-hand book!

Noote

I'm sorry, my lord, it was thoughtless. I just saw the book in a glass case beside the tomb with a plaque—

Bishop

A plaque?

Noote

Saying you had presented it.

Bishop *thoughtfully*

You mean— with my name?

Noote

Yes. Something like "Presented by Bishop Hever".

Bishop
Yes, or "Generously presented by Bishop Hever".

Noote
Yes. It would always stand there as a sort of... Well, as a memorial to your time here—

Bishop *thoughtfully*
You mean it would assure me of a place in the history of the Cathedral?

Noote
Yes, my lord, exactly. But as you say it's impossible—

Bishop
My dear Noote, nothing is impossible! Let's see— *(Looks at his watch.)* It is now half-past eight. We will catch the nine o'clock train to London.

Noote
But what about...?

Bishop *overriding him*
We shall arrive at Victoria at twenty to eleven. What time does the sale start?

Noote
Er— *(Looks at advertisement)* Eleven o'clock, my lord. *(Anxiously)* But what about...?

Bishop *continuing*
Eleven o'clock. That gives us twenty minutes to get to Bond Street. We shall go by bus, of course.

Noote *interested in spite of himself*
Bus? Isn't it quicker by tube?

Bishop *appalled*
Quicker by tube! Do you realise that to get from Victoria to Bond Street by tube you have to go to South Kensington on the District Line, then change on to the Circle Line — quite the worst in London, by the way. Change again at Notting Hill Gate on to the Central Line: the journey can take up to an hour! No, no. We shall take the dear twenty-five bus — straight to the top of Bond Street in about ten minutes. We shall stroll down to the saleroom — arriving in all probability several minutes before the sale begins— buy this interesting relic, have lunch at the Athenaeum, wander in the park and feed the pelicans and catch the four o'clock train home. Now, Noote, who said it was impossible?

Noote
You did, my lord.

Bishop *surprised*
Did I?

Noote
Yes, you said we've got all this work to do: the questionnaire, the six hundred envelopes to be addressed, stamped and tucked in— the delegation from the St Ogg's Ladies Guild—

Bishop *dismissively*
That? Oh, never mind all that. We'll soon find someone to do that. The important thing is to hurry. We've only got half an hour.

Noote
But it may not be so easy to find someone at short notice.

Bishop
Nonsense—

Archdeacon *(OOV) calling*
Anyone at home?

Bishop
What did I tell you? *(Calls)* Come in, Henry.

The **Archdeacon** *enters*

Archdeacon
Morning, Bishop. The door was open so I thought I'd pop in.

Bishop
Glad you did, Henry. I've got a little job for you.

Archdeacon
A job? Oh, in that case, I'll pop out. *(Turns back to door.)*

Bishop
Nonsense, Henry, you'll do nothing of the kind.

Archdeacon
But, Bishop, I was planning to go—

Bishop

Never mind what you were planning. You can do this little job for me, surely? There's nothing to it.

Archdeacon *relieved*

Oh, isn't there ?

Noote

No, Archdeacon. It's just a matter of addressing, stamping and tucking in six hundred envelopes and entertaining a delegation from the St Ogg's Ladies Guild who are coming to spend the day at the Palace.

*The **Archdeacon** reacts.*

Archdeacon *appalled*

Little job? I say, Bishop? *(With heavy irony)* You're sure there is nothing else you'd like me to do?

Bishop

Well, if you could manage to write two hundred words on Fellowship for the *Diocesan Newsletter*— Come on, Noote, or we'll miss the train.

*On the **Archdeacon**'s reaction, mix to:*

Scene 2
Studio / Interior / Day

*A first-class railway compartment. The **Bishop** enters followed by **Noote**.*

Bishop

Here we are, Noote. I told you we'd make it.

Noote

Yes, my lord, but don't you think you should have told the Archdeacon where we are going?

Bishop

Henry? Oh, no, Noote, no. Better keep it a secret— then it will be a complete surprise for them all. Now, which is back to the engine?

Noote

This side, my lord.

Bishop
Good, I shall sit there.

He points to the corner seat by the window. A briefcase lies on the seat.

Noote *seeing briefcase*
I'm afraid you can't, my lord.

Bishop
Why not ?

Noote
There's a briefcase on that seat.

Bishop
But I must have a corner seat back to the engine. I have to work.

Noote
Well, what about that one?

Points to corner seat by the corridor.

Bishop
No, it's too dark. I'll sit there. *(Indicates seat by the window.)*

Noote
But what about the briefcase?

Bishop
Oh, stop fussing, Noote! We'll move it, of course. You don't think I'm going to sit on it, do you? Are you suggesting I don't respect other people's property?

Noote *persevering*
But I think the person who put it there meant it to signify that he had reserved the seat, my lord.

Bishop
Reserved the seat? What nonsense. To reserve a seat in advance, you have to apply to the stationmaster and pay a fee of two shillings. Come on, let's go and have some coffee. I must say I'm beginning to enjoy myself— don't forget to move that case.

Exit **Bishop.**

Noote *unwillingly*
Well, if you insist, my lord

Noote moves the case to the seat by the corridor.

Mix to:

Scene 3
Studio / Interior / Day

The dining car.

*The **First Waiter**, an elderly man, comes to greet the **Bishop**.*

First Waiter
Morning, your lordship. Two for coffee?

Bishop
Yes please, waiter.

First Waiter
I've got two nice ones up here.

*First Waiter leads the way to a four-seater table. In the far corner a man sits reading a newspaper, in a way that obscures him completely from view. The paper is the St Ogg's local paper. On the front page the **Dean**'s photo is clearly visible.*

First Waiter
There we are, gentlemen, coffee won't be a moment.

Bishop
Thank you, waiter. (**Bishop** and **Noote** make themselves comfortable.) I must say it's nice to get away for a few hours.

Noote
Oh, isn't it, my lord?

Bishop
We live in a very narrow world round the Cathedral. We see too much of the same old faces— (*Notices the photo of the **Dean** and reacts violently.*) Ah!

Noote
What is it, my lord?

Bishop
That same old face!

Noote
Where?

Bishop *whispering*
There! That face— that baleful face!

Noote
Oh, the Dean's face?

Bishop
Yes, the Dean's face. Can one never get away from it?

*The paper is lowered, revealing the **Dean**.*

Dean
Good morning, my lord.

The whistle blows and the train starts.

Bishop *recovering*
Er, Dean— this is a surprise. We were just talking about you, weren't we, Noote?

Noote
Yes, Dean. The Bishop was saying that your face…

Bishop *hastily interrupting*
That your face is on the front of the newspaper.

Dean
My wife tells me it is a reasonable likeness.

Bishop
Oh, I agree.

Dean
You have no doubt seen the Editorial?

Bishop *vaguely*
Editorial? No, I don't think I have.

Noote
But you did, my lord. You read it out loud to me, you said…

Bishop *hastily*
Oh, yes. Now that my chaplain reminds me, Dean. I did notice something. But I'm afraid I've been too busy with the affairs of the diocese to read the details. You know what it is like being a bishop— well, of course, you don't— but I can assure you that one is kept constantly busy. One hardly ever gets a chance to read the papers.

Dean
You surprise me, my lord.

Bishop *patronisingly*
Do I? Yes, a lot of people think that being a bishop is easy.

Dean
I mean I am surprised that you do not make a detailed study of the press. I should have thought it was an important part of your work. Ah, coffee.

Second Waiter *entering*
Black or white, gentlemen?

All three turn their cups the right way up.

Bishop
White for me.

Noote
And me.

Dean
Black, if you please.

Second Waiter *pours coffee. The **Bishop** unwraps the lumps of sugar in the saucer and puts them in his coffee.*

Bishop
You don't want your sugar, do you, Noote?

Noote
Well, I did rather, my lord.

Dean *handing sugar*
You may have mine, my lord. I never take it.

Bishop
Oh, thank you, Dean.

*The **First Waiter** enters with a tin of biscuits.*

First Waiter
Biscuits, gentlemen?

Bishop
Please. I like the chocolate wholemeal ones.

***First Waiter** hands a packet to the **Bishop**.*

First Waiter
I see you've found a friend.

Bishop
A friend?

First Waiter
They say "Birds of a feather", don't they? *(Chuckles.)*

Bishop *coldly*
Do they?

First Waiter *to **Noote***
Biscuits for you, sir?

Noote
Do you have any "Petits Beurres"?

First Waiter
Yes, sir. *(Hands packet.)*

Noote
Oh, I can't eat a whole packet.

Bishop
Never mind, I'll help you out.

***Noote** takes packet.*

First Waiter *to **Dean***
Biscuits for you, sir?

Dean
No thank you.

First Waiter *pleasantly*
Oh, watching your waistline, are you, sir?

Dean
I do not care for biscuits.

First Waiter *jocularly to* **Bishop**
I should have thought you were the one who needed to worry— eh, my lord?

The **Bishop** *about to bite a biscuit reacts. The* **First Waiter** *chuckles and exits. The* **Dean** *smiles pleasantly.*

There is a pause.

Noote
You don't often go to London, do you, Dean?

Dean
No. I do not like London.

Bishop
May one ask what takes you up there today?

Dean *suddenly evasive*
Today? Oh, er, just shopping, private shopping. *(Hastily changes the subject.)* What a beautiful day it is!

Noote and the **Bishop** *look surprised.*

Noote
But it's raining, Dean.

Dean *nonplussed*
Really? I hadn't noticed. *(Hastily)* Er, tell me, my lord, what takes you to London today?

Noote *confidentially*
Well, actually it's rather exciting. You see we're going to…

Bishop *hastily interrupting*
Going to do some shopping — just shopping: a little spree, you know. We thought we'd take the day off.

Dean *surprised*
Indeed? And what about the affairs of the Diocese? Have you abandoned them?

Bishop
I can assure you Dean, that the affairs of the Diocese are at this moment being looked after exactly as if I were there myself.

Cut to:

Scene 4
Studio / Interior / Day

The study.

*A large pile of circulars and a pile of envelopes lie untouched. In an armchair sits the **Archdeacon** with a cup of coffee and a biscuit. He is listening to "Music and Movement".*

Scene 5
Studio / Interior / Day

The railway compartment.

*The **Bishop** enters, followed by **Noote**.*

Bishop
Really, Noote, can't you take a hint?

Noote
But I hadn't finished my coffee, my lord.

Bishop *sitting in the corner seat by the window*
Couldn't you see I wanted to get away from him?

Noote *sitting on the opposite side, by the corridor, opposite the briefcase.*
But why? You seemed to be getting on so well.

Bishop *sourly*
Did we? Tell me, Noote— did anything in the Dean's behaviour strike you as odd?

Noote
Yes, my lord; he didn't have any sugar in his coffee.

Bishop *impatiently*

Not that! Didn't he seem to you to be avoiding something?

Noote *thoughtfully*

Well, now you mention it— he was, wasn't he?

Bishop *triumphantly*

You noticed it too! Can you say what it was?

Noote

Yes, my lord— putting on weight. He didn't have any of those nice biscuits.

Bishop

Not the biscuits, Noote. He was avoiding telling us where he is going and I think I know why!

*Enter the **Dean**.*

Dean

Ah, there you are, my lord. I've brought you this. *(Hands the local paper to **Bishop**.)* I thought you would like to read the Editorial.

Bishop

Oh— but Dean, I can't deprive you of your paper. What will you read?

Dean

I have the Sunday paper.

Bishop *suspiciously*

The Sunday paper?

Dean

Yes, it was something I noticed advertised in it this morning that is the cause of my journey. Well, well, I must go and find my seat.

*Exit **Dean**.*

Bishop

Now Noote, did anything strike you in that little interchange?

Noote

It certainly did! It takes the Dean three days to read the Sunday paper.

Bishop *exasperated*
Noote— can't you see that it is proof incontrovertible that he is after Bishop Gurdon's sermons?

Noote *surprised*
Oh, do you think so, my lord?

Bishop
I'm certain!

Noote *pleased*
Oh, good! You can get together and buy them between you.

Bishop *indignantly*
What? And have his great long name on my plaque? No, Noote, we must stop him.

Noote
Stop him? But how?

Bishop
I don't know. I must sit here and think.

Noote *anxiously*
But you can't do that!

Bishop
Why not?

Noote
You've got to read the Editorial.

Bishop *furious*
This? I can tell you what I'm going to do with this! *(Begins to crumple paper.)* I'm going to, to—

*Enter the **Dean**.*

Dean
Enjoying the Editorial, my lord?

Bishop *hastily smoothing out the paper*
Yes, Dean, yes. Just getting to grips with it.

Dean
Good, good.

Noote
Why have you come back, Dean?

Dean
It is odd, but I cannot find my seat.

Bishop
Why not sit somewhere else? *(Hastily)* Not here, of course— Er, Noote and I are working— we'd disturb you.

Dean
No, I must find it. I left my briefcase there.

Noote *alarmed*
Briefcase? Did you say briefcase?

Dean
Yes, why have you seen it?

Noote *agitated*
Seen it? No, no I haven't seen a briefcase. There's no briefcase here.

Dean
I didn't suppose there was. I left it on my seat to reserve it.

Noote *earnestly*
But, Dean, you can't reserve a seat with a briefcase.

Dean *sharply*
What do you mean?

Noote
You have to see the Stationmaster in advance and pay a fee of two shillings.

Dean
Are you feeling all right, Noote?

Noote
Me? Oh, yes, thank you.

Dean
You look very flushed, suddenly.

Noote
Oh, I'm all right, Dean, I haven't got a briefcase— er, a temperature.

Dean
Good. Well, as I cannot find my seat, I think I'll sit here until the guard comes round.

*The **Dean** sits opposite **Noote**.*

Noote
Oh, no! Don't do that, Dean. I shouldn't do that!

Dean
Oh dear, I appear to have sat on—*(Pulls out the briefcase)* this briefcase. *(Examines it)* But it's my briefcase! This is my briefcase!

Noote *unhappily*
Oh, no. It can't be!

Dean
But it is. It has my initials on it.

Bishop *brightly*
Well, well, Dean. So you have found your seat after all.

Dean
But this is not the seat I put my briefcase on.

Bishop *innocently*
Isn't it?

Dean
No. I put it on that seat, where you are sitting, my lord.

Bishop
How extraordinary. Someone must have moved it.

Dean *grimly*
I wonder who could have done that.

Bishop
I wonder.

*They both look at **Noote**.*

Noote *hastily*
So do I, so do I.

Dean
So I'm afraid I must ask you to move, my lord.

Bishop
Me? Move? Whatever for?

Dean
I wish to work.

Bishop
But so do I.

Dean *firmly*
That is why I particularly reserved that seat.

*A pause. The **Bishop** loses the struggle.*

Bishop *crossly*
Really, all this fuss about a seat. It's too absurd. I can assure you I don't mind where I sit. Noote!

Noote
Yes, my lord?

Bishop
Come on.

***Noote** gets up and the **Bishop** sits in his seat. **Noote** sits between the **Bishop** and the **Dean**.*

Dean *courteously*
Thank you, my lord.

*The **Dean** sits. Watched by the **Bishop** and **Noote**, the **Dean** takes a street directory out of his briefcase and searches in it.*

*The **Bishop** and **Noote** crane over to see what he is looking for. The **Dean** looks up and the **Bishop** and **Noote** quickly look the other way. The **Dean** pulls out the map and looks for a reference. He looks puzzled.*

Noote
Er, Dean—

Dean
Yes, what is it?

Noote
I think the Bishop is wondering what you are doing.

*The **Bishop** reacts.*

Bishop *hastily*
I was wondering if you need any help, Dean?

Dean
Help? Well are you familiar with London, Noote?

Noote
Oh, yes, Dean. I have an aunt in Eccleston Square.

Dean
Then perhaps you can tell me the quickest way to get from Victoria Station to
Bond Street?

***Bishop** and **Noote** react.*

Noote
Bond Street? Oh, well— yes— the quickest way is to go by—

Bishop *quickly*
By tube! You want to go by tube, Dean.

Noote
But my lord, you said—

Bishop
Quiet, Noote! Leave this to me.

Dean
Tube? But isn't there a convenient bus?

Bishop
A bus? What an idea! No, Dean, now, listen carefully. Take the District line
from Victoria and when you get to South Kensington, change on to the Circle
line for Notting Hill Gate. When you get to Notting Hill Gate, you change
again on to the Central line—

*The **Dean** nods as he takes in the instructions.*

Mix to:

Film

Victoria Station.

*The **Bishop** and **Noote** come through the barrier with the **Dean**. The **Bishop** points to the Underground sign. The **Dean** goes towards it. The **Bishop** and **Noote** turn in the opposite direction.*

Shot of Hyde Park Corner with the buses going round.

Street sign: "Bond Street"

***Bishop** and **Noote** alighting from a bus. **Bishop** and **Noote** walking down Bond Street. They arrive at the entrance to Christerby's.*

Noote *(His attention is focused on the architecture.)*
Have you noticed, my lord, every time one comes to London, the buildings seem to get higher?

Bishop *(Looking at passing girls wearing miniskirts.)*
Yes, Noote— and not only the buildings. *(Looks at watch.)* Come on, the sale's just starting.

They turn and enter.

Mix to:

Scene 6
Studio / Interior / Day

Book auction at Christerby's. The room is not large. At one end there is a rostrum with a desk beside it and, in front of it, a horseshoe-shaped table covered with worn green baize, around which are chairs. The walls are covered with bookcases and shelves.
*The **Auctioneer** on the rostrum is leaning down talking to the **Clerk** who sits at the desk. A few dealers are either sitting at the table or examining books. A porter in a buff-coloured dustcoat is arranging books.*
Little knots of people stand about talking. By the door is a sign: "Brice-Parkinson Collection".

*The **Bishop** enters with **Noote** behind him. **Noote** carries a catalogue.*

Noote
The catalogue, my lord. (*Hands catalogue to* **Bishop**.)

Bishop
Good. Which lot is it?

Noote
Lot thirty-nine.

Bishop
Excellent. The Dean can't possibly get here by then. (*Looks at watch.*) I wish they'd start, though. It's eleven by my watch.

Noote
Oh, isn't it exciting? Are all these books to be sold this morning?

Bishop
I imagine so— Sh! He's starting—

The **Auctioneer** *straightens up.*

Auctioneer
Good morning, ladies and gentlemen. Today we are selling the Brice-Parkinson collection. I shall first read the conditions of the sale set out in the front of the catalogue: "The highest bidder is to be the buyer; and if any dispute arise between two or more bidders, the lot so in dispute shall be immediately put up again and resold."

Noote *whispering*
Oh, wouldn't the Archdeacon enjoy this?

Bishop
Henry? Oh, no. He's much better off where he is.

Mix to:

Scene 7
Studio / Interior / Day

The study at the Palace. Envelopes and questionnaires remain untouched.

The **Archdeacon** *pours himself a glass of sherry.*

Radio announcer
And now, "Music While you Work".

The *Archdeacon* sips sherry contentedly.

The doorbell rings.

The *Archdeacon* puts down his sherry and exits to hall.

Scene 8
Studio / Interior / Day

The hall.

The *Archdeacon* enters from the study and crosses to the front door. He opens it to reveal a party of middle-aged ladies.

Archdeacon
Oh, er, Ladies?

First Lady
Good morning, Archdeacon. We are from the St Ogg's Ladies Guild.

Archdeacon
I'm afraid the Bishop is out.

Second Lady *surprised*
Really?

Archdeacon
Yes, I'm just— holding the fort.

First Lady
I see. Well, reinforcements have arrived! Come on, girls.

The Ladies surge forward, pushing the *Archdeacon* back against the doorpost.

Archdeacon
But what am I going to do with you all?

Small lady with Scots accent *bringing up the rear*
Never mind, Archdeacon. We'll think of something! *(She winks.)*

On the *Archdeacon's* reaction, mix to:

Scene 9
Studio / Interior / Day

Christerby's book auction. **Noote** *stands stock still, looking at the floor.*

Auctioneer
One thousand and fifty guineas, one thousand and fifty guineas. The bid is on the right of the room, there. One thousand and fifty guineas.

A scruffy-looking man beside the **Bishop** *picks his nose.*

Auctioneer
One thousand and sixty guineas, one thousand and sixty guineas. *(Addressing a smart man in the front row)* The bid is against you, sir.

The smart man shakes his head.

Auctioneer
One thousand and sixty guineas for the last time. *(He pauses and brings down the gavel.)* Sold to Lord Chrichton. *(The scruffy man looks pleased.)* Lot thirty-eight. Fifty guineas, sixty, seventy, eighty ninety...

Noote *whispering*
We're next, my lord.

Bishop
Good. Can you see the Dean?

Noote
I daren't look up, my lord.

Bishop
Why ever not?

Noote
It might look as though I'm bidding.

Auctioneer *taking bids*
Two hundred, two hundred and ten, two hundred twenty, thirty, forty, fifty...

Bishop
Nonsense! The auctioneer knows quite well who is bidding. You can talk, move around— do anything you like.
(He makes a large gesture to prove his point.)

Auctioneer
Three hundred guineas. Was that a bid, sir?

Bishop *looking round for the* **Dean**
Well he's not here.

Auctioneer
Are you bidding, sir? The clerical gentleman, at the back?

Everyone looks at the **Bishop**.

Bishop
Er, what?

Auctioneer
Are you bidding, sir?

Bishop *flustered*
No, no. Certainly not.

Auctioneer
Three hundred guineas on the left of the room still.

The **Bishop** *stands, like* **Noote**.

Auctioneer
Selling at three hundred guineas— *(He brings down the gavel.)* Lot thirty-nine...

The **Bishop** *nudges* **Noote**. *They look expectantly towards the Auctioneer.*

The **Clerk** *stands up and confers with the* **Auctioneer**.

Auctioneer
Lot thirty-nine has been withdrawn from the sale.

The **Bishop** *and* **Noote** *react.*

Mix to:

Scene 10
Studio / Interior / Day

The study. A pile of stamped and addressed envelopes. The **Archdeacon** *sits comfortably with a glass of sherry.* **Second Lady** *approaches him and in the background we see all the ladies seated at the table busily dealing with the circulars.*

Second Lady
Everything all right, Archdeacon?

Archdeacon
Yes, thank you. No complaints.

Mix to:

Film

Victoria Station. The clock at one minute to four.

Station announcer
The train standing at platform twenty-seven is the St Ogg's express. Passengers for Ringmold and Tatley change at Hawley Junction. Tea will be served on this train.

The **Dean** *comes through the entrance to the platform.*

Mix to:

Scene 11
Studio / Interior / Day

Railway carriage. **Bishop** *and* **Noote** *sit gloomily.*

Bishop *bitterly*
It's an outrage, an absolute outrage. Dragging us all the way to London and then withdrawing the wretched book from the sale. I don't know who this Brian Parkins thinks he is—

Noote *patiently*
Brice-Parkinson, my lord. Brice-Parkinson. He's a millionaire.

Bishop
Is he? Well I've a good mind to write and ask him to pay for my fare.

Noote
But my lord—

Bishop
And yours, Noote, yours as well.

Noote
But perhaps he couldn't help it.

Bishop
What do you mean?

Noote
Well, he may simply have found he was so fond of the book that he could not bear to part with it.

Bishop
Huh! More likely someone offered him a good price and he thought he'd pocket the auction fee!

Noote
Oh, I'm sure a famous collector like him would never do such a thing.

Bishop
Are you? Well I should just like to know where that book is at the moment.

*The **Dean** enters.*

Dean *cheerfully*
Ah, there you are, my lord.

Bishop *taken aback*
Oh, Dean—

Dean
I trust you had a good day.

Noote
Oh, no. We've had the most—

Bishop
Moderate, Dean, moderate. What about you?

Dean
Me? Oh, a most successful day, my lord.

Bishop
You have?

Noote *amazed*
But you weren't even at the—

Bishop *covering up*
Club for lunch— we expected to see you at the Athenaeum, Dean.

Dean
I had lunch in a restaurant, my lord.

Bishop
Oh, where was that?

Dean
In Bond Street.

Noote
Oh, you got there, then?

Dean
Of course I got there. Though I must tell you, my lord, the tube is not the quickest way.

Bishop *innocently*
Oh, really? You do surprise me.

Dean
The twenty-five bus is much quicker.

Bishop *enjoying himself*
Well, well. I'll remember that in the future.

Dean
Indeed, the tube this morning took nearly an hour. I was late for my appointment.

Bishop
I'm sorry to hear that, Dean. It must have been very inconvenient?

Dean
No, it was all right. As it happened, I was able to make a telephone call from South Kensington. Well, well. I'm going to have tea. *(He takes a plain*

brown-paper parcel from his pocket and puts it on his seat.) I trust no one will disturb this if I leave it here to reserve my seat?

Noote *anxiously*
Oh, no. I'm sure they won't, Dean. I'm absolutely certain.

Dean
Are you having tea, Noote?

Noote
Oh, well, Dean, it sounds a splendid idea.

Bishop
Splendid, indeed but, alas, we have already had tea.

Noote *taken aback*
We have, when?

Bishop *suavely*
At the hotel, Noote. Surely you can't have forgotten?

Noote
Er, er— I'm afraid I have, my lord.

Bishop
Really, your memory! *(To **Dean**)* His memory is appalling, Dean. However, don't let us hold you back. Go and enjoy your tea.

Dean
I fully intend to, my lord. I shall not be long.

Bishop
No need to hurry.

*Exit **Dean**. **Bishop** watches him go.*

Bishop *bursting to speak*
What about that?

Noote *confused*
I'm sorry, my lord, but I really can't remember. Which hotel was it?

Bishop
Not that, Noote. I mean the Dean getting the book!

Noote *more confused*
The Dean? The book?

Bishop *trying to be patient*
He was laughing at us, don't you see?

Noote
No my lord. I'm awfully sorry, but I don't seem to be seeing anything just at the moment.

Bishop
Oh, Noote! The Dean realised we were after the book, too— he pretended to believe all that stuff about the tube being quicker than the bus— and as soon as we were out of sight, he rushed to a phone box, rang the saleroom and bought the book from under our noses.

Noote
Gracious! *(Considers.)* No, my lord. I'm sure you are wrong.

Bishop
Why?

Noote
If he'd bought it, he'd have it with him.

Bishop
He has. There! *(Points to parcel.)*

Noote
That? Oh, no.

Bishop
If you don't believe me, open it!

Noote
Open the Dean's parcel! My lord, what are you saying?

Bishop
If you won't, I will.

Noote
But you can't— you mustn't!

Bishop *seizing parcel defiantly.*
Mustn't I? And why not?

Noote *beside himself*

Other people's property, my lord— "Thou shalt not covet thy neighbour's goods— his ox, nor his ass— nor anything that is his".

Bishop *looking inside parcel*

What on earth?

Noote

"Nor thy neighbour's wife, nor his servant, nor his maid…"

Bishop

Oh, shut up, Noote!

Noote

But it's the Tenth Commandment, my lord— all the things of thy neighbour's thou shalt not covet—

Bishop

I'm perfectly familiar with the Tenth Commandment, Noote, and it certainly does not cover the contents of this parcel.

Noote

Why, what is it?

Bishop

An Adonis Body Belt. And there is nothing in the Tenth Commandment about coveting thy neighbour's corsets!

Mix to:

Scene 12
Studio / Interior / Day

The barrier at St Ogg's railway station. Passengers are coming from the train. The **Dean** *comes through, clutching his parcel, followed by the* **Bishop** *and* **Noote***.*

Noote

Do you think he suspected?

Bishop

No, you packed them much too well.

Noote

I do hope you're right. I should not like to think he thought we knew.

Bishop
Don't worry, he'll never guess— though it is going to be difficult to stop one-self from trying to spot if he's wearing them!

*The **Archdeacon** enters.*

Archdeacon
Hullo, Bishop.

Bishop *warmly*
Henry, old friend! Have you come down specially to meet us?

Archdeacon
Well, not entirely, Bishop.

A porter enters with a brown-paper parcel.

Porter
Is this it, Mr Archdeacon?

Archdeacon *takes parcel and reads*
"Venerable H. Blunt, Christerby's, Bond Street." Yes, thank you.

Porter
Ah, sign here, will you?

*The **Archdeacon** signs and takes the parcel. **Bishop** and **Noote** exchange a glance.*

Bishop
Henry? What have you got there?

Archdeacon
Oh, only Bishop Burdon's sermons.

Bishop
What?

Noote
You bought them, Archdeacon?

Archdeacon
No, I've been given them.

Bishop
Who by?

Archdeacon
The owner.

Noote
Mr Brice-Parkinson?

Archdeacon
That's the chap, I rang him up.

Bishop
But what made him give them to you, Henry?

Archdeacon
I offered to put them in a glass case in the Cathedral with his name on it.

Noote
Oh, Archdeacon, how clever of you!

Archdeacon
Not really. Some people are so vain they'll do anything to see their name on a plaque. Won't they, Bishop?

Bishop *ruefully*
They will, Henry. And talking of vanity, did you know that— *(lowers his voice)* the Dean…

*The **Bishop** puts his arm on the **Archdeacon**'s shoulder and they walk away, followed by **Noote**, as the credits roll.*

The Bishop Learns the Facts

Pauline:

AGAG was recorded on Sunday evenings at the BBC Television Centre in Wood Lane, Shepherd's Bush, in front of a studio audience. The use of studio audiences has always been contentious. On the one hand they can irritate the viewer, but on the other their reactions are an enormous help to actors when playing comedy.

Using a studio audience always necessitates a 'warm-up', which Edwin and I often did. Contrary to popular belief, a warm-up is not to tell people when to laugh, but to have a friendly presence – or in our case two friendly presences – explaining what is going on, entertaining them during breaks in the recording, and not letting them become too distracted by all the technical paraphernalia.

However, it soon became clear that my being part of the warm-up created a problem: the audience were uncomfortable in my presence. I was unusual; no woman had ever written situation comedy for television before, either in this country or, so I was told, in any other part of the world either, and they were confused about my being there – which, as the entire purpose of the warm-up was to put them at ease, made things difficult. So what was I to do? I was after all the co-writer of the series, so I could hardly sit quietly in a corner with a bag over my head. It was a problem I never satisfactorily resolved – but a comparatively small one compared to the problem I had with the Light Entertainment department of the BBC, whose members were all men. They simply could not come to terms with the fact that a young woman they knew as an actress was the co-author of a successful situation comedy. So whenever I put in an appearance, there was a great deal of shuffling of feet, clearing of throats and talking loudly among themselves. The only exception to this was Frank Muir, who was always open and helpful, but who was replaced by Michael Mills, who conformed to type. He did – was obliged to – acknowledge my presence, but could only manage to do so by saying that, as I was around, I'd better have an affair with him. An invitation I politely declined.

Edwin:

The Bishop Learns the Facts sprang from an advertisement we saw on the back page of the *Church Times* for long-sleeved polo shirts made in black nylon with white collars, designed as a practical alternative for the clergy to wear instead of a stock and starched clerical collar. We decided that Noote should have one, and when he did so the rest of the story fell into place.

The Bishop Learns the Facts

Series Three
First transmitted on BBC One, 1 January 1969

Scene 1
Studio / Interior / Day

The study.

The **Bishop** *sits on the sofa. He is wearing glasses and is trying to thread a needle. On his knee lies a shirt with a hole in it.*

Bishop *calling*
Noote, Noote—

Noote enters dressed in flannels, a sports jacket and clerical collar.

Noote
Yes, my lord?

Bishop
Come and thread this for me, will you? Your eyes are younger than mine.

Noote
Right, my lord. *(He takes needle.)*

Bishop
Look at this shirt, I don't know how I'm going to mend it. The hole is enormous.

Noote
You should have tackled it before — "A stitch in time saves nine".

Bishop
I don't want a lecture, Noote, I simply want you to thread that needle.

Noote
Certainly— I just hope it won't make me late. *(He tries to thread needle.)*

Bishop
Late? But you're not going to Scouts yet, are you?

Noote
No my lord. I'm meeting someone for tea.

Bishop
Oh? Who's that?

Noote
Just an old friend—

Bishop
I see. *(Suddenly)* Have you done the laundry?

Noote
No, I forgot. Never mind it can go tomorrow.

Bishop
But I'm down to my last two collars.

Noote
Well you should invest in one of these— *(Pulls at his collar, which is soft.)*

Bishop
What on earth is that?

Noote *proudly*
The latest thing, a black roll-topped shirt with a white clerical collar in Bri-Ny-lon, we're all wearing them.

Bishop
Whatever for?

Noote
They're so easy, they never wear out. I just pop it into hand-warm water, rinse it, then hang it on a coat hanger overnight, and it's ready to wear the next morning.

Bishop
Really, Noote, you sound like a commercial.

Noote
But I don't have to iron it, or anything.

Bishop
So I see. But I have always worn a properly starched linen collar— and I intend to go on doing so.

Noote
Well I'm sorry, but if you want the laundry sent today, you'll have to do it your-self. It's my afternoon off. *(He hands back the threaded needle.)*

Bishop
And I suppose you haven't prepared tea, either?

Noote *on his dignity*
I have laid the tray, buttered the scones, put the tea in the pot, filled the kettle, and put it on the stove. All you have to do is wait for it to boil, make it and drink it. Good afternoon, my lord.

*Exit **Noote**.*

Bishop
Really! How unnecessary!

He picks up the needle and thread and carefully ties a knot in the end of the cotton, then inserts the needle into the shirt and pulls it out quickly. The thread comes out of the needle.

Bishop
Confound it!

*The **Dean** enters.*

Dean
Good afternoon, my lord. Noote let me in. He said you would be pleased to see me.

Bishop
Oh, did he? *(He is embarrassed by the shirt and tries to put it under a cushion.)*

Dean
What is that?

Bishop
This? Oh just a shirt with a hole I'm trying to mend.

Dean
Ah, the price of bachelorhood.

Bishop
I seem to spend half my life trying to mend shirts and sending collars to the laundry.

Dean

You should find yourself a wife, my lord.

Bishop

Wouldn't it be cheaper to buy a new shirt?

Dean

I assure you, my lord, one gets far more from marriage than merely having one's shirts repaired.

Bishop *concentrating on threading the needle*

Well as a bachelor, I wouldn't know about any of that.

Dean *looking at him searchingly*

Really? Wouldn't you?

Bishop *putting down needle and giving his attention to the* **Dean**

Now, Dean, what can I do for you?

Dean

Tomorrow is my wife's birthday.

Bishop

Please offer her my felicitations.

Dean

Thank you, my lord. I have arranged for her present to be delivered here.

Bishop

Why?

Dean

So that it will be a complete surprise. I will come and collect it.

Bishop

Of course Dean, of course. When will it arrive?

Dean

By parcel post, tomorrow afternoon. You don't mind, my lord?

Bishop

My dear Dean, we are sent into this world to help each other.

Dean

My sentiments entirely, my lord!

Bishop

In that case, would you mind threading this needle for me. *(He hands needle to Dean.)*

On the Dean's reaction, mix to:

Scene 2
Studio / Interior / Day

The Cathedral Tea Rooms. Ladies in hats sit at the tables, for the most part accompanied by clerical gentlemen. The Archdeacon sits at a table in the window, having a good tea. The Waitress approaches.

Waitress

Do you want your bill, sir?

Archdeacon

Yes please, Mary.

Waitress

Let's see— *(She scans the table and is surprised.)* Just the one plate of pastries today?

Archdeacon

Yes. I had a late lunch.

Waitress

I see. So it's just the pastries, two toasted teacakes, buttered toast, scones, and a pot of tea for one. *(Tears off bill and puts it on the table.)* There we are. *(Exits.)*

Archdeacon

Thank you. *(He rises and places tip under plate.)*

Noote enters accompanied by a very attractive young woman of about the same age as himself. Conversation in the tea rooms ceases and all heads turn to look at them both.

Noote

Hello, Archdeacon.

Archdeacon

Good afternoon, Noote. *(He looks at the girl appreciatively.)*

Noote
May I introduce you to a very old friend of mine?

Archdeacon
Yes, please.

Noote
We lived next door to each other as children. Julia, this is the Archdeacon.

Julia
How do you do!

Noote
Julia has just come back from Singapore, and I must say I'm very pleased to see her again.

Archdeacon
I don't doubt it.

Julia
And I'm very happy to see dear Mervyn again. *(She and **Noote** smile at each other, as the **Archdeacon** watches them with great interest.)*

Archdeacon
How very nice. *(He continues watching them, then pulls himself together.)*
Well, well, I must be going. A pleasure to meet you, my dear. A great pleasure. Goodbye Noote. Have a good tea. *(Exits.)*

Julia
Goodbye, Archdeacon.

Noote
Let's sit over here, shall we? *(Watched by everyone, **Noote** escorts **Julia** to a table, nodding as he does so to various acquaintances.)*

Noote
I'm terribly sorry I didn't introduce you properly to the Archdeacon, but I've forgotten your married name.

Julia
That's all right. I haven't got used to it myself yet. It's Kendrick.

Noote
Yes, of course. Tea and a slice of cake?

Julia
Thank you.

Noote *calling* **Waitress**
Mary.

Waitress *entering*
Yes, sir?

Noote
Tea and two slices of cake, please.

Waitress
Right. *(She stops.)* Excuse me, but—

Noote
What is it?

Waitress
The Archdeacon left without paying for his tea.

Noote
Don't worry, I'll pay for him. I don't suppose it's very much.

Waitress *handing bill*
Well it's certainly less than usual.

Noote *(taking bill)*
Oh, good. *(He looks at the bill and reacts.)* Oh, Moses!

On **Noote**'s *reaction, mix to:*

Scene 3
Studio / Interior / Day

The study.

The **Bishop** *sits on the sofa, darning awkwardly. There is a tea tray on the table beside him.*

Doorbell.

He puts down the shirt and in doing so pulls the thread out of the needle. With a sigh of impatience he exits to hall.

Scene 4
Studio / Interior / Day

The hall.

*The **Bishop** enters and opens the front door, revealing the **Archdeacon**.*

Bishop
Hello, Henry. You're just in time for tea.

Archdeacon *beaming*
Am I really? *(Enters.)*

Bishop
Come along into the study.

They exit.

Scene 5
Studio / Interior / Day

The study.

*The **Bishop** and **Archdeacon** enter.*

Bishop *pouring tea*
Sit down, Henry. Have a scone?

Archdeacon
I won't say no, Bishop. *(He makes himself comfortable on the sofa and takes a scone.)*

Bishop *putting a cup of tea in front of him*
There you are. I expect you can do with that. *(He sits beside the **Archdeacon** and picks up the shirt.)* You don't mind if I get on with this darning, do you?

Archdeacon *buttering scone*
No Bishop, certainly not. Is there any jam?

Bishop *indicating jam on tray*
Noote is out to tea with a friend.

Archdeacon
Yes, I've just met her.

Bishop
Her? He didn't say it was a woman.

Archdeacon *appreciatively*
Oh yes, Bishop. Definitely!

Bishop
Really Henry? Well, well.

Archdeacon
If you ask me— it's a match.

Bishop
Henry! You astonish me. Are you sure?

Archdeacon
You should see them together, Bishop.

*On **Bishop**'s reaction, mix to:*

Scene 6
Studio / Interior / Day

*The Cathedral Tea Rooms. **Julia** and **Noote** are having tea.*

Julia
More tea, Mervyn?

Noote
Yes please. Oh isn't all this tremendously jolly!

Julia *seriously*
Mervyn, there's something I want to ask you to do for me.

Noote
Really ? What is it?

Julia
Will you marry me?

Noote *concerned*
I couldn't possibly do that. It would be bigamy.

Julia
No, marry me to Ben, my husband.

Noote
But you are married to Ben.

Julia
Yes, but not properly.

Noote
Oh Julia, I am sorry.

Julia
We were married out in Singapore in a Registry Office, but now we're home I want to be married properly in a church and I'd like you to conduct the ceremony.

Noote
I see. I thought you meant… *(He starts to laugh loudly. The clergymen in the Tea Room turn and look at him. He becomes embarrassed, stops laughing and lowers his voice.)* Of course, I should be delighted to. I've never married anyone before.

Julia *speaking quietly*
But you know how to, don't you?

Noote
Yes, I think so.

Julia
Well you aren't short of people to advise you.

Noote
What do you mean?

Julia
Look. *(She indicates the clergymen who are watching them.)*

Noote
I see what you mean. *(He laughs loudly. The clergymen hurriedly look away.)*

Cut to:

Scene 7
Studio / Interior / Day

The study.

*The **Bishop** and **Archdeacon** as before.*

Bishop
And you really think he's keen on this girl, Henry?

Archdeacon
I tell you it's a match.

Bishop
But Henry, he's always terrified of women.

Archdeacon
Not this one, Bishop.

Bishop
Really, this is most inconvenient. Just as I've got him trained. To have to look for another chaplain—

Archdeacon
Why? Is he leaving?

Bishop
He'll have to, Henry. I can't have a married chaplain. A woman around the place. What would she do with herself all day?

Archdeacon
Well she could mend your shirts for a start.

Bishop
Yes, so she could. And she could do the laundry and make the tea—

Archdeacon
Why not? If she'd like to.

Bishop
And they needn't live in. I could have the old stables done up for them— Henry old friend, what a splendid idea. Have another cup of tea, and please finish this last scone. *(He passes plate to **Archdeacon**.)*

Archdeacon
I'm sorry, Bishop. I don't think I can manage it.

Bishop *aghast*
Henry! What's the matter? Aren't you well?

Archdeacon *reassuringly*
I'm fine Bishop, don't worry about me. It's just something I've eaten.

Cut to:

Scene 8
Studio / Interior / Day

The Cathedral Tea Rooms.

Noote and ***Julia*** *are talking confidentially.*

Julia
And Ben gets home on Tuesday— so any time after that will do.

Noote
Right. I'll find out about the licence and arrange with the Dean about having the Cathedral. How many guests will you have?

Julia
Oh, just Mother and Aunt Jane, we want it to be very quiet.

Noote
Who's giving you away?

Julia
Our Bank Manager. As soon as he heard, he asked if he could. Isn't that kind of him?

Noote
Well, I think that's taken care of everything.

Julia
Are you sure you know what to do?

Noote
Yes— don't worry, I'll ask the Bishop for a few tips— he's done it hundreds of times. *(He looks at his watch.)* Golly, is that the time? I must rush! I've got to go

to Scouts. *(They get up to go, as **Noote** begins to laugh.)* I say, I've just thought of something…

Julia
What's that?

Noote
Here am I going to marry you, and all the time you are married! *(He laughs loudly as all eyes in the tea rooms turn to look at him.)*

Cut to:

Scene 9
Studio / Interior / Day

The study.

*The **Bishop** and **Archdeacon** are as before.*

Bishop *enthusiastically*
Marriage will be the making of him, Henry. And who knows— in the fullness of time— to hear this old house echo to the sound of childish laughter— *(He stops suddenly.)* But no— it's impossible.

Archdeacon
Why, Bishop?

Bishop
Well you know Noote, Henry. Can you honestly imagine that shy, nervous, innocent creature plucking up the courage to propose to a girl? It's out of the question.

*The front door slams and **Noote** enters breezily.*

Noote
Oh, there you are, my lord. Good afternoon, Archdeacon.

Archdeacon
Hello, Noote, old chap

Noote *cheerfully to **Bishop***
How have you got on? Had a nice afternoon? Done your darning?

Bishop *looking at* **Archdeacon**
You seem very cheerful, Noote.

Noote
Oh I am, my lord. Very.

Bishop
The Archdeacon tells me you have been having tea with a young lady.

Noote
Julia? Yes, she's an old friend. And you'll never guess what she's asked me to do.

Bishop
What?

Noote
Marry her!

Bishop
Marry? My dear Noote!

Archdeacon
And what did you reply?

Noote
I told her I'd be very happy to do so. We're going to try and fix it for next week. No point in hanging about, is there? Well, I can't stay here I must go and change for Scouts, or I'll be late. See you later on.

Noote exits, humming the wedding march. The **Bishop** and **Archdeacon** look at each other dumfounded.

Bishop
My dear Henry, it seems that you were right.

Archdeacon
I knew it was a match, Bishop.

Bishop
But one could hardly have expected it to happen so quickly. Though, mark you, no one could have anticipated that the lady would propose to him.

Archdeacon
No, and it's not even Leap Year!

Noote enters and goes to desk.

Noote
Sorry, I think I've left my whistle in this drawer. Oh yes, here it is.

Bishop
My dear Noote, we were just discussing this very exciting news you've just given us.

Noote
Exciting? Well yes, I suppose it is a bit exciting. You know it's my first time, don't you?

Bishop *taken aback*
Yes, of course I do.

Noote
Between ourselves, I'm a bit apprehensive.

Bishop *reassuringly*
I'm sure there's no need to be, Noote. What's worrying you?

Noote
Well— I'm not quite sure what I have to do— I mean— I know in principle, but I'm not too sure of some of the details. Anyway, I must go and change.

*Exits humming the wedding march. The **Bishop** and **Archdeacon** exchange a look.*

Bishop
What did I tell you? The boy's very innocent.

Archdeacon *shaking his head gravely*
So it seems, Bishop.

Bishop
We shall have to give this some thought. We can't let him marry in a state of ignorance. We shall have to get someone to talk to him. I wonder who?

Archdeacon
Can't you do it?

Bishop
Me?

Archdeacon
Well, you're his Bishop.

Bishop
Well yes, I am, but it might be rather embarrassing. There must be another way.

Archdeacon
There's a Swedish film on in London.

Bishop
But we can't send the poor boy to a thing like that all by himself!

Archdeacon *generously*
I wouldn't mind going with him— to help him out.

Bishop
No, Henry. I tell you what. When he comes down, before he goes to Scouts, you, as the older man, can have a little chat with him.

Archdeacon *rising hastily*
No, Bishop. I've just remembered. I must go home at once.

Bishop *surprised*
Must you, Henry? Why?

Archdeacon
My housekeeper will be expecting me.

Bishop
Whatever for?

Archdeacon
She'll have got my tea! *(Exits hurriedly.)*

The **Bishop** *shakes his head and picking up shirt tries to thread the needle. There is the sound of* **Noote** *rushing downstairs.*

Bishop *calling*
Noote, can you spare a minute?

Noote enters in scout uniform, short trousers, etc.

Noote
What is it, my lord?

Bishop *embarrassed*
I want to talk to you about something.

Noote
Oh, have you changed your mind about those black roll-necked shirts with the white collar? Do you want to know where to buy one?

Bishop
No, Noote. Nothing like that. This is— this is difficult for me.

Noote *understandingly*
Of course! You want me to thread your needle for you.

Bishop *thinking quickly*
Yes, that's it. Would you mind, old chap?

Noote
No my lord, I've got a moment. *(He takes needle and cotton.)*

Bishop *patting the seat beside him*
Do sit down, Noote.

Noote
Oh thank you, my lord. *(He sits beside **Bishop**.)*

Bishop
Noote, this young lady…

Noote
Julia?

Bishop
Yes, Julia. When am I going to meet her?

Noote *surprised*
Oh. Do you want to, my lord?

Bishop
I think I ought to, don't you? If you are going to marry her.

Noote
Very well, I'll bring her to tea tomorrow.

Bishop
Splendid! *(Pause. He clears his throat.)* Noote, you mentioned just now that

there are— there are one or two things about marriage you aren't too sure about.

Noote *cheerfully*
That's right, some of the details.

Bishop
Yes, well I was wondering if we could have a little chat about— the details.

Noote
Yes please, my lord. I'd love a few tips.

Bishop *taken aback*
I don't know about tips exactly— but I thought if we discussed the matter, man to man, it might remove some of your apprehensions.

Noote
It would, my lord. I'd be most grateful.

Bishop
Right then. Where shall we begin?

Noote
Why don't you give me a blow by blow account of exactly what happens?

Bishop *hastily*
I don't think there's any need for that! I tell you what, you tell me what you think should happen and I'll do my best to fill in the gaps.

Noote
Right, my lord. If that's what you'd prefer.

Bishop
It is, Noote. *(Kindly)* And Noote—

Noote
Yes, my lord?

Bishop
There's no need to be embarrassed.

Noote *surprised*
No, my lord?

Bishop *firmly*
No. Certainly not.

Noote *puzzled*
Oh, right.

Bishop
Fire away then. What do you think happens?

Noote
Well, let me see. The man stands on the left and the woman stands on the right.

Bishop *guardedly*
Go on.

Noote
And in this case, of course, the Bank Manager will be standing just behind.

Bishop
The Bank Manager?

Noote
Yes, my lord. He's asked if he can.

Bishop *bewildered*
You can't have the Bank Manager there.

Noote
But someone's got to give her away, my lord.

Bishop
Give her away? My dear Noote, are you talking about the ceremony?

Noote
Yes, my lord. Aren't you?

Bishop *hastily covering up*
Yes, Noote. Of course I was. *(He tries again.)* But I suppose we must give a little thought to what happens afterwards.

Noote
Really? I thought once the ceremony was over I'd done my stuff.

Bishop *deeply worried*
Did you, Noote, did you really? So you haven't given any thought to what will happen afterwards?

Noote
No, my lord. I can't say I have. *(He threads needle.)* There you are— there's your needle.

Bishop
Thank you, Noote.

Noote *rising*
Not at all, my lord. Well, I must rush. Can't be late for Scouts. Goodbye, my lord. *(He exits hurriedly.)*

Bishop *troubled*
Goodbye, Noote.

He shakes his head. Starts to darn shirt, but pulls the cotton out of the needle once more. On his exasperated reaction, mix to:

Scene 10
Studio / Interior / Day

The hall.

The sound of a clock striking three. A parcel is pushed through the front door.

__Noote__ hurries downstairs, dressed in flannels and sports coat. He is humming the wedding march. He sees parcel, picks it up, reads the address, looks puzzled and exits to study.

Scene 11
Studio / Interior / Day

The study.

The __Bishop__ sits darning shirt. __Noote__ enters with parcel.

Noote
My lord?

Bishop *kindly*
Noote, my dear boy, what is it?

Noote
This has just arrived, but it's addressed to Mrs Pugh-Critchley, care of the Palace.

Bishop
Yes, it's her birthday present. The Dean said it would arrive this afternoon. Put it on the desk, will you.

Noote
Yes, my lord. I'm just off to fetch Julia for tea.

He puts parcel on the desk and goes to the door.

Bishop
Noote, one moment—

Noote
Yes, my lord?

Bishop
Nothing. I was just wondering— Did you do Nature Study at school?

Noote
No, my lord, I had piano lessons instead.

Bishop
What a mistake— (**Noote** *opens the door.*) Noote—

Noote
Yes, my lord?

Bishop *hopefully*
You didn't keep rabbits, I suppose?

Noote
No, my lord.

Bishop
That's a pity.

Noote
Is that all, my lord?

Bishop
Yes, yes dear boy. Off you go.

Noote
Right, my lord.

Bishop
And Noote.

Noote
Yes, my lord?

Bishop *kindly*
Don't despair.

Noote *puzzled*
No, my lord, I won't. Thank you very much.

Exit **Noote.**

Bishop *(He sighs and goes to the bookcase and takes out a volume.)* "The Origin of the Species." *(He thumbs through it and shakes his head.)* Too obscure. *(He replaces it and takes out another book.)* "Modern Anthropology." *(Thumbs through it.)* Far too obscure. *(He puts it back and takes a third book, which he looks at.)* Not obscure enough! *(Replaces it hastily on shelf.)*

The **Archdeacon** *enters. He carries a book wrapped in brown paper.*

Archdeacon
Afternoon, Bishop.

Bishop
Henry! Am I pleased to see you. Come and sit down. *(They sit side by side on the settee.)* The situation is a great deal worse than we imagined. The boy's ignorance is profound.

Archdeacon *surprised and interested*
Really? Doesn't he even know— *(He makes a gesture.)*

Bishop
He knows nothing, Henry. And what's worse, he doesn't even appear to be interested.

Archdeacon
Bless my soul!

Bishop
It really is the most appalling comment on our Education System. I'm thinking of bringing it up in the House of Lords.

Archdeacon
Haven't you talked to him?

Bishop
I've tried to, Henry, but faced with such total incomprehension it's difficult to know where to begin. And, after all, I'm a bachelor. If I were a married man it might be easier— it's a nightmare.

Archdeacon
Well, Bishop, your worries are over.

Bishop
My dear Henry, what do you mean?

Archdeacon *indicating his parcel*
I've just bought this in the bookshop. Give it to him and you'll have no more trouble.

Bishop
What is it?

Archdeacon
"Lady Chatterley's Lover"!

Bishop
But, Henry, I can't give him a book like that! It would be so embarrassing.

Archdeacon *puts book on coffee table.*
But the Bishop of Woolwich says it's very good.

*The **Dean** enters.*

Dean
Ah, my lord, there you are. Has it arrived?

Bishop
What? Oh yes, Dean. Noote put it on the desk.

Dean *(He crosses to desk and picks up parcel.)*
Excellent. Good afternoon, Archdeacon.

Archdeacon
Hello, Dean.

Dean
This is most kind and my wife thanks you for your good wishes.

Bishop
I hope she is enjoying her birthday.

Dean
Yes, my lord— though this *(He pats his parcel.)* is the *pièce de résistance.*

Bishop
Really? What is it, Dean?

Dean
The Book of the Rose. Peculiarly suitable for dear Grace, don't you think, Archdeacon?

Archdeacon
Yes, Dean— peculiarly.

Bishop
Let me show you out, Dean.

Dean
Thank you, my lord. *(He moves towards the door.)*

Archdeacon *quietly to* **Bishop**
Bishop— the Dean is a married man— you know— *(Winks and nods at the* **Bishop.***)*

Bishop *puzzled*
A married man? *(Realises.)* Of course. Dean, I wonder if you can help me.

Dean *turning back into the room*
I shall be pleased to try, my lord.

Bishop
Well, it's like this— I would *(He is embarrassed.)*— Won't you sit down?

Dean
Thank you, my lord. *(He puts his parcel on the coffee table and sits on sofa.)*

Bishop
It's rather difficult to know how to begin.

Dean *seeing shirt*
Do you want me to thread this needle for you?

Bishop
What? Oh yes, of course. That would be very kind.

Dean
A pleasure, my lord.

Bishop *choosing his words carefully*
Dean— how would you convey to someone embarrassing information they don't possess without— without—

Dean *helpfully*
Embarrassing them?

Bishop
Precisely.

Dean *thoughtfully threading needle*
Well, my lord, it would depend on who the "someone" was.

Bishop
Well, a bachelor, say.

Dean *looking at the **Bishop** keenly*
A bachelor?

Bishop
Yes. How would you, as a married man, set about it without causing him embarrassment?

Dean
I should try to show him.

Bishop *surprised*
Show him? Show him what?

Dean
The principles, my lord. Explain them to him, man to man.

Bishop
I see. Well, thank you very much, Dean.

Dean
Not at all, my lord. *(He hands threaded needle to **Bishop**.)* Your needle.

Bishop
Thank you.

Dean *(Rises and picks up the wrong parcel from the coffee table.)*
My parcel.

Bishop
Thank you very much for your advice, Dean. Let me show you out.

Dean
Please don't worry, I'll show myself out— *(He goes to the door then turns back to the **Bishop**.)* And, my lord—

Bishop
Yes, Dean?

Dean *gently*
Don't despair.

*Exit **Dean**.*

*On **Bishop**'s puzzled reaction, mix to*

Scene 12
Studio / Interior / Day

The hall.

*Noote is entering from the front door as the **Dean** enters from the study.*

Noote
Hello, Dean. Have you got your parcel?

Dean
Yes, thank you, Noote.

Noote *opening the front door for him*
Wish Mrs Pugh-Critchley "Many Happy Returns of the Day" for me, will you?

Dean
Thank you, Noote, thank you.

*Exits hurriedly. **Noote** shuts the front door and exits to the study.*

Cut to:

Scene 13
Studio / Interior / Day

The study.

*The **Bishop** and **Archdeacon** sit side by side on the sofa. **Noote** enters.*

Noote
I'm back, my lord.

Bishop
But where is the young lady, Noote? You were bringing her for tea.

Noote
She sends her apologies, my lord, but she's not well.

Bishop
Dear me. Nothing serious, I hope?

Noote
No, no, my lord. Shall I go and put the kettle on?

Archdeacon *firmly*
Yes, please.

Noote
Right. *(He goes towards the door, but the **Bishop** stops him.)*

Bishop
No, Noote, not yet.

Archdeacon
But Bishop, it's tea time!

Bishop
But we've got something to do first, haven't we?

Archdeacon *puzzled*
Have we?

Bishop
You know we have.

Archdeacon
Oh, so we have. *(He picks up parcel.)* Here you are, Noote, a present for you.

Noote
Oh Archdeacon, how very kind.

Bishop *hastily*
Not that, Henry. Please don't open that, Noote

Noote
But the Archdeacon has just given it to me

Bishop
But I want to talk to you. Come and sit down.

Noote
Do you want me to thread your needle again? *(He sits.)*

Bishop
No thank you. Now, Noote, you remember what we were discussing just before you went out?

Noote
Yes, my lord. You asked me if I'd ever kept rabbits.

*The **Archdeacon** bursts out laughing.*

Bishop
Please, Henry!

Archdeacon
Sorry, Bishop.

Bishop
I mean before that.

Noote
Oh, about the wedding? Julia and I have just been discussing that.

Bishop
You have?

Noote
Yes, about what's to happen afterwards.

Bishop *brightening*
Afterwards? Ah, you mean the honeymoon?

Noote
There isn't going to be a honeymoon.

Bishop
No Honeymoon? Did you hear that, Henry?

Archdeacon *philosophically*
Perhaps it's just as well— under the circumstances.

Bishop
But my dear boy, why isn't there going to be a honeymoon?

Noote
Julia says that she wants to save the money for the baby.

Bishop *brightening gently*
The baby? So you expect there to be a baby, do you Noote?

Noote
Yes, my lord. Of course I do.

Bishop *very gently*
And tell me, my boy, what exactly leads you to think that Julia will have a baby?

Noote
Because the doctor says its due in seven months.

Bishop *aghast*
Seven months? But this is appalling!

Noote
No it's not. She's delighted— and so is her husband.

Bishop
Husband? But she hasn't got a husband.

Noote

Of course she has. They were married in a Registry Office last year— that's why I'm marrying them properly in the Cathedral.

Bishop

You mean that you are to conduct the service?

Noote

Of course. What did you think I meant?

Bishop

I know it sounds absurd, Noote— but the Archdeacon and I had the idea that you were going to marry her yourself.

Noote

Me? Marry Julia? *(He starts to laugh, then stops as he suddenly thinks of something.)* How very embarrassing!

Bishop

Don't be embarrassed please. It was a simple mistake— you see the Archdeacon saw you with her— and then you came and told us she'd asked you to marry her— and...

Noote *interrupting*

I'm sorry, my lord, but I always find anything like this acutely embarrassing. *(Suddenly)* What was all that you kept asking about after the wedding?

Bishop *embarrassed*

Nothing, Noote, Absolutely nothing!

Noote

And about babies— that was nothing, either?

Bishop

Nothing. Nothing at all! Don't give it another thought.

Noote

Right then. In that case I'll just undo this present the Archdeacon has just given me. *(He starts to undo string.)*

Bishop *hastily*

No. No don't undo that!

Archdeacon

You won't need it now.

Noote
Why not?

Bishop
Because you won't like it!

Noote
I think I must be the judge of that, my lord. *(He opens parcel.)* Oh, Archdeacon thank you so much. It's what I've always wanted.

Bishop
What?

Archdeacon
It is?

Noote
"The Book of the Rose". How lovely.

Bishop
The book of the what?

Noote
The rose, my lord— Oh, and there's a card inside. *(He reads card:* "To Slyboots from Cheeky". *(He looks at the **Archdeacon** bashfully.)* Oh, Archdeacon, you shouldn't have. Thank you.

Archdeacon
Steady on, Noote

Bishop
Slyboots from Cheeky? This must be the Dean's birthday present to Mrs Pugh-Critchley!

Archdeacon
He must have taken the wrong parcel.

Bishop
So he has. And you realise what this means, Henry?

Archdeacon
It undoubtedly means, Bishop, that the Dean is giving Mrs Pugh-Critchley a copy of "Lady...

Dean *(OOV)*
My lord! My lord! *The **Dean** enters with parcel.*

Dean
There appears to have been some mistake, my lord. The bookseller has sent the wrong book.

Noote
No Dean, it's here. You took the wrong one.

Dean *holding up parcel*
Then to whom does this belong?

Noote
Well, Dean, the Archdeacon gave it to …

Bishop *interrupting hastily*
Me— Dean. He gave it to me. It's mine. It belongs to me. *(He grabs the book from the **Dean**.)*

Dean *surprised*
It's yours, my lord?

Noote
But it isn't— the Archdeacon—

Bishop
Quiet, Noote. Yes, Dean. It's mine.

Dean
Have you read this book, my lord?

Bishop *embarrassed*
No, Dean I haven't. Not yet.

Dean
But you intend to?

Bishop
Yes, Dean. I most certainly do.

Dean *thoughtfully*
I see. Well the Bishop of Woolwich does say it's very good. Here you are, my lord. *(He hands book to **Bishop**.)*

Bishop
Thank you Dean. *(He takes book from the **Dean** and puts it on the sofa, on top of the shirt.)* Now if you will excuse me, I have two more shirts to mend, so I must get on.

Dean *keenly*
Really, my lord? Two more?

Bishop
Well you know how it is for us bachelors, Dean. So here is dear Mrs Pugh-Critchley's "Book of the Rose". I'm sure you want to rush back and give it to her.

Dean *calmly*
No my lord. Not yet.

Bishop
Why not?

Archdeacon
Does she prefer the other one?

Dean
No, Archdeacon. I wish to speak to the Bishop alone.

Bishop
Me, Dean?

Dean
Yes, my Lord. Alone!

Bishop *alarmed*
Alone? Just, you and me?

Dean
So if you will excuse us, gentlemen.

Noote
Yes, of course, Dean.

Archdeacon *reluctantly*
If you insist.

Dean
I do, Archdeacon.

*The **Archdeacon** and **Noote** move unwillingly to the door. The **Dean** follows them. They turn and see him directly behind them. **Noote** exits hurriedly. The **Archdeacon** remains mutinous.*

Dean
Archdeacon, please leave the room.

Archdeacon *cracking*
Oh very well— Cheeky!

*Exit **Archdeacon**.*

*The **Dean** closes the door behind him.*

Bishop *uneasily*
Dean, what is all this about?

Dean *gently*
I thought it would be less embarrassing if we were alone.

Bishop *nervously*
What do you mean?

Dean *(Moving the shirts out of the way, he sits on the sofa.)*
Won't you come and sit down, my lord?

Bishop
But, Dean, really I—

Dean
Come along now. *(He pats the seat beside him.)*

Bishop
I'd rather stand.

Dean
There's no need for embarrassment, my lord.

Bishop *deeply embarrassed*
I'm not embarrassed.

Dean
Then please sit down.

Bishop
Oh, very well. *(He perches on sofa arm.)*

Dean
Now then, I wish to have a little chat with you.

Bishop *rising hurriedly*
My dear Dean, there's no need. No need at all.

Dean
Please sit down, my lord.

*The **Bishop** sits.*

Dean
There is just something I feel you should know.

Bishop
No, there isn't Dean. I assure you I know all I need to know.

Dean *kindly*
But I am afraid it is obvious that you do not. And my wife agrees it is my duty to enlighten you.

Bishop *rising horrified*
Your wife?

Dean
Please don't feel uncomfortable about this, my lord. Sit down. *(He pats the sofa.)* Let us discuss this, man to man.

Bishop *sitting reluctantly*
But, Dean—

Dean *rising*
Now then, I just want you to sit there and watch. *(He takes off his coat.)*

Bishop
What on earth are you doing, Dean?

Dean
I have something I wish to show you.

Bishop
Show me? I'd rather you didn't.

Dean
But it is something as a bachelor you really should know about.

Bishop *frantic*
No Dean, no! Certainly not. Not on any account!

Dean
I insist, my lord. Look! *(He points to the clerical collar of his shirt.)* Look, it is a black roll-necked shirt with a white collar in Bri-Nylon, they never wear out— *(On the **Bishop**'s relieved reaction begin to roll credits as the **Dean** continues.)* You just pop them into hand-warm water, rinse them out and hang them on a coat hanger overnight and they are ready to put on in the morning…

The Bishop is Hospitable

Pauline:

The Bishop is Hospitable was part of the third series, first shown in 1969, and Robertson Hare, who was now eighty years old, was beginning to have problems remembering his lines. When we suggested he have them written on a board held out of shot so he could read them, he said that wouldn't work because he couldn't act in his reading glasses. This made things very difficult for everyone concerned, particularly during studio day as, apart from other considerations, a great many of the technical cues are taken from the actor's lines. The only positive aspect of the situation was that, during the recording, Bill Mervyn and Derek Nimmo were concentrating so hard on getting Bunny through it that their usual antipathy towards each other was temporarily put aside.

Edwin:

To say that Bill and Derek did not get on would be a euphemism: they detested each other. At the end of a scene during rehearsal, they would each turn away in opposite directions and never spoke to each other except when it was necessary.

To understand why this was the case, one has to remember that they had come from very different sides of the theatre. Bill was a traditional actor and was used to working and associating with the theatre stars of the day. Derek, on the other hand, had worked in insurance before doing National Service, after which he had a job as a paint salesman and became involved in organising concerts in Penny Lane, Liverpool. Amateur acting led to his getting into a repertory company in Bolton, after four years of which he took his chance in London, where he and his family lived in a caravan. For a time he worked for Lew Grade in his theatrical agency and he was road manager for the singer Al Martino. This varied experience was highly unusual for actors at that time and gave Derek a detached view of 'show business' and of his place in it, enabling him to manage his career far more adroitly than most actors.

He was, for example, always on the lookout for publicity, and if there was outside filming did not hesitate to behave in a way that would attract the attention of the press; and he always had his fan club at recordings. For Bill, such behaviour was brash: actors in his world were gentlemen and behaved with decorum. Another problem was that Bill saw the Bishop as the principal role, with many good laugh lines. But when rehearsals began, he found this young quick-witted comic buzzing round, taking laughs off him that he had never realised were there. In the West End, at that time no young actor would have dared to do such a thing to an established star, and he found it intolerable, while to Derek his attitude was incomprehensible.

Pauline:

Regrettably, in this script, the Dean's wife, Grace Pugh-Critchley, makes her only appearance in this book. She was the best female character in AGAG, and we had enormous fun inventing her.

A gaunt woman of about six foot two, she saw herself as captivatingly small and feminine; and her husband the Dean, who was also about six foot two, saw her that way as well.

She was played superbly by Joan Sanderson, a gifted actress, whose career included major roles with the Royal Shakespeare Company. Among Joan's many contributions to the show was always choosing a hat that enhanced the situation in which Grace found herself.

The Bishop is Hospitable

Series Three
First transmitted on BBC One, 22 January 1969

Film

*The forecourt of St Ogg's railway station. A bus pulls up. Among the people who get out and hurry into the station are the **Dean** and **Mrs Pugh-Critchley**. The **Dean** carries a suitcase.*

Cut to:

*The booking hall. The **Dean** has just bought a ticket, which he hands to **Mrs Pugh-Critchley**, who is standing beside him.*

Dean
Here you are, my love.

Mrs Pugh-Critchley
Thank you, Lionel. Now remember, your dinner is on the kitchen table, I've locked up everywhere and the keys are in the—

Dean
Yes, yes, in a minute— Come along, my love, or you'll miss the train. It's just arrived. *(He picks up the suitcase and they hurry through the barrier.)*

Cut to:

The platform. The train is waiting.

*The **Dean** hurries through the barrier ahead of **Mrs Pugh-Critchley** and opens the door of a carriage, turning as he does so to look for her, but his attention is caught by the sound of giggling and he turns back to the carriage.*

Four gorgeous girls with suitcases and make-up boxes are getting out as he holds open the door.

*The **Dean**, with an expression on his face not wholly devoid of carnal interest, follows their progress until he finds himself face to face with his wife. She is not amused.*

Mrs Pugh-Critchley *coldly, taking suitcase*
Thank you, Lionel. *(She gets into carriage as the **Dean** looks once more in the direction of the girls.)* Now, Lionel, listen. The keys are on the— *(She stops as she sees he is not paying attention.)* Lionel! *(The **Dean** turns to her.)*

Dean
Enjoy the Reunion, my love. Remember me to your old headmistress.
*(He closes the carriage door and looks again at the departing figures of the girls. Seeing him, **Mrs Pugh-Critchley**, turns her back on him and sits in the corner seat as the guard blows his whistle and waves his flag. The train moves off. The **Dean** waves to her absentmindedly, then turns and follows the girls out through the barrier.)*

Cut to:

*Forecourt of station. The **Dean** comes out of booking hall. He sees the girls getting into a small car helped by the **Archdeacon**. The **Archdeacon** gets into the driving seat and waving to the **Dean** drives off.*

*The **Dean** reacts with disapproval, then his eye is caught by a large poster: "The St Ogg's Theatre, A sizzling Revue. All Nudes is Good Nudes".*

*On the **Dean's** reaction, mix to:*

Scene 1
Studio / Interior / Day

The study.

*The telephone is ringing. **Noote** hurries in and picks up the receiver.*

Noote
The Palace, St Ogg's. Yes, this is the Bishop's chaplain speaking. I see. Very well, I'll tell his lordship. Thank you, goodbye. *(He puts the phone down as the **Bishop** enters.)*

Bishop
Who was that, Noote?

Noote
The *Church Times*, my lord.

Bishop *anxiously*
About the interview? They haven't cancelled it, have they?

Noote
No, they just wanted to check that it would be all right for tomorrow morning.

Bishop
Excellent. In that case get out all my speeches from the Lambeth Conference, will you?

Noote
Certainly. *(He opens drawer of desk and taking out bulky file looks through the contents.)* They're all here. This is your speech on Church unity. *(Produces a thick typescript.)*

Bishop *taking it*
Ah yes— I remember— this is rather good.

Noote *producing a similar typescript*
Your proposals for the "Admission of Women to the Priesthood".

Bishop *taking it from him*
Splendid. I took a very strong line.

Noote
And this one is your speech suggesting "The Redistribution of Wealth Within the Church".

Bishop *taking script*
Ah, yes. This contains some really radical thinking. *(He holds up all three type-scripts and looks at them lovingly.)* Not a bad contribution to the Conference, was it, Noote?

Noote
No, my lord, certainly not. It's just a pity you didn't get a chance to say any of it.

Bishop
Never mind. If I can get to say some of it in this interview tomorrow morning, my work won't have been entirely in vain. I'll just read through them to refresh my memory, and then you can just make some copies—

Noote
Copies? You want me to copy all that lot?

Bishop
Certainly, Noote. You are my chaplain, and I must have copies to give to this journalist.

Noote
But when am I going to find the time? I've got so much to do tomorrow and the rest of the week.

Bishop
What's wrong with tonight?

Noote
But it's my one free evening.

Bishop
Precisely. Now I must get on with my preparation.

Noote
But why do you need to do all this preparation? Just for an interview.

Bishop
My dear, Noote, you obviously don't understand. An interview like this can have far reaching results. After the Bishop of Barming's was published, not only was he invited to preach at Windsor Castle, he was also asked to stay the weekend!

Noote
Well, yes, but the Bishop of Barming's interview was rather different, wasn't it my lord?

Bishop *indignantly*
I hope you are not suggesting that I am not capable of giving as an intelligent interview as the Bishop of Barming.

Noote *hurriedly explaining*
No, my lord, of course not— but it wasn't the interview itself that was so special— it was the piece at the end— you know, "The View of a Colleague".

Bishop
Really?

Noote
Oh yes. The person they asked to do that said some very nice things— in fact he described the Bishop as "almost a modern saint".

Bishop
Really? And who was this person they asked?

Noote
His chaplain.

Bishop
I see.

Noote *enigmatically*
So do you still want me to copy out all those speeches?

Bishop *thoughtfully*
What? Oh, well, I'm not too sure— Noote, tell me, has the reporter from the *Church Times* made an appointment to see you tomorrow morning?

Noote
No, my lord.

Bishop
Then of course I want you to copy out all those speeches. *(The doorbell rings.)* Was that the doorbell?

Noote
Yes, my lord.

Bishop
Then tell them to go away. I'm far too busy to see anyone this afternoon.

*The **Archdeacon** enters.*

Archdeacon *anxiously*
Bishop, I'm so glad I found you in.

Noote
Why Archdeacon, what's the matter?

Archdeacon
I need a bed, urgently

Bishop *rising anxiously*
My dear Henry— Noote, quickly— a chair.

Noote
Yes, my lord. *(He gets a chair and takes it to the **Archdeacon**, and he and the **Bishop** sit him in it.)*

Archdeacon *puzzled*
Thank you very much.

Noote
Can I get you something, what about a nice hot cup of tea?

Bishop
How about some brandy?

Archdeacon *surprised*
Isn't it a bit early in the afternoon for brandy?

Bishop
Please Henry. Let me get you something. I insist.

Archdeacon
Well, Bishop, if you put it like that. I'll have a sherry.

Bishop
Excellent. Quick, Noote— a sherry.

Noote
Right, my lord— a sherry. *(He rushes to the decanter and pours a glass of sherry.)*

Bishop *worried*
Do you think you've got a temperature?

Archdeacon *surprised (He feels his head.)*
I don't think so.

Noote
Sherry, Archdeacon. *(He picks up the **Archdeacon**'s hand and gently puts his fingers around the glass.)* Can you manage?

Archdeacon
Yes thank you, Noote.

Bishop
No talking, Henry. Just drink.

Archdeacon
If you say so. Cheers. *(He drinks. The **Bishop** and **Noote** watch anxiously.)*

Bishop
How do you feel?

Archdeacon
Very nice, thank you. *(He hands empty glass to **Noote**, who refills it.)*

Noote
My lord, should we get the doctor?

Bishop
Yes, I think we should. Don't you, Henry?

Archdeacon
What? Oh certainly— if someone is ill. Cheers.

Bishop *surprised*
Someone?

Noote
You are, Archdeacon. Aren't you?

Archdeacon
Me? I never felt better in my life.

Bishop
But you said you needed a bed urgently.

Archdeacon
So I do; there's a big show opening at the theatre tomorrow night and they've roped me in to help find places for people to stay.

Noote
Oh Archdeacon, of course— you're theatre chaplain, aren't you?

Archdeacon
Yes. And I've been meeting people off the train all day.

Bishop
Really, Henry. You might have explained all this. I'm very busy.

Archdeacon
Sorry, Bishop. But do you know of any spare beds?

Bishop
No I don't. And I have to prepare for a most important press interview tomorrow morning.

Archdeacon *rising*
Of course, Bishop— the *Church Times*— I quite understand. I'll go and try the
Mitre Hotel. Sorry to hold you up.

Bishop
What's that, Henry? You know about the interview?

Archdeacon
Yes, Bishop. The opinion of a colleague— I know all about it.

Noote
Oh my lord, the Archdeacon must be the…

Bishop *quickly interrupting*
All right, Noote. Henry, old friend, don't be in such a hurry to go away.

Archdeacon
But Bishop, you're busy.

Bishop *genially*
So I am, so I am, but I've always got time for an old colleague like you. Now
then, what's all this about beds?

Archdeacon
Well, I've just got one more to find, but don't you worry. *(He goes to door.)*

Bishop *leading him to sofa*
Nonsense. Your worries are my worries, Henry. They must come here.

Archdeacon
You're sure, Bishop?

Bishop
Absolutely certain, Henry. I insist.

Archdeacon
I'm sure she'll be delighted, Bishop. Thank you very much.

Bishop
She? You didn't say it was a "she", Henry.

Archdeacon
Didn't I? It's just one of the girls.

Noote
We couldn't have a girl here.

Bishop
Why couldn't we have a girl here?

Noote
Not an actress girl.

Archdeacon
Don't worry, Noote, she's not an actress.

Noote
Well, a singer, then.

Archdeacon
She's not a singer either.

Bishop
Then what is she, Henry?

Archdeacon
Well, she moves about the stage.

Bishop *puzzled*
Moves about the stage?

Archdeacon
That's right. Then she stands still.

Bishop *still puzzled.*
Really? Then what happens?

Archdeacon
The lights go out.

Bishop
Henry! You don't mean—

Archdeacon
That's right, Bishop.

Bishop *nonplussed*
Oh. I see.

Archdeacon
They say it's very artistic.

Bishop *thoughtfully*
Do they?

Archdeacon
And she's got to stay somewhere.

Noote *firmly*
Well, I don't think she should stay here. Even if she is a ballet dancer!

Bishop and Archdeacon exchange looks.

Bishop
Noote, she is not a ballet dancer.

Noote
But she must be, my lord. If she's not an actress, not a singer, but moves about the stage, and then stands still and the lights go out, then she can only be a— *(He realises.)* Oh no, Archdeacon, no we couldn't, we really couldn't!

Bishop
But she's got to stay somewhere, Noote.

Noote
But, my lord—

Bishop
When shall we expect her, Henry?

Archdeacon
Are you quite sure, Bishop?

Bishop
If it will help you, Henry, yes!

Archdeacon
Tell you what. I'll try at the Mitre, and if they can't help— I'll send her round.

Doorbell.

Bishop
See who that is will you, Noote?

Noote
Very well, my lord.

*Exit **Noote**.*

Archdeacon
Are you going to the show tomorrow night, Bishop?

Bishop
Me, Henry? I don't think I can afford to go to a show like that.

Archdeacon
That's a pity. I hoped I'd see you there.

Bishop
I don't want to meddle in your affairs, Henry, but do you think *you* can afford to go?

Archdeacon
My word yes, Bishop. I've got a free seat.

***Noote** enters with the **Dean**, who looks harassed.*

Noote
The Dean, my lord.

Bishop
Ah, Dean. Good afternoon.

Dean
Good afternoon, my lord— Archdeacon.

Archdeacon
Hello, Dean. We meet again.

Dean *coldly*
So it would seem, Archdeacon.

Archdeacon *to* **Bishop**
The Dean was at the station.

Bishop
Really Dean? Why was that?

Dean

I was seeing my wife off.

Noote

The Dean tells me that Mrs Pugh-Critchley has gone to her "Old Girls" at Broadstairs.

Archdeacon *(Politely)*

I didn't know your mother-in-law lived at Broadstairs, Dean.

Dean

My wife was at school in Broadstairs, Archdeacon. She is going to her "Old Girls" reunion.

Bishop

What'd you want to see me about, Dean? I am rather busy.

Dean *surprised*

Really? I thought this was a celebration.

Bishop

A celebration?

Dean

The Archdeacon has a glass in his hand.

Archdeacon

This? Oh this is nothing.

Bishop

No— It was a mistake.

Dean

In my opinion drinking is always a mistake.

*The **Bishop** and the **Archdeacon** exchange a look.*

Archdeacon *draining glass*

Well I'll be off then, Bishop. I'll go and try my hand at the Mitre.

Dean

I should not have thought that even the Mitre would serve alcohol at this time in the afternoon, Archdeacon.

Archdeacon *on his dignity*
It so happens, Dean, that I am not going to the Mitre in search of alcohol.

Dean *disbelieving*
Really, Archdeacon?

Archdeacon
Really, Dean! I am going to try and fix up a girl for the night.

He makes a dignified exit.

Noote *hurriedly*
I'll just see the Archdeacon out, my lord.

Exit **Noote.**

Bishop
The Archdeacon is having difficulty in finding accommodation for the girls from the theatre. In fact he has asked me to help him out.

Dean
I trust you refused.

Bishop
Refused? Why should I?

Dean
Are you aware of the nature of the entertainment at the theatre this week, my lord?

Bishop
I most certainly am— more or less.

Dean
Then you can hardly sanction having one of these shameless creatures in your house, and neither would any other right-thinking person.

Bishop
You seem to have very strong feelings about it, Dean.

Dean
I certainly do. I consider these entertainments highly undesirable and I would have a very poor opinion of anyone who encouraged them in any way.

Bishop *uneasily*
I see. Well Dean, I'm sure I don't know how I can—

Dean *interrupting*
However, it is not about that I have come to see you.

Bishop *relieved*
Good.

Dean *anxiously*
In the bustle of her departure, my wife has unhappily omitted to tell me where she has put the Deanery keys.

Bishop
But don't you have a key of your own?

Dean
I have a front door key, but my wife's security precautions include locking the interior doors. I haven't had any lunch, and my dinner is on the kitchen table.

Bishop *dismissively*
Well, I'm sure you'll manage somehow. *(He looks at his watch.)* Good gracious, is that the time!

Dean
Alas, going without my dinner is not the worst of it, my lord. My real problem is tomorrow morning.

Bishop
You mean breakfast as well?

Dean
I mean that my study door is also locked and I need to work.

Bishop
I'm sorry Dean, but I don't know what you expect me to do about it.

Dean
I thought you might lend me a room here.

Bishop
Naturally I'd love to, but I really am going to be very busy tomorrow—

Dean
St Paul said a Bishop should be given to hospitality, my lord.

Bishop

St Paul said a lot of things. Why not take the morning off?

Dean

Normally under such circumstances I would. However, it is impossible, as I have an appointment with a journalist and I need somewhere to receive him.

Bishop

Well I'm sorry Dean but I don't see how I can— *(He stops.)* A journalist?

Dean

From the *Church Times*. They wish me to give them my personal opinion of you.

Bishop *aghast*

Your opinion? But I thought that the Archdeacon—

Dean

I have already asked the Archdeacon, but he says that he hasn't a room either. *(He turns to go.)* Well my lord, I am sorry you cannot help me. *(Moves toward the door.)* Good afternoon.

Bishop

Dean, don't go please. You can use my study tomorrow morning.

Dean

I should not wish to inconvenience you.

Bishop

Inconvenience me? A colleague, like you? Impossible! And you must stay to dinner as well.

Dean

No, my lord. This is too much. I cannot trespass on your hospitality in this way.

Bishop

Nonsense, Dean, if you haven't had any lunch I insist you stay for dinner.

Dean

Well, since you mention it, I must confess to being somewhat hungry.

Bishop

Then please think nothing of it. As you said yourself, "A Bishop should be given to hospitality." *(He puts his arm around the **Dean**'s shoulder and smiles at him.)*

*On the **Dean**'s reaction, mix to:*

Scene 2
Studio / Interior / Night

The dining room.

*The **Bishop**, **Noote** and the **Dean** have just finished the main course. The **Dean** has obviously been speaking for some time. **Noote** is very bored, but the **Bishop** is hanging on his every word.*

Dean
...so that, although Glow Fast Nuts undoubtedly maintain a steady heat, both Cosy Glow and Stovite share the merit of producing the minimum of clinker. However, in spite of these undeniably important considerations, my own pre-dilection, bearing in mind the eccentricities of the Cathedral boiler, is for Sunbright Doubles—

Bishop
Really, Dean, how very interesting.

Dean
You think me capricious?

Bishop
Certainly not. I had no idea that the subject was so exhaustive.

Dean
And I have hardly scratched the surface, my lord.

Noote
Golly! And you've been talking about it for hours.

Dean *sharply*
Am I boring you?

Bishop
Boring us? Good gracious, what an idea! On the contrary, I can't tell you, Dean, what a pleasure it is to have you with us.

Dean
Really? Well, for my part, my lord, this evening is of enormous value to me.

Bishop
Value?

Dean
For the interview tomorrow morning— It has shown me another side of your character, my lord: your domestic side.

Bishop
Domestic? Yes, course. *(Rising)* Let me take your plate.

Dean
Thank you. *(Hands plate to **Bishop**.)*

***Noote** rises holding his plate and puts out his hand for the **Bishop**'s plate.*

Bishop
What are you doing, Noote?

Noote *surprised at the question*
Taking the plates out, my lord.

Bishop
No, no. Give me your plate. I shall take them out.

Noote *shattered*
You take the plates out!

Bishop
Certainly, Noote.

Noote
But you never—

Bishop
Now, Noote, we have a guest, remember. I'll just take these plates to the kitchen, Dean. *(He piles up plates, side plates, serving dishes, etc.)* Noote, kindly open the door for me.

***Noote**, amazed, opens the door. The **Bishop** goes out past him, nodding and winking at him to follow.*

Noote
Have you got something in your eye, my lord?

Bishop
Certainly not! Will you please come and— er— open the kitchen door.

Noote
But it is open.

Bishop
Noote, will you please do as I say!

Bishop exits to hall.

Noote
Oh very well. Excuse me, Dean. *(He exits after the **Bishop**.)*

Cut to:

Scene 3
Studio / Interior / Night

The hall.

*The **Bishop** enters with the plates, followed by **Noote**.*

Noote *indicating kitchen door*
There you see? It is open.

Bishop
Never mind all that. You are sure you rang the Archdeacon and told him on no account to send this girl?

Noote
He wasn't in, but I spoke to his housekeeper, Mrs Banner.

Bishop
And you're absolutely certain she fully understood the message?

Noote *reassuringly*
Absolutely my lord. You mustn't worry. After all if this girl was coming she'd be here by now, wouldn't she?

Bishop *relaxing*
Yes, of course she would, Noote, you're quite right. Well then, I'll just go back to the Dean. It's all going splendidly! *(He turns to re-enter the dining room.)*

Noote
But what about those plates, my lord?

Bishop
What? *(He realises he is still holding the plates.)* Oh, right. Take them out to the kitchen, will you? *(He hands plates to **Noote** and exits to dining room. **Noote** sighs and goes towards the kitchen door.)*

Doorbell.

***Noote** turns, looking for somewhere to put the plates, but can't find anywhere, so goes to the front door, opening it with difficulty.*

Cut to:

Scene 4
Studio / Interior / Night

The dining room.

*The **Bishop** enters.*

Dean
Ah, there you are, my lord. People have suggested that I might consider changing to a gas system, but I cannot say that the notion entirely appeals, for several reasons. Firstly— *(There is the sound of china being dropped.)* What was that?

Bishop
I dread to think.

Cut to:

Scene 5
Studio / Interior / Night

The hall.

***Noote** stands at the open front door, surrounded by broken crockery. He is talking to a very attractive girl who has a suitcase and make-up case.*

Girl
I'm terribly sorry I startled you, but the Archdeacon said that the Bishop would be pleased to see me.

Noote reacts and glances anxiously towards the dining room.

Cut to:

Scene 6
Studio / Interior / Night

The dining room.

Dean
Shouldn't you go and see what has happened, my lord?

Bishop
What? And miss your reasons for not changing to gas?

Dean *flattered*
Really, my lord, I hadn't realised how interested your were in the subject.

Bishop
Ah, Dean, there's a great deal you don't know about me.

Dean
I'm beginning to realise there is, my lord.

Noote enters.

Noote *frantically*
My lord, my lord!

Bishop
Noote, please be quiet. The Dean is speaking.

Noote *distraught*
But it's happened, my lord, it's happened.

Bishop
Yes, Noote, we heard it happen. And I hope you've cleared it up.

Noote
No, no. There's more to it.

Bishop
Of course there's more to it. You'll jolly well have to pay. Now please sit down and allow the Dean to continue.

Noote
But the message, my lord. The message didn't get through!

Bishop *exasperated*
Noote, will you please sit down— *(He realises what **Noote** has just said.)* The message? *(**Noote** nods his head frantically.)* You mean it didn't get through? *(**Noote** nods his head even more frantically.)*

Dean
Is there something wrong, my lord?

Bishop *rising*
No Dean, no. Not at all— just a slight domestic problem— the pudding giving trouble— please excuse me.

*****Bishop** and **Noote** exit hurriedly.*

Cut to:

Scene 7
Studio / Interior / Night

The hall.

*The **Bishop** and **Noote** enter from the dining room. The **Bishop** closes the door carefully behind him.*

Bishop *whispering*
Where is she?

Noote *whispering back*
In the study.

Bishop
She can't stay here. The Dean might see her. You must tell her to go away.

Noote
But I can't do that— she's nowhere to go.

Bishop

This is a nightmare— what can we do? *(Suddenly)* I know!

Noote

Yes?

Bishop

Put her in the guest room. *(He turns to go back to the dining room.)*

Noote

But what happens if she won't stay there?

Bishop

You must make her, forcibly if you must. She has to stay upstairs until the Dean goes. Tell her to have a bath. *(He exits to dining room.)*

Noote

A bath? Oh Moses!

On his reaction, cut to:

Scene 8
Studio / Interior / Night

The dining room.

*The **Bishop** enters nervously and sits at the dining table.*

Dean

Is everything all right, my lord?

Bishop *smiles reassuringly*

Yes, thank you, Dean. Everything is under control.

Dean

How about the pudding?

Bishop *blankly*

Pudding? Oh, the pudding is off, I'm afraid.

Dean *disappointed*

Dear me.

Bishop
Are you still hungry then?

Dean
I am a little, my lord.

Bishop *pushing some cheese biscuits towards him*
Have a biscuit.

Dean *gratefully*
Thank you. *(He takes a very small biscuit.)*

Bishop
Have some butter.

Dean *buttering biscuit*
Will you join me?

Bishop
Me? No thank you. *(He looks at his watch.)* Good gracious, is that the time?

Dean *looking at his watch*
It's half-past eight.

Bishop
My bedtime!

Dean *very surprised*
Bedtime?

Bishop
I like to turn in early.

Dean
But surely not this early?

Bishop
I'm afraid so. I find I can't do my work properly if I sit up half the night. Have some cheese. *(He pushes the cheese plate towards the **Dean**.)* You said you were hungry.

Dean
Thank you, perhaps I will. *(He picks up his knife to cut some cheese)* I must confess, my lord, that I am surprised you take such a diligent attitude to your pastoral duties.

Bishop
If you think it wise.

Dean
Wise?

Bishop
Nothing worse than cheese late at night!

Dean
I hadn't thought of that. *(He puts his knife down.)*

Bishop
Better not take the risk. *(He pushes the cheese plate away.)* Well, well. *(He suppresses a yawn. The **Dean** glances at him, then picks up the biscuit, as the **Bishop** yawns again.)*

Bishop
Sorry, Dean.

Dean *reluctantly putting biscuit down*
Perhaps I should go, my lord.

Bishop *rising quickly*
Did you have a coat?

Dean *picking up his napkin to wipe his mouth*
Yes, my lord. I did.

Bishop *putting his arm round the **Dean**'s shoulder and leading him towards the door*
I'll get it for you. I expect you'll be glad to turn in after such a long day. *(He hustles the **Dean** into the hall.)*

Cut to:

Scene 9
Studio / Interior / Night

The hall.

*The **Bishop** and **Dean** enter. The **Dean** is still holding his napkin.*

Bishop
Now then, where's your coat?

Dean
On the chair, my lord.

Bishop
So it is. *(He picks up the **Dean**'s coat and helps him into it.)* Allow me.

There is the sound of a bath running.

Dean *putting his right arm into the coat*
Is someone having a bath?

Bishop
A bath? Oh, that will be Noote.

Dean *transferring napkin to his right hand in order to put his left arm into coat*
He goes to bed early as well, does he?

Bishop
Pressure of work, you know. Pressure of work. *(He does up the **Dean**'s coat buttons.)* There we are.

Dean
I really had no idea, my lord.

Bishop *opening front door*
Well, Dean, I hope you've enjoyed your evening with us. *(He holds out his hand.)*

Dean *changing napkin to his left hand*
Indeed, my lord. Most instructive! I've seen a side of you I didn't know existed.

They shake hands.

Bishop
Excellent! Well, my study will be ready for you tomorrow morning for your interview with the journalist from the *Church Times*.

Dean
Thank you, my lord.

Bishop *ushering him out of the front door*
A pleasure, Dean, a pleasure. Goodnight, sleep well. *(He closes the door and leans against it with relief.)*

There is the sound of knocking.

Bishop *(Puzzled, he reopens the door.)*
What is it now?

*The **Dean** stands in the doorway, napkin in hand.*

Dean
This, my lord. *(He hands napkin to **Bishop**.)*

*The **Bishop** takes the napkin and closes the front door as **Noote** comes down the stairs.*

Noote
Has he gone?

Bishop
Yes, at last! Now then, how is she?

Noote
Hungry!

Bishop
Well there's no dinner here, the Dean's eaten it.

Noote
There's a bit of bacon and eggs.

Bishop
That's for breakfast.

Noote
I thought we could make a sacrifice.

Bishop
Did you? Well, I'm not making any sacrifices, Noote. This Salome may have wound you round her little finger, but she won't wind me!

Toni *(OOV)*
May I come down?

Toni Rogers comes down the stairs. She wears an attractive dressing gown. The **Bishop** is impressed.

Bishop
Good evening, my dear.

Toni
Good evening, my lord. I'm Toni Rodgers. It's so kind of you to put me up.

Bishop
How do you do? I expect you're hungry. I'm afraid we've only got bacon and eggs.

Noote reacts.

Toni
Bacon and eggs would be wonderful. Thank you very much.

Bishop
You're very welcome. They will be waiting for you in the dining room when you come down. Now is there anything else you would like?

Toni
No thank you. Your chaplain has been looking after me. I'll just go and have my bath. I won't be long.

Noote
I'll come with you to check if everything is all right.

Bishop
No, Noote. You go and cook the bacon and eggs. I'll go with Miss Rogers and check if everything is all right.

Toni
There's no need. I'm sure everything is fine.

Noote *protesting*
But, my lord—

Bishop
Do as you are told, Noote.

Noote
Very well. *(He exits unwillingly to kitchen.)*

Bishop *smiling at* **Toni**
He's only a boy, but willing. *(The doorbell rings.)* Go on upstairs, will you. I'll just deal with this.

Toni
Right. See you in a moment. *(Exits upstairs.)*

The **Bishop** *opens the front door, revealing the* **Dean**.

Dean
Ah, I've caught you!

Bishop *guiltily*
Caught me?

Dean
You haven't gone to bed yet.

Bishop
No, I was just— just locking up.

Dean
I'm afraid I must trespass on your hospitality a little longer, my lord. My wife has locked all the bedroom doors.

Bishop
Do you want to borrow some blankets so you can sleep in the bath?

Dean
Alas, the bathroom is also locked, my lord. I have no alternative but to sleep here.

Bishop *floundering*
But, Dean, we— we've only got the one guest room.

Dean
But it's not in use.

Bishop
No, no of course it isn't— but

Dean *going towards the stair*
Then if I may— I am rather tired. It's been a difficult day.

Noote enters.

Noote
Was that the bell? Dean! I thought you'd gone home.

Dean
And I thought you were having a bath.

Bishop
He's had it Dean.

Dean
Really? That was quick.

Bishop
Yes, he is quick— at some things.

Dean
But he's dressed again.

Bishop
Has he? He's quicker than I thought he was.

Dean
Really? Well, I mustn't keep you from your beds. It's the first door on the left along the landing, isn't it? *(He moves towards the stairs.)*

Bishop
No, no, Dean, you can't— the room's not ready. Look, you wait in the study. *(He takes the **Dean**'s arm and leads him towards the study.)* Have a look at the paper, Noote will get you a cup of tea.

Dean
Very well, my lord, if you insist. But I don't want to keep you up.

Bishop
Don't worry about that. Just as long as you're comfortable. There you are. *(He pushes the **Dean** into the study and closes the door.)*

Noote *whispering*
Why did he come back?

Bishop *whispering*
Mrs Pugh-Critchley has locked all the bedroom doors, so he wants to sleep here.

Noote
But he can't. There's only one guest room, and he'll meet Miss Rogers.

Bishop
Not if we keep our heads. We'll put Miss Rogers in my room.

Noote *deeply shocked*
My lord, I most profoundly object! My conscience will not allow me to stand idly by while you embrace depravity—

Bishop
Shut up, Noote. I won't be in it.

Noote
Then where will you sleep?

Bishop
Your room, of course. (***Noote** reacts.*) Now then, listen carefully. When Miss Rogers comes down after her bath and goes to the dining room, you nip upstairs and take her things out of the guest room and put them in my room.

Noote
But what about the Dean?

Bishop
While she's having her supper, you take the Dean upstairs. He has his bath, goes to bed, and when he's asleep we take Miss Rogers up to my room. What do you think of that?

Noote
Of course, it's obvious, isn't it?

Bishop
Come along, then. Let's go and get these bacon and eggs. And remember, Noote, as long as we keep our heads, everything will be all right. (*Both exit to kitchen.*)

***Toni** enters down the stairs. She comes to the middle of the hall and stands uncertainly for a moment, then moves towards the study as the **Bishop** enters with a tray of crockery.*

Bishop
Stop!

Toni
What's the matter?

Bishop
You mustn't go in there.

Toni
Why not?

Bishop
Because the Dean— the dining room is here. *(He shepherds her across the hall to the dining room door.)*

Toni
Oh, I see.

Bishop
Would you mind just taking this in. *(He hands her the tray.)*

Toni
Yes, of course I will.

Bishop
Thank you so much. I won't be a moment.

*Toni exits to dining room with tray. The **Bishop** closes the door behind her as **Noote** enters from the kitchen carrying a plate of bacon and eggs covered with a silver cover.*

Noote
The bacon and eggs, my lord.

Bishop *lifting lid*
Ah, that smells good. Now give it to me, and I'll take it into her while you go upstairs and move her things to my room.

Noote
Right, my lord.

Bishop
And hurry up. The Dean will be getting impatient.

Noote
Yes, my lord. I'm on my way. Leave everything to me.

*He exits quickly upstairs. The **Bishop** turns towards the dining room as the **Dean** enters from the study, sniffing.*

Dean
Do I smell bacon and eggs?

Bishop
Well yes, Dean, you do. In a manner of speaking.

Dean *lifting lid with relish*
For me? How very kind. I must confess I am extremely hungry.

Bishop
No, Dean, it's not for you. *(He replaces the lid, much to the **Dean**'s distress.)* Its— it's for breakfast!

Dean
Do you usually cook breakfast at night?

Bishop
Yes. It saves time in the morning.

Noote enters downstairs.

Noote
Ready, my lord.

Bishop
Excellent. Your room is ready, Dean, if you'd like to go upstairs.

Dean
Thank you, my lord. *(He looks longingly at the bacon and eggs.)*

Noote
This way, Dean, if you'd like to come along with me. *(He leads the **Dean** towards the staircase.)*

Bishop
Do have a bath, Dean. Make yourself comfortable.

Dean *going upstairs*
Thank you, my lord. I will. *(He stops.)* Ah, one moment.

Bishop
What's wrong?

Dean
I have no night attire.

Noote
Don't worry about that, Dean. I'll lend you some pyjamas.

Dean *severely*
I do not wear pyjamas. I consider them unhealthy.

*The **Bishop** and **Noote** react.*

Bishop
Really? Good gracious. Well, I expect Noote can fix you up with something, can't you, Noote?

Noote
Can I, my lord?

Bishop
Certainly you can. Goodnight, Dean. Sleep well.

Dean
Goodnight, my lord. And thank you for your hospitality.

*The **Bishop** watches **Noote** and the **Dean** go upstairs, then exits to the dining room.*

Cut to:

Scene 9
Studio / Interior / Night

The dining room.

***Toni** sits at the table. The **Bishop** enters with tray.*

Bishop
Here we are, my dear, your bacon and eggs. Sorry to have been so long.

Toni *taking plate and starting to eat*
I'm sorry to have put you to so much trouble.

Bishop *beginning to relax*
It's no trouble at all. It's a pleasure, though I'm afraid you'll find us rather dull.

Toni
Dull?

Bishop
After the glamorous life you lead.

Toni
It's not as glamorous as you'd think. It's just hard work.

Bishop *gently*
Tell me, my dear, what makes a girl like you do a job like yours?

Toni *thoughtfully*
Well, I first became interested in it at school.

Bishop *surprised*
Dear me. What sort of school was it?

Toni
A convent.

Noote enters.

Noote
Everything is under control, my lord.

Bishop
Excellent. Come and sit down, Noote

Noote
Thank you, my lord. *(He sits and smiles at **Toni**.)* Are your bacon and eggs all right?

Toni
Yes, they're delicious.

Noote *relaxing*
Good. The eggs come from a little farm not far from here. *(He smiles at **Toni**.)* I always think that eggs from a farm—

Bishop *interrupting*
Miss Rogers was just telling me about her job, Noote.

Noote *rising, embarrassed*
Oh! Wouldn't she rather have some coffee?

Toni
Yes, please.

Noote *relieved*
Good, I'll just go and make it.

He hurries to the door and opening it starts to exit, but stops and quickly closes it again.

Noote
My lord, my lord!

Bishop *rising*
What is it? *(To **Toni**.)* Excuse me, my dear.

Noote
On the stairs, the stairs!

Bishop
What? What's on the stairs? *He opens the door and exits to hall followed by **Noote**.*

Cut to:

Scene 10
Studio / Interior / Night

The hall.

*The **Dean** is coming downstairs. He wears a surplice, and is deeply troubled. **Noote** and the **Bishop** enter from the dining room.*

Bishop *sternly*
Dean! Why aren't you having a bath?

Dean
I am just about to, my lord, but before I do so I have something for your chaplain.

Noote *puzzled*
For me, Dean?

Dean
Something you apparently left in the bathroom.

Noote
Something of mine?

Dean *embarrassed*
It appears, Noote, that when you dressed after your bath, you did not dress completely. I believe these must be yours.

*He holds up a pair of ladies knickers. On **Noote**'s reaction, fade to:*

Scene 11
Studio / Interior / Night

Noote's bedroom.

*A small room with a narrow bed and a desk with a wooden chair, and nothing else. **Noote** in dressing gown and pyjamas is turning down the bedcover.*

*The **Bishop** enters, also wearing dressing gown and pyjamas. He carries a sponge bag and his Lambeth speeches.*

Noote *quietly*
Is everything all right, my lord?

Bishop
Yes. They are both in their rooms.

Noote
But will they stay there? The Dean has been out four times already!

Bishop
Well surely he can't want anything else.

Noote
Not even— you know— in the night?

Bishop
Certainly not, Noote. I drew his attention to the fact that the room is properly furnished. *(He yawns.)* Well, I'm ready to turn in. *(He sits on the bed and takes off his slippers.)*

Noote *bowing to the inevitable*
So you're having the bed, are you?

Bishop
I have to be fresh for the morning.

Noote
Then I'll just have to sleep on the sofa in the study.

Bishop
No, Noote, you can't go downstairs. They might hear you.

Noote *indicating chair*
Well I can't sleep on that!

Bishop
Don't worry, Noote. You won't have time to sleep.

Noote
Why not?

Bishop
Because you've got all these speeches to copy out!

*On **Noote**'s reaction, mix to:*

Scene 12
Studio / Interior / Night

The landing.

*There are four doors: the bathroom is near the top of the stairs, the **Bishop**'s room, with a discreet mitre on the door, is opposite the guest room; **Noote**'s room, with a light showing under the door, is at the other end of the stairs.*

*The grandfather clock strikes three. A light goes on under the guest room door, it opens and the **Dean** enters. He goes quietly to the top of the stairs and exits. After a moment a light goes on under the **Bishop**'s door, which opens and **Toni** enters. She goes to the bathroom and exits.*

Cut to:

Scene 13
Studio / Interior / Night

The hall.

*The **Dean** enters quietly down the stairs and exits to the dining room.*
Cut to:

Scene 14
Studio / Interior / Night

The dining room.

*The **Dean** enters and putting on the light, goes to the table and lifts the silver cover on the dish, and sees that the plate is empty, except for a couple of bacon rinds. Bewildered and disappointed he eats the rinds.*

Cut to:

Scene 15
Studio / Interior / Night

The landing.

***Toni** comes out of the bathroom. As she gets to the **Bishop**'s door, the **Dean** enters behind her at the top of the stairs. Without seeing him, she exits to **Bishop**'s bedroom.*

*Appalled by what he has just seen, the **Dean** notices the light under **Noote**'s door and hurries towards it.*

Cut to:

Scene 16
Studio / Interior / Night

***Noote**'s bedroom.*

***Noote** is dozing at the desk over copying the speeches. The **Bishop** is asleep and snoring loudly. The sound of knocking.*

Dean *(OOV)*
Noote, are you there? Open this door at once!

Noote *waking*
What? Who's that?

Dean *(OOV) banging on door*
Pugh-Critchley. I wish to speak to you immediately!

Bishop *waking*
What— what was that?

Noote *whispering*
It's the Dean, my lord. He wants to speak to me.

Bishop *whispering*
He mustn't know I'm here!

Dean *(OOV) bangs on door and rattles the knob*
Open this door at once, do you hear. At once!

Noote *whispering*
What shall I say?

Bishop *whispering*
Anything, as long as you make him think I'm in my bedroom! *(He pulls the blankets over his head.)*

Noote
Golly!
He goes to the door and carefully opens it a few inches.

Cut to:

Scene 17
Studio / Interior / Night

The landing.

Dean, *at* **Noote**'s *door. The door opens a slit, and* **Noote**'s *anxious face appears in the narrow gap.*

Noote *politely*
Good evening, Dean. Can I help you?

Dean
Where is the Bishop?

Noote
In his bedroom.

Dean
Are you absolutely certain?

Noote
Absolutely. Without a shadow of doubt!

Dean
Then I have to inform you that I am appalled.

Noote
Are you, Dean? Why's that?

Dean
Because I have just seen a woman go in there.

Noote
Oh Moses! Have you?

Dean
Are you aware that there is a woman in the Palace?

Noote *unhappily*
As a matter of fact, yes, Dean, I am— but it isn't as bad as you think— really
it isn't.

Dean
Then you know all about it? Has it been going on long?

Noote
No, Dean. The Bishop is only doing it to oblige the Archdeacon. She's from
the theatre.

Dean
The theatre? This is too much. I am going back to the Deanery.

Noote
But I thought all the doors are locked.

Dean
So they are, but I would rather sleep on the stairs than spend another minute
under this wicked roof.

Noote
But what shall I tell the Bishop?

Dean
You may tell him that I have indeed seen another side of his character. *(He exits
along the landing, watched by **Noote**.)*

Cut to:

Scene 18
Studio / Interior / Night

Noote's bedroom.

Noote closes the door and turns towards the bed.

Noote
My lord. *(He sees that the bed is empty and looks round for the **Bishop**.)* My lord? *(The **Bishop**'s head emerges from under the bed.)* Ah, there you are. I expect you heard all that, didn't you?

*On the **Bishop**'s reaction, mix to:*

Scene 19
Studio / Interior / Day

The hall.

*The **Bishop** enters wearily down the stairs, wearing his dressing gown. **Noote** enters from the study.*

Noote
Good morning, my lord.

Bishop
Is it, Noote?

Noote
Well no, actually it isn't. There's no breakfast.

Bishop
That, Noote, is the least of my worries.

Noote
Shouldn't you be dressed, my lord? Your interview is in half an hour.

Bishop
Interview? The interview is cancelled.

Noote
But what shall I tell the journalist when he arrives?

Bishop
Tell him I'm ill. Very, very ill!

Noote
But you've set such store by this interview— you know, the Bishop of Barming, the invitation to Windsor Castle—

Bishop
By the time the Dean has given his opinion of me, Noote, the only invitation I'm likely to get is to the Tower of London!

Noote *indignantly*
But I've been up all night copying all those speeches.

Doorbell.

Bishop *turning to go upstairs*
If that's the journalist, tell him I'm ill.

Noote opens the door, revealing the **Archdeacon**.

Archdeacon *cheerfully*
Morning, Noote!

Noote
Good morning, Archdeacon. Won't you come in?

Archdeacon
My word, it's a beautiful morning. Is the Bishop in?

Bishop
Yes Henry, I am. And I've got something to say to you—

Archdeacon
There's no need, Bishop. What are friends for? I knew you'd be pleased.

Bishop
Pleased!

Archdeacon
For sending the journalist. Attractive young woman, isn't she?

Bishop
Henry, you don't seem to realise what a mess you have caused— *(He stops.)* What did you say?

Archdeacon
I said she was very attractive.

Noote
You said she was a journalist.

Archdeacon
So she is. Toni Rodgers. She works for the *Church Times.*

Bishop
But I thought she was from the theatre.

Archdeacon
No, no. I met her at the Mitre last night, and she told me she had come to interview you this morning, but had nowhere to stay as they were full up, so I—

Noote
So you sent her here— Oh my lord, if only we'd known.

Bishop
If only, Noote.

Toni enters by the front door carrying a carrier bag.

Toni
Good morning, everyone.

Archdeacon
Good morning, my dear.

Toni
Archdeacon, thank you for sending me here. I've had a most interesting time.

Noote
I didn't know you were up, Miss Rogers.

Toni
Yes, I got up early. I had to go and see the Dean.

Bishop
The Dean!

Toni
What a strange man he is. Does he always sleep on the stairs?

Noote
Only when his wife's away.

Bishop
And did he give you his opinion of me?

Toni
No, I went to tell him not to bother.

Bishop
Why?

Toni
Because the Archdeacon gave me his last night.

Bishop *brightening*
Really? *(He beams at the **Archdeacon**, who beams back and winks reassuringly.)*
Well, I expect you'd like to interview me now?

Toni
Can't we have some breakfast first?

Noote
There isn't any, I'm afraid.

Toni
Yes there is. I've just bought some.

Noote
You have?

Toni
It's the least I could do, after eating yours last night. I've got eggs, bacon and sausages.

Bishop *taking carrier bag from Toni*
Thank you very much, my dear. Here you are, Noote. See how quickly you can cook that.

Noote
Right, my lord. Shan't be a jiffy. *(Exits to kitchen.)*

Bishop
Come along, my dear. Let's go into the dining room. Henry, old friend, have you had breakfast?

Archdeacon *reluctantly*
I'm afraid so, Bishop

Toni
Couldn't you eat some more? I bought lots.

Archdeacon *cheering up*
I could try, couldn't I?

Bishop *putting his arm round his shoulder and leading him towards the dining room*
So you could, Henry. And knowing you, I expect you'll succeed. *(He turns to Toni.)* Now, there are some speeches of mine, I've had specially copied for you that I expect you'd like to glance at…

Roll credits as they go into dining room.

The Bishop Takes a Holiday

Edwin:

This episode was one of several in which we took the characters out of the Cathedral Close and brought them face to face with the rustic community in the diocese. It was fun to write and I enjoyed recalling memories of the figures I had known during my country childhood in east Kent.

In *The Bishop Takes a Holiday*, the senior clergy of St Ogg's discover for themselves that in the country if you don't understand and respect local customs you soon find yourself in trouble.

Pauline:

When, after the second series, Stuart left to join Frank Muir at London Weekend Television, our new director was John Howard Davies. John had had a hugely successful career as a boy actor, playing, at the age of nine, the title role in David Lean's 1948 film *Oliver Twist*. He joined the BBC in 1966, and his first job was as floor manager on our N.F. Simpson series. I remember wanting to take him under my wing, as he seemed still to have vestiges of Oliver Twist about him.

As our director he was pleasant and helpful, but we didn't have the same close relationship with him that we had had with Stuart, nor did he, at that time, have the experience he later gained.

When the series ended, we asked him what he was doing next and he replied that he was to do a show with a group of undergraduates, which he didn't think would catch on. It was *Monty Python*. He went on to do *Faulty Towers* and later became Head of Light Entertainment at the BBC.

The Bishop Takes a Holiday

Series Three
First transmitted on BBC One, 5 February 1969

Scene 1
Studio / Interior / Day

The study.

*A morning in early autumn, the sun pours in through the windows, the **Bishop** sits at his desk in shirtsleeves. **Noote** enters with letter and postcard.*

Noote
The mail, my lord.

Bishop
Anything interesting?

Noote
Yes, my lord. One of those visitation questionnaires you sent out to the parish clergy asking for church attendance figures.

Bishop
Who's this one from?

Noote
The Reverend Arthur Cox, my lord, the incumbent at Little Wickham. *(He hands envelope to **Bishop**.)*

Bishop
Is there anything else?

Noote
Only another postcard from the Dean.

Bishop
Oh? Another view of the prison?

Noote
Yes, my lord. He says "Weather perfect, discipline good, wish you were here."

Bishop
Huh. Who else but the Dean would think of relieving the chaplain of the local prison for a holiday!

Noote
Shall I put it with the others, my lord?

Bishop
Yes, you'd better. He's bound to come looking for them when he gets back.

Noote *putting the card with a row of identical cards on the chimneypiece*
He's certainly been lucky with the weather.

Bishop *sourly*
That's what makes it so galling. When I think of the way it rained when I spent my holiday in Torquay. *(He takes letter out of envelope.)*

Noote
Well, at least you did get a holiday, which is more than I did.

Bishop *outraged*
Holiday? Let me tell you, Noote, that fourteen days in a hotel lounge playing Scrabble with my sister is not my idea of a holiday!

Noote *sympathetically*
Oh no, of course it wouldn't be, not with your spelling.

Bishop *reading the letter*
What a disgrace!

Noote *pleasantly*
Oh, I wouldn't call it that, it's just you never remember "i" before "e" except after "c"—

Bishop *sharply*
I am not talking about my spelling, I'm talking about this— *(Brandishing letter)* This parish of little Wickham is a disgrace— the church attendance has dropped by half. What's the Reverend Cox playing at?

Noote
Doesn't he give an explanation, my lord?

Bishop *reading, mystified*
He says "My dear Lord Bishop, sorry about these figures, it's all a case of Genesis chapter twenty-five, verse twenty-three"— *(He looks baffled.)*

Noote *knowingly*
Oh, of course. "Two nations are in thy womb", my lord.

Bishop *startled*
I beg your pardon?

Noote
You know, "Two manner of people shall be separated from thy bowels".

Bishop
Really Noote, there's no need to be offensive.

Noote
You know, my lord— it's what Isaac's wife, Rebekah, was told by the Lord when she was expecting Esau and Jacob.

Bishop
Oh, that! Of course I know that.

Noote *encouragingly*
There you are. I thought you would.

Bishop *indicating letter*
The point is, what's it got to do with these figures dropping?

Noote
I've no idea.

Bishop
Thank you, Noote, you've been a great help.

Noote *beaming*
That's all right, my lord— it's a pleasure.

*The **Archdeacon** puts head round door.*

Archdeacon
May I come in?

Bishop
Henry of course!

Noote
Good morning, Archdeacon.

*The **Archdeacon** enters. He wears tropical suit with clerical collar and carries a Panama hat.*

Bishop
My word, you look smart. Have you come to say goodbye?

Noote
Just leaving for the airport, Archdeacon?

Archdeacon *gloomily*
No, it's all off, I'm afraid.

Noote *horrified*
Not your week in Spain, Archdeacon?

Archdeacon
Yes. I've just heard. They've made a mess of the bookings.

Bishop
But haven't they offered you another date, Henry?

Archdeacon
Yes, next week, but that will be too late.

Bishop *surprised*
Too late Henry? Why?

Archdeacon
The sherry festival will be over.

Noote
Oh, Archdeacon— how disappointing.

Bishop
What rotten luck, Henry. I am sorry. Still, perhaps it's for the best. Remember what happened the last time you went to a sherry festival!

Noote
Oh, yes, Archdeacon, you were dreadfully ill.

Archdeacon
That was the water.

Bishop *doubtfully*
Well, Henry, I know you said it was the water.

Archdeacon
It was, Bishop, definitely; I used it for cleaning my teeth. *(Thoughtfully)* Mark you, I would have known better this time—

Bishop
Well, I'm very sorry about it. Still, all I can say is you're in good company. Noote and I were just lamenting the fact that our holidays went wrong. Weren't we, Noote?

Noote
Yes, my lord. Still, we can all be glad for the Dean, can't we?

*Pause. The **Bishop** and **Archdeacon** exchange a look.*

Bishop
Well Henry, I must say you've come to see us at just the right moment.

Archdeacon *brightening*
Have I, Bishop? Oh, thank you very much. *(He goes to decanter and pours sherry.)*

Bishop
That isn't quite what I meant.

Archdeacon *stopping, decanter in hand*
Isn't it? *(Looks at glass.)* Oh I beg your pardon. *(Beams. Pours some more and lifts glass.)* Cheers!

Bishop
I meant, Henry, that I've had a visitation return from Little Wickham.

Archdeacon *sitting down happily*
Little Wickham? Oh, a charming spot.

Noote
The incumbent is the Reverend Arthur Cox, Archdeacon.

Archdeacon
Yes, I know. He's got a splendid cook. She's very good at toad-in-the-hole.

Bishop
He may have a good cook, Henry, but his church attendance figures are a disgrace.

Archdeacon

Well, he's got a bit of a problem there.

Noote

Yes, Archdeacon— "Two nations are in thy womb and two manners of people shall be separated from thy bowels".

Archdeacon *startled*

I say— steady on!

Bishop

Do you know what the problem is Henry?

Archdeacon

Yes, Bishop. There's a new man at the Methodist chapel, and he's a very good preacher.

Bishop

What? You mean he's poaching the congregation?

Archdeacon

Yes, Bishop.

Bishop

Dear me, this is serious.

Noote

Is it, my lord? After all, does it really matter which church the people go to, so long as they actually go?

Bishop *outraged*

What *do* you mean, Noote? Of course it matters.

Noote

But after all it's been suggested we should join up with the Methodists.

Bishop *reprovingly*

No, Noote. It's been suggested that the Methodists should join up with us! Henry, something must be done and quickly.

Archdeacon *eagerly*

Do you want me to go over there, Bishop?

Bishop

Well, would you mind?

Archdeacon
Mind? I'd be delighted.

Bishop *surprised*
Really? Is Little Wickham as nice as all that?

Noote
Oh, yes, my lord. I went there once, and there's a lovely little early Norman church with a beautiful barrel-vault roof, and the font's a perfect treasure—isn't it, Archdeacon?

Archdeacon
Yes, and so's the cook.

Bishop
You keep talking about this cook, Henry.

Archdeacon *apologetically*
Do I? Sorry, Bishop.

Bishop
Is she really that good?

Archdeacon *solemnly*
Well, until I had eaten her toad-in-the-hole, I'd never been able properly to imagine the afterlife.

Bishop *impressed*
Really? As good as that!

Archdeacon
And then there's the vicarage itself, with its garden and little stream.

Bishop *interested*
Ah, a stream. No fish, I suppose?

Archdeacon
Only brown trout.

Bishop
Really? Do you know, Henry, I suddenly see the solution to this problem.

Noote
You do, my lord?

Bishop

Absolutely. Noote, take a letter—

Noote *hurriedly picking up pad and pencil*
Right, my lord— who's it to?

Bishop
The Reverend Arthur Cox, Little Wickham— My dear Cox, I fully appreciate your problem and suggest you take a fortnight's holiday starting tomorrow. I have decided to take over your parish personally and, with the aid of my staff, am confident I shall be able to fight this battle for you and win it.

Noote
Golly. But how my lord?

Bishop *decisively*
House-to-house visiting, Noote: to get them back into the church, and then, once they're there, I shall preach.

Noote *anxiously*
But my lord, can we go off and leave the Cathedral like this— while the Dean is away? Is Little Wickham so important— such a small village?

Bishop *reprovingly*
The Church today, Noote, is not so strong that it can afford to see its membership dwindle in this alarming manner without a battle.

Noote
I suppose not.

Bishop
And it will be a battle, make no mistake, but a battle that is our bounden duty to fight. Don't you agree, Henry?

Archdeacon
Absolutely Bishop! Especially if you like toad-in-the-hole.

Cut to:

Film / Morning

The archway of the Cathedral Close.

To the theme of "Onward Christian Soldiers", simply played on the organ, the **Archdeacon** *drives his open Morris 1000 through the arch and into the high street* of St Ogg's. The **Bishop**, dressed in tweeds and clerical collar, sits beside him, and **Noote** is crammed in the back among cases and fishing tackle.

Car drives through street, leaving the main road for a minor one, then the minor one for a country lane. The music builds as the car goes deeper and deeper into the country, then suddenly comes to a grinding halt as it meets a herd of cows blocking the way. The car stops and the clerics wait. Eventually the cows clear the lane, which reveals a sign: "Little Wickham". The **Archdeacon** starts the car as the music begins again.

Main Street of Little Wickham. Car approaches and drives down road. "Onwards Christian Soldiers" rises to a crescendo. **Noote** draws the **Bishop**'s attention to the Methodist church, which stands in the main street and is a galvanised iron shed. In front of it stands the Minister; he smiles and waves at the **Bishop**, who ignores him.

The **Archdeacon** draws the **Bishop**'s attention to the lych-gate, beside which stands **Loder**, the sexton, and **Mrs Plummer**. **Loder** bows respectfully and **Mrs Plummer** bobs a curtsey. The **Bishop** waves graciously as they turn into the drive of the Vicarage.

The Vicarage is a most inviting house, with **Mrs Shoebridge** in her apron waiting outside the open door.

The car stops and with it the music, which is replaced by birdsong and country noises.

The clerics get out of car, and **Mrs Shoebridge** takes the **Bishop** and **Archdeacon** into the house leaving **Noote** to deal with the luggage.

Scene 2
Studio / Interior / Day

The hall of the Vicarage.

The **Bishop** and **Archdeacon** enter, followed by **Mrs Shoebridge**.

Mrs Shoebridge
His Reverence said I was to make you comfortable, my lord.

Bishop
Thank you, my good woman.

Archdeacon
We can rely on you, Mrs Shoebridge.

Mrs Shoebridge
Thank you, Mr Archdeacon. He said he hoped you'd enjoy your holiday, my lord.

Bishop
Holiday? Oh, this is no holiday, we are here to work. I have a sermon to concentrate on.

Noote enters with fishing equipment.

Noote
I'll just stick your fishing rods down here, shall I, my lord?

Bishop *reacting*
What? Oh, yes.

Mrs Shoebridge *firmly*
Not there, sir, if you please. In the corner. I'll see to them later.

Noote *put in his place*
Oh. Yes, of course. *(He hurriedly puts equipment down where indicated.)*

Mrs Shoebridge *opening study door*
If you will go into the study, gentlemen.

Bishop
Oh, thank you, Mrs Shoebridge.

*Exeunt **Bishop** and **Archdeacon**.*

Scene 3
Studio / Interior / Day

The study at Little Wickham.

A comfortable, unpretentious country room. It has two deep-set windows with shutters and window seats. From one the church can be clearly seen, the other overlooks the garden. Bookcases line the walls containing well-read books. There are two comfortable armchairs with faded floral loose covers, bleached almost white by the sun, which streams in through the windows.

Design note: *The room should be the sort of low-pitched eighteenth-century room that has white panelling and an old tiled floor that you have to step down into and mind your head. A roll-topped desk, faded framed photographs, a portrait in oils* *of an eighteenth-century parson, and amateur watercolours. A sense that it has all happened, rather than been arranged.*

Bishop *and* **Archdeacon** *enter.*

Bishop *approvingly*
What a delightful room. *(Glancing out of the window)* And you can see the garden from here, with the stream.

Archdeacon *sitting in chair*
What did I tell you, Bishop? My word, this chair is comfortable.

Bishop *sitting, impressed*
Oh— so is this one.

Noote *enters and goes to window overlooking church.*

Noote *appreciatively*
Oh, what a little honey!

Archdeacon *rising, interested*
Really? Where?

Noote
The church, Archdeacon.

Archdeacon *losing interest*
Oh yes, very nice. *(He sits back in chair.)*

Mrs Shoebridge *enters.*

Mrs Shoebridge
Now, gentlemen— about lunch.

All *expectantly*
Yes, oh yes, lunch, etc.

Mrs Shoebridge
I haven't got anything special.

All *disappointed*
Oh.

Mrs Shoebridge
Only toad-in-the-hole.

All *brightening*
Ah!

Mrs Shoebridge
It will be ready in about an hour. I've got to go to the shop, so if you'd like to make yourselves comfortable.

Bishop
Thank you, dear lady, we will.

Mrs Shoebridge *at door*
I shan't be long.

Noote *politely*
Right. Well, I'll just take the cases upstairs.

Mrs Shoebridge *firmly*
Thank you, sir. I'd rather you left them alone. I'll deal with them.

Noote *squashed*
Oh yes— of course.

Mrs Shoebridge *cheerfully*
I'll be off then. *(Exits.)*

Bishop
Well, we've got an hour, Henry.

Archdeacon
Yes, Bishop: an hour till lunch.

Noote *eagerly*
Just time to start house-to-house visiting, my lord!

Bishop
Good idea, Noote.

Archdeacon *gloomily*
Oh dear, must we?

Bishop
No, Henry, don't you disturb yourself—

Archdeacon *gratefully*
Oh, thank you, Bishop.

Noote
So it's just you and me, my lord?

Bishop
No, it's just you, Noote. Off you go. I have a great deal of work to do preparing my sermon for Sunday.

Archdeacon
Do you want me to leave you alone?

Bishop *casually*
No, Henry, you stay where you are and have a rest. I shall go and work down by the stream. *(Exits.)*

Scene 4
Studio / Interior / Day

The hall.

Bishop *enters and picks up fishing rods.*

Noote *entering*
Oh, are you taking your fishing rods with you, my lord?

Bishop
Yes, Noote. They'll help me to think.

Noote *reacts. Cut to:*

Film

The gate of the Vicarage.

Mrs Shoebridge *with shopping basket comes out of the gate and goes up street.*

Mrs Plummer, *with a basket of eggs and bunch of chrysanthemums, who has clearly been on the lookout, waits till she is out of sight, then hurries up the drive.*

Cut to:

Scene 5
Studio / Interior / Day

The hall.

*The **Bishop** selecting fly from box.*

Bishop *thoughtfully*
A Zulu or a butcher? The Zulu, I think.

Noote *pointedly*
Yes, that should help you to think, my lord.

*The **Bishop** reacts.*

Doorbell rings.

Bishop
Who can that be?

***Noote** opens door, revealing **Mrs Plummer**.*

Noote
Oh, good morning.

Mrs Plummer
Good morning, sir. I'm Mrs Plummer.

Bishop
How do you do, madam, won't you come in?

***Mrs Plummer** enters eagerly. She looks round with great interest.*

Mrs Plummer *bobbing eagerly*
Thank you ever so much, my lord. We heard you were coming.

Bishop *flattered*
Really?

Mrs Plummer
So I thought I'd just pop round to welcome you.

Noote
Isn't that charming, my lord?

Bishop
Yes, indeed. Most kind.

Mrs Plummer *indicating basket*
I've brought you some eggs for your tea.

Bishop *taking them*
Really? Eggs— how delicious!

Mrs Plummer
I've just collected them from right under the hen.

Bishop
Feel them, Noote— they're still warm.

Noote *not liking to touch them*
Oh look, my lord— there's a feather.

Mrs Plummer
I don't expect you see anything like this in the town.

Bishop *enthusiastically*
We certainly don't, do we, Noote?

Noote
No my lord. And look at those beautiful flowers.

Mrs Plummer
I thought you might like them too, my lord, to cheer you up.

Bishop
How kind. But why don't you put them in the church?

Mrs Plummer *a gleam in her eye*
Really? May I?

Bishop *amused*
Of course, dear lady.

Mrs Plummer
Oh, how lovely. I'll just pop through your garden, shall I? Now, this minute?

Bishop *graciously*
But of course. At once.

Mrs Plummer
Well then, I'll say ta-ta, your lordship.

Noote
Oh, ta-ta— I mean, good morning.

Bishop
Good morning. And thank you for calling.

Mrs Plummer
It was a pleasure, your lordship. *(Exits.)*

Noote
Oh, wasn't that charming, my lord?

Bishop
Charming, absolutely charming. *(He opens study door and calls out.)* Henry. *(He exits to study.)*

Scene 6
Studio / Interior / Day

The study.

Bishop *enters with eggs, followed by* ***Noote.***

Bishop
Henry, look at these.

Noote
They're from a hen, Archdeacon.

Archdeacon
Really? Who'd have thought it?

Bishop
A dear woman brought them.

Noote
And some lovely chrysanthemums.

Archdeacon
Where are they?

Bishop
I told her to put them in the church.

Archdeacon
Was that wise?

Noote
What do you mean, Archdeacon?

Archdeacon
It may not be her job.

Bishop
What's that got to do with it, Henry?

Archdeacon
Well, people are funny in the country, you know.

Bishop *crossly*
Nonsense— people in the country are extremely sensible. After all— they are close to nature.

Archdeacon
Yes, Bishop— sometimes a bit too close.

A knock on the study door.

Bishop
Hullo? Another caller, to make us welcome.

*Noote opens door, revealing **Loder**, cap in hand.*

Loder *(respectfully)*
Morning, my lord. I'm Loder, the sexton.

Bishop
Ah, sexton, how do you do?

Shakes hands.

Loder
I'm well— thank you kindly, my lord. His Reverence said I was to see you all right and wanting for nothing.

Bishop
Oh, how kind. *(Front doorbell rings.)* My word, we are popular this morning.

Noote
I'll go, my lord. *(Exits.)*

Scene 7
Studio / Interior / Day

The hall.

Noote *enters from study and opens the front door, revealing* ***Urchin***.

Noote
Yes?

Urchin
Mr Loder? I want Mr Loder.

Noote
Can I give him a message?

Urchin
Mum said tell him young Tommy's gone.

Noote
Gone?

Urchin
Snuffed it.

Noote
Oh, dear. I am sorry.

Urchin
Mum said run all the way and you'd give me something.

Noote
Oh, did she?

Urchin *firmly*
Yes.

Noote *feels in pocket*
Well, here you are then.

Hands coin.

Urchin
Cor!

Looks at coin, spits on it and exits running. **Noote** *exits to study.*

Scene 8
Studio / Interior / Day

The study.

Noote *enters.*

Noote
Mr Loder— I'm afraid I have bad news.

Loder
Not young Tommy? (**Noote** *nods.*) I feared this might happen. Will you excuse me, my lord? I must go and ring the passing bell.

Bishop
Of course, of course, I'm so sorry.

Loder
We shall have to arrange the funeral.

Bishop
Of course, of course.

Exit **Loder.**

Bishop
How sad.

Archdeacon
Very sad, Bishop.

Noote
Most sad. What is the passing bell, my lord?

Bishop
One of those quaint old customs, Noote. They toll the bell, for the number of years the deceased has lived.

Noote
I see. One fears that young Tommy will not require many tolls.

Bishop
One fears not, Noote.
Bell begins to toll.

Bishop
Oh, there it is now.

They rise.

Noote *counting*
One, two, three—

Cut to:

Scene 9
Studio / Interior / Day

A corner of the Belfry.

Loder tolling bell.

Cut to:

Scene 10
Studio / Interior / Day

The study.

Noote
Nineteen, twenty, twenty-one—

Bishop
We can rejoice he reached manhood, Henry.

Archdeacon
Indeed, yes, Bishop.

Cut to:

Scene 11
Studio / Interior / Day

The Belfry.

Loder *tolling bell.*

Cut to:

Scene 12
Studio / Interior / Day

The study.

Noote
Forty-five, forty-six, forty-seven—

Cut to:

Scene 13
Studio / Interior / Day

The Belfry.

Loder *tolling bell.*

Cut to:

Scene 14
Studio / Interior / Day

The study.

Noote
Seventy-eight, seventy-nine, eighty—

Cut to:

Scene 15
Studio / Interior / Day

The Belfry.

Loder *tolling bell.*

Cut to:

Scene 16
Studio / Interior / Day

The study.

The clerics are sitting down.

Noote
One hundred and four, one hundred and five, one hundred and six.

Bell stops.

Noote *impressed*
One hundred and six— Moses!

Cut to:

Scene 17
Studio / Interior / Day

The Belfry.

Loder *is drinking glass of beer and replacing it on tray held by the* **Urchin.**

Cut to:

Scene 18
Studio / Interior / Day

The study.

Bishop *brightening*
Perhaps it's not quite so sad after all, Henry?

Door flies open, and **Mrs Shoebridge** *enters in hat and coat.*

Bishop *rising*
Ah, Mrs Shoebridge.

Archdeacon *rising*
Is lunch ready?

Mrs Shoebridge
No, and it won't be.

Bishop
I beg your pardon?

Mrs Shoebridge
I'm leaving.

Noote
But you can't!

Mrs Shoebridge *fiercely*
Don't you tell me what I can do, you young whippersnapper!

Noote reacts and goes behind Bishop.

Bishop
But, my good woman, what's wrong? What's upset you?

Mrs Shoebridge
You have.

Bishop *taken aback*
Me?

Mrs Shoebridge *indignantly*
Telling that woman to put her nasty chrysanths in my church. The cheek of it!

Bishop
What?

Mrs Shoebridge
If my flowers don't suit you— you can do without my cooking as well, and good riddance!

Exits, banging door.

Archdeacon *despairingly*
Bishop, what have you done?

Noote *reproachfully*
Oh, my lord—

Bishop *defensively*
Well— there are other cooks.

Archdeacon
Not like her, Bishop!

Noote
No, my lord— remember what the Archdeacon said about the afterlife and toad-in-the-hole.

Bishop
Oh, I'd forgotten that.

Archdeacon *emphatically*
We've got to get her back!

Bishop
Well, there's only one way. We shall just have to take those flowers out of the church. Come on.

Mix to:

Scene 19
Studio / Exterior / Day

The lych-gate, with path to the church behind.

Loder stands with spade. **Bishop, Archdeacon** and **Noote** *enter.*

Loder
Did you hear the bell, my lord?

Bishop
We did, sexton. Right, Noote, go and get them.

Noote
Very well, my lord.

Exit **Noote**.

Bishop
I thought you said he was *young* Tommy.

Loder

That's right, my lord. *Old* Tommy's son. Will it be all right to hold his funeral at two o'clock on Saturday, my lord?

Bishop

Of course, of course. Will many people attend?

Loder

All his family, my lord.

Bishop

What about the rest of the village?

Loder

Oh, yes. Harry Smart will be there too.

Bishop *surprised*

Harry Smart? You mean everyone else in the village is related to the deceased?

Loder *nodding*

Everyone, my lord! His wife had twelve children, you see. Then there was thirty-nine grandchildren, so naturally there was seventy-five great-grandchildren—

Bishop

But even so, there are more people than that in this village.

Loder *agreeing*

Of course, my lord, I said his *wife* had twelve children.

Bishop reacts.

Loder

Well, I must go and dig the grave.

Noote enters with flowers.

Noote

Here they are, my lord.

Bishop

Oh, give them to me, Noote.

Loder

Here, just a moment.

Bishop
What's the matter?

Loder
Aren't they the flowers Elsie Plummer just put in there?

Bishop *firmly*
Yes, and that's why they are going straight out again. I'm taking them to the rubbish heap myself.

Loder *his manner changing*
Then you'd better take this, my lord, you'll need it. *(Hands spade.)*
Bishop
Whatever for?

Loder
To dig the grave. I'm not doing it.

Noote
Oh, Mr Loder, why ever not?

Loder
Because Elsie Plummer is my sister!

Exit **Loder**.

Archdeacon
Oh, Bishop, you've done it again.

Bishop
Well, how was I to know? Anyway, at least Mrs Shoebridge will come back.

Noote *eagerly*
Oh, yes, and I'm really ready for some toad-in-the-hole.

Bishop
And you'll need it for this afternoon, Noote.

Noote *puzzled*
This afternoon? Oh, you mean my visiting?

Bishop
Not visiting, Noote— digging. Here.

Hands spade.

Noote
Oh, my lord.

*On **Noote**'s reaction, mix to:*

Scene 20
Studio / Interior / Day

The study.

***Bishop** and **Archdeacon** sit in armchairs. Front door slams, they rise eagerly.*
Archdeacon *excitedly*
That's her, Bishop!

Bishop
At last. *(Calls)* Mrs Shoebridge, Mrs Shoebridge?

***Mrs Shoebridge** enters.*

Mrs Shoebridge
Did you call, my lord?

Bishop *happily*
I certainly did.

Archdeacon *happily*
You've come back.

Mrs Shoebridge
Yes— to get my things.

Bishop
But we've taken the flowers out.

Mrs Shoebridge *softening*
Have you?

Bishop
Yes, we threw them away.

Archdeacon
Right away.

Bishop
Far away!

Archdeacon
As far as possible!

Mrs Shoebridge
Really?

Bishop
Yes, so you'll come back now, won't you?

Mrs Shoebridge
I'm sorry, I can't. I've got another job.

Bishop
What? But you can't have—

Archdeacon
Where?

Mrs Shoebridge
At the Manse. The Methodist Minister's asked me to look after him and do the flowers in his chapel.

Bishop *horrified*
Oh, no. Won't you change your mind?

Mrs Shoebridge
Sorry, my lord, it's all arranged. I must get my things.

Exit **Mrs Shoebridge**.

Bishop
Henry, this is a disaster.

Archdeacon
It's more than that, Bishop— it's almost a calamity.

Bishop
I don't know how we're going to face Cox. One thing's certain, we've got to get the congregation back now.

Archdeacon *rising gloomily*
I suppose we'd better start this house-to-house visiting.

Bishop
There's no need for that, Henry.

Archdeacon *relieved*
Isn't there? Good. *(He sits down again.)*

Bishop
No, they'll all come to the church for the funeral.

Archdeacon
Of course— and that's when you'll preach a sermon?

Bishop
A sermon? Not just *a* sermon, Henry, I shall preach the finest sermon of my entire ministry. A sermon which will ensure that when Cox returns he will find a congregation the size of which he has never even dreamed.

Archdeacon *admiringly*
Well done, Bishop. So there's nothing more to worry about?

Bishop
Nothing, Henry, nothing. *(Pauses.)* Well, just one thing.

Archdeacon
What's that?

Bishop
I haven't written it yet.

Mix to:

Film

The church clock striking two.

Scene 21
Studio / Exterior / Day

The lych-gate.

Bishop and ***Archdeacon*** *wearing their vestments.*

Bishop *looking at watch*
Two o'clock, Henry, the cortège should be here by now.

Archdeacon
Have you got your sermon, Bishop?

Bishop *indicating sermon notes*
Rather, Henry. And— although I say it myself— it is the best one I've ever written.

Archdeacon
Well done— you've certainly worked hard.

Bishop *groaning*
Oh, don't! To be here in this beautiful place, with my fishing rods and that lovely little stream— and not to get near it once! Still, Henry, there are more important things in life than enjoying oneself, aren't there?

Archdeacon
So they say, Bishop.

Noote enters. He is also wearing his vestments and is bent almost double.

Noote
I've put the books out, my lord, but you'll have to announce the hymns— I couldn't reach up to the hymn board.

Bishop
Really, Noote, can't you stand up any straighter than that? You look ridiculous.

Noote
No, my lord, I'm absolutely locked.

Bishop
All this fuss over a bit of digging!

*The **Urchin** enters.*

Urchin
Hullo.

Bishop *taken aback*
Oh, hullo, my child.

Urchin
You waiting for the funeral?

Bishop
Yes. Have you seen them?

Urchin
They're coming up the road. There's lots of them.

Bishop *pleased*
Oh, are there?

Archdeacon
That's good.

Noote
Oh yes, isn't it?

Urchin
Here they come! Look!

Film

The cortège with the coffin on a cart pulled by an old horse, followed by a crowd of people, approaches.

Cut to:

Scene 22
Studio / Exterior / Day

The lych-gate.

The clerics adopt suitable expressions in anticipation of the funeral.

Cut to:

Film

The cortège passes in front of the lych-gate and the clerics without stopping.

Scene 23
Studio / Exterior / Day

The lych-gate.

The clerics look at each other in consternation.

Bishop
What on earth...?

Archdeacon
Where are they going?

Noote
Oh, look what they're doing!

Cut to:

Film

*The **Methodist Minister**, in gown and bands, comes out of the chapel. The cortège stops opposite him.*

Cut to:

Scene 24
Studio / Exterior / Day

The lych-gate.

Bishop *aghast*
But they can't—

Archdeacon *gloomily*
It looks as though they have, Bishop.

Bishop *exasperated*
Oh, this really is too much! *(Sighs heavily and looks at his sermon.)* All that hard work for nothing! *(He tears up his sermon notes to pieces and flings them on the ground, where they land in a puddle of water.)*

Noote
Oh, I call that mean, I really think they might have told us. To go to the Methodist chapel like that—

Urchin *protesting*
But they ain't—

Bishop *reacting*
What?

Archdeacon
Why ain't they?

Noote
Where are they going then?

Urchin
The pub.

Bishop *mystified*
The pub?

Noote *explaining*
Short for public house, my lord.

Bishop *irritably*
I know that! But whatever for?

Urchin
He wanted to be carried past it.

Noote
Oh, look, my lord. Look!

Archdeacon
Bishop, do you see what they are doing?

Cut to:

Film

The cortège is turning round and returning to the church.

Cut to:

Scene 25
Studio / Exterior / Day

The lych-gate.

Noote *happily*
Look, my lord, they're coming back. Isn't that perfectly splendid of them?

Archdeacon
So you'll be able to preach your sermon after all.

Bishop *happily*
So I will, Henry, so I will— *(He is confused.)*— But my sermon? Where is it?
It's gone.

Archdeacon
But you were holding it just now.

Bishop *in panic*
I know, it was in my hands— but where is it now? Noote, where have you put
it?

Noote
I haven't put it anywhere, my lord. You had it.

Bishop
Then where is it?

They begin to search each other, turning round in circles.

Urchin
You said you didn't want it no more. You chucked it away. *(He points to the
sodden remains of the torn sermon in the puddle.)*

*On **Bishop**'s horrified reaction, mix to:*

Scene 26
Studio / Interior / Day

The hall of the Vicarage.

*Close up of black hat on hat stand, **Bishop**, **Noote** and **Archdeacon** enter, chat-
ting happily, they all carry hats.*

Noote *warmly*
Oh, it was a splendid sermon, absolutely splendid!

Bishop *grudgingly*
Well I suppose it did the trick.

Noote
I'm certain it did, my lord. The things everybody said about it afterwards!

Archdeacon
And they're all coming to Matins tomorrow, Bishop.

Bishop *grudgingly*
So they are, Henry, so they are! Well our visit here has born the fruit we hoped for, although not quite in the way I anticipated. But thank you, Henry, for stepping into the breach.

Archdeacon *modestly*
That's all right, Bishop, think nothing of it. My sermon on turning water into wine always goes with a bang.

Bishop *drily*
So I observed. However, let us rejoice that the sheep are returning to the fold.

Archdeacon
All except one!

Bishop
Mrs Shoebridge. Yes, well it's a pity about that, but you can't have everything can you?

Ring at doorbell.

Bishop
Who can that be?

*Opens door to reveal **Mrs Shoebridge** with case.*

Bishop
Mrs Shoebridge!

Archdeacon
Mrs Shoebridge!

Noote
Mrs Shoebridge!

Bishop
Have you come back to collect something?

Mrs Shoebridge
Yes, my lord. My old job!

Bishop
What?

Mrs Shoebridge *beaming*
Well, my lord, when you went and took those flowers out of the church I realised it had been a mistake— and then, today, when you preached that lovely sermon Archdeacon, well— I just had to come back.

Bishop
Dear lady, we're most grateful you've changed your mind.

Archdeacon
We certainly are.

Mrs Shoebridge
Right, well I'll just get my hat and coat off, tidy up the church and start getting dinner.

Archdeacon *excitedly*
Really? What will you get?

Mrs Shoebridge
I hadn't thought— What about toad-in-the-hole?

Archdeacon *ecstatically*
What indeed!

Mrs Shoebridge
Right. I shan't be long. *(Exits.)*

Bishop
Well, Henry, hang up your hat, and we'll go and sit down. *(Looks at hat stand, sees hat.)* Oh, you have.

Archdeacon *producing hat*
No, I haven't.

Bishop
Oh, is that yours, Noote?

Noote *producing hat*
No, my lord.

Bishop
Then who's is it?

Noote
It must be Mr Cox's, my lord.

Bishop
But it wasn't there when we went out.

Archdeacon
He must have come home, Bishop.

Noote
Oh yes— while we were in church…

Bishop
But he's not due back for a week.

Archdeacon *beaming*
Never mind, Bishop, let's go and tell him the good news.

Noote *excitedly*
Oh yes, my lord. Do let's, do let's, do let's!

Bishop *opening study door*
Right! Come on.

Exeunt to study.

Scene 27
Studio / Interior / Day

The study.

Clerics enter, in a chair with his back to the door is a figure.

Bishop *graciously*
Ah— Mr Cox. Good afternoon—

*The figure rises and turns, it is the **Dean**.*

Dean
Good afternoon, my lord.

Bishop *nonplussed*
Dean— what are you doing here?

Dean *grimly*
I might ask the same question.

Archdeacon
Have you come out of gaol?

Noote
Did you enjoy your holiday?

Dean
Until yesterday.

Bishop
Oh, did it rain?

Dean
Yesterday, I heard to my amazement that you, my lord, had deserted the Cathedral and with the whole of your staff had come out here for a holiday.

Bishop *indignantly*
A holiday? This isn't a holiday.

Dean
Isn't it?

Noote *rubbing back*
Oh no, Dean, we haven't had a holiday.

Dean
Then why have you come out here?

Bishop *warmly*
Because the Church's interests required we should, Dean. This parish was in an extremely run down state, and I realised that only my immediate and personal intervention could stop the rot.

Dean
And have you stopped it?

Noote *warmly*
Oh yes, Dean. We have, you see the Archdeacon—

Bishop *interrupting*
I think we can say we have succeeded, Dean.

Dean
Then I appear to have been misinformed.

Bishop
I think you have, Dean.

Dean
Do you intend to stay on, my lord?

Bishop
Oh, well— Yes— Henry, I think we should stay another week, don't you?

Archdeacon *firmly*
Now, Bishop— definitely.

Bishop *(to Dean)*
Just to see everything is all right.

Dean
Very well, I will return to St Ogg's. *(Goes to door.)* I owe you an apology, my lord.

Bishop
Not at all, Dean. A slight misunderstanding, nothing more. Let me show you out.

Dean
Thank you. *(Stops.)* I must just get my eggs.

Noote
Eggs?

Dean
Ah yes— here they are. *(He picks up basket of eggs.)*

Bishop
Where did you get those?

Dean
While I was waiting for you, my lord, a dear woman brought them to the door.

Bishop *suspiciously*
Really?

Archdeacon *anxiously*
She didn't bring anything else, did she?

Dean
Only some flowers, Archdeacon.

Noote *alarmed*
Flowers?

Bishop *anxiously*
What did you do with them?

Dean
I suggested she should wait until the service was over and put them in the church.

Bishop
What?

Noote
Oh, no!

Archdeacon
Oh, Bishop.

They turn and rush to door, fling it open to reveal Mrs Shoebridge in hat, buttoning up her coat.

Bishop *pleading*
We can explain—

Noote
It was a mistake—

Archdeacon
Oh, don't go— please don't go!

Without a word she turns and goes.

Roll credits.

*The clerics turn menacingly and look at the **Dean**. The **Dean** backs away, round the room. They follow him into hall. He backs out of door.*

The Affair at Cookham Lock

Edwin:

The character of the Dean of St Ogg's, the Right Reverend Lionel Pugh-Critchley D.D., was forged from two people. The first was the Venerable Julius Hare D.D. (1795–1855), Vicar of Herstmonceux and Archdeacon of Lewes, a former Cambridge don, long remembered for preaching incomprehensible sermons lasting several hours to the country people of his parish in an unheated church in winter; the second was the neighbour who lived in the flat above us, a company secretary who had been an officer in the navy, who seemed to have the impression that, because we lived underneath him in our basement flat, we were under his command, so was forever sending us notes and making rules. I remember a particular correspondence about the water tank on the landing going on for several months.

So when we were fitting the Dean into the plot, we only had to ask ourselves how Archdeacon Hare or our neighbour would behave for the Dean's comportment to become clear.

Pauline:

This script was part of the third series, transmitted in 1968, long before the advent of home recording. In it our clerics are anxious not to miss the last episode of a thriller they have been watching on television, during which the name of the murderer will be revealed.

We based *The Affair at Cookham Lock* on the highly successful and long-running Paul Temple radio series broadcast over many years on the BBC Home Service. All episodes of Paul Temple were set in the Thames Valley, where it was always summer, and tea was in the garden under the weeping willow. The plot involved the rituals of the middle class being interrupted by a man with a foreign accent moving into the village for mysterious and unsavoury reasons, and a few peripheral baddies to muddy the waters. This state of affairs was unfailingly resolved by the gifted amateur sleuth, Paul Temple, accompanied by his wife, Steve, and his loyal assistant (who provided character interest with his working-class accent) – so by the end of each series, between the three of them, the nasty foreigner would be safely behind bars.

The Affair at Cookham Lock

Series Three
First transmitted on BBC One, 12 February 1969

Scene 1
Studio / Interior / Day

The study.

*Through the French windows the Cathedral is seen to be floodlit. The **Bishop** and the **Archdeacon** enter. **The Bishop** carries a tray with coffee, cups, cream jug etc.*

Bishop
You don't mean it, Henry?

Archdeacon
I do, Bishop. It all came out last week when you were taking the Confirmation class at Ringmold.

Bishop
Dr Prentis not properly qualified— well, well. *(Suddenly)* Then how's he managed to treat his patients?

Archdeacon
That's where he's been so clever; he's been reading it up at nights.

Bishop
Of course! That's why he always looks so tired!

Archdeacon *solemnly*
You realise what this means, Bishop?

Bishop *shocked*
Henry! You're not suggesting Dr Prentis murdered Mrs Winters?

Archdeacon *firmly*
I certainly am.

Bishop
But the afternoon she was killed, Dr Prentis went to Maidenhead. Otto Klein saw him in the antique shop.

Archdeacon
He only saw him from behind. He could have been mistaken.

Bishop
No, Henry. You are quite wrong. Still, there's only one way to find out.

*The **Bishop** goes to the television set – an early model – and switches on.*

Archdeacon *eagerly*
Is it half-past already, Bishop?

Bishop
No, but the old set takes a bit of time to warm up. Will you have some coffee?

Archdeacon
Please, Bishop. I always enjoy your coffee.

Bishop *pouring coffee*
No, I can't believe it was Dr Prentis. I still think it was that lock-keeper.

Archdeacon
No, Bishop, he was working the lock all the afternoon. People saw him.

Bishop
It could have been his wife. Remember, Henry, it was raining and they said he was wearing oilskins and a sou'wester— and she is a tall woman.

Archdeacon *appreciatively*
Yes, a fine woman, most striking.

Bishop
That was not quite what I meant. Your coffee. (***Bishop** about to hand coffee to **Archdeacon** looks out of the window. He stops and puts coffee back on the tray.*) Hullo, it's gone wrong again.

Archdeacon *disappointed*
Is the cream off?

Bishop *excitedly*
No, the cathedral floodlighting, it is blinking again.

Archdeacon *chuckles*
Oh dear, the Dean will be upset!

Bishop *mischievously*
Won't he? I think I'd better ring and tell him, don't you?

Archdeacon *beaming*
Oh, I say, isn't that a bit hard, Bishop?

Bishop
Well he deserves it! *(Goes to phone and dials.)* I told him to get a proper firm of lighting engineers in, but no— he could do it himself— and what's the result? It's gone wrong four times in the first two days. *(Into phone)* Hullo? Dean? I'm sorry to disturb you, but I've happened to notice that the floodlighting has gone wrong again. *(Winks at **Archdeacon**.)* Yes, I'm sure it is only teething troubles— but had you called in a proper firm of lighting engineers as I suggested— hardly economy, Dean, if it keeps going wrong! And another thing, that light you put in my mulberry tree is shining directly into my bedroom window. Not at all, Dean. I thought you would like to know. Good evening, Dean. *(Smiling broadly, the **Bishop** replaces receiver.)* How about that, Henry?

Archdeacon
You certainly told him, Bishop.

Bishop
I did, didn't I? And I enjoyed it! Oh, I know I shouldn't, but even a Bishop is human.

Archdeacon *solemnly*
Well, I call it a scandal.

Bishop *anxiously*
Really? Have I gone too far? Should I ring back and apologise?

Archdeacon
No, Bishop, the light— shining in your bedroom window.

Bishop
Oh, that?

Archdeacon
Yes, keeping you awake all night.

Bishop *chuckling*
Don't worry, it doesn't. I can sleep through anything, but don't tell the Dean!

*They both chuckle as the door opens. Enter **Noote**.*

Noote *anxiously*
Has it started?

Bishop
No, Noote. You are all right.

Noote
Oh, thank goodness! Scouts went on rather late tonight. I couldn't bear to miss the last episode. I must see how they catch him.

Archdeacon
Him? Do you know who it is, then?

Noote
Of course, Archdeacon: the insurance agent.

Bishop
The insurance agent?

Archdeacon *puzzled*
But he can't have done it.

Bishop
Of course not: he was in Australia.

Noote *knowingly*
Well he did it, my lord. You look at his eyes!

Archdeacon
His eyes? What's wrong with his eyes?

Noote
They're too close together, Archdeacon. My Grandmother used to say "Never trust a man whose eyes are too close together."

Bishop
Really, Noote!

Noote *firmly*
But she was always right, my lord. She said you couldn't trust Hitler.

Bishop
How very perceptive of her. Now do come and sit down.

Noote
Is there anything to eat?

Bishop
I don't think so. You finished up the pudding, didn't you, Henry?

Archdeacon *pointedly*
Yes, and now we are having coffee, aren't we, Bishop?

Bishop
What? Oh, of course Henry. *(Hands the cup of coffee he has poured to the **Archdeacon**.)*

Noote *taking it from him.*
Oh well, I'll just have to make do with this.

Archdeacon *protesting*
But that's my cup!

Noote
It's all right, Archdeacon. I'm not fussy. *(Drinks.)* Delicious coffee, my lord.

Archdeacon
So glad you're enjoying it.

The doorbell.

Noote
Shall I see who it is?

Bishop
Yes, Noote— and get rid of them. It's just about to start.

Noote puts down cup and exits.

Scene 2
Studio / Interior / Night

The hall.

*Noote enters from study and goes to front door. He opens it, revealing the **Dean**, who carries a tool bag and looks worried.*

Dean
I wish to see the Bishop.

Noote
He's in the study, Dean. Will you go in?

Dean *handing tool bag to* **Noote**
Thank you.

Noote
Is this a tool bag?

Dean
It is.

Noote
Isn't that lucky?

Dean
Why?

Noote
Well, on my way home, I noticed the floodlighting has gone wrong again.

The **Dean** *reacts.*

Scene 3
Studio / Interior / Night

The study.

The **Bishop** *is adjusting the television.*

Bishop
How's that for a picture, Henry?

Archdeacon
Perfect, Bishop.

The **Dean** *enters.*

Dean
My lord, Archdeacon.

Bishop
Oh, Dean—

Dean
Am I interrupting something?

Bishop
Interrupting? Well, no— of course not. That is to say—

Dean
Yes?

Bishop
We were just about to watch something on the television.

Dean *puzzled*
This evening? I was not aware of anything on television worthy of notice.

Bishop
My dear Dean, do you mean you haven't been watching this excellent programme? Why, it's the best thing since— Henry, when did they last show us
anything as exciting?

Archdeacon
Last November, Bishop.

Bishop
Really, what was that?

Archdeacon
The Miss World Competition.

Bishop
Yes, well this is quite different. Really first-class.

Dean
But what is it, my lord?

Bishop
It's a thriller.

Dean
A thriller? Ah, nothing worthy of notice.

Bishop
Well, what can I do for you, Dean?

Dean

I have come to thank you for telephoning me so promptly about the flood-lighting.

Bishop

Oh, think nothing of it, Dean. It was a pleasure. *(Winks at **Archdeacon**.)*

Dean

I am aware of that.

Bishop *taken aback*

What?

Dean

I am aware, my lord, that you are hostile to my efforts to save this Cathedral money by installing the floodlighting myself.

Bishop

Nonsense, Dean, Nonsense. Still, you must admit it does keep going wrong.

Dean

I admit no such thing. The fault has been rectified.

Bishop

What was it? The whole thing wrongly assembled?

Dean

It was simply a loose connection at the junction box.

Bishop

Oh, so everything is all right now?

Dean

Yes, my lord.

Bishop

Until the next time.

Dean

There will be no next time.

Bishop

Really? I wish I had your faith.

Archdeacon
What about the light in the Bishop's bedroom?

Bishop *delighted*
I'm glad you reminded me, Henry. Now that, Dean, that is far from satisfactory.

Dean *defensively*
It is the spotlight for the spire. It's positioning is very difficult.

Bishop
No doubt it calls for the sort of expertise that only a professional firm of lighting engineers can be expected to possess.

Dean
Couldn't you draw your curtains?

Bishop
And sleep in a stuffy bedroom? *(Firmly)* No, Dean, I must insist something is done!

*The **Bishop** winks at the **Archdeacon** who winks back.*

Dean *worried*
Well, my lord, if you will show me exactly what is happening.

Bishop
With pleasure. *(Going to door.)* Will you come up and see now?

Archdeacon
Er, Bishop—

Bishop
What, Henry?

Archdeacon
There isn't time.

*The **Archdeacon** points to the television and indicates his watch.*

Bishop
Gracious, I nearly forgot. Noote, show the Dean where my room is, will you?

Noote
Me, my lord? But I don't want to miss the start.

Bishop
Don't worry, we'll call you. Now off you both go.

Archdeacon *pointedly*
I'll say goodbye now, Dean.

Dean
I beg your pardon, Archdeacon?

Bishop *understanding*
Oh, yes. The Archdeacon means there's no need to bother to say goodbye, Dean. Just show yourself out when you want to.

Dean
Thank you, my lord.

Bishop
Not at all. I expect you will want to get home and solve the problem.

Dean *troubled*
If it is capable of solution.

Bishop *brightly*
Well, if it isn't, you can still call in a professional firm, can't you?

Dean *tartly*
There will be no need for that. If it is possible to do something, rest assured I shall do it.

*Exit **Dean**.*

Bishop
Lucky you remembered, Henry.

Archdeacon
Had you really forgotten, Bishop?

Bishop
Well you know how it is when you're enjoying yourself. *(Chuckles.)* I think it will be some time before we have any more trouble with the Dean. *(He looks towards television set.)* Hullo! It's starting.

Announcer *(OOV)*
And now the final episode of our thriller serial, "The Affair at Cookham Lock". Episode thirteen, "The Killer Exposed".

Thriller music.

Bishop
Here we go. I've been looking forward to this all the week.

Archdeacon *fervently*
Oh, so have I!

Bishop
Still think it's Dr Prentis, Henry?

Archdeacon
Certain, Bishop.

Bishop
Well, I'm afraid you are in for a disappointment.

Noote enters hurriedly.

Noote *dismayed*
Oh, its started. Why didn't you call me?

Bishop *testily*
All right, all right. You haven't missed anything.

Noote
But you promised—

Bishop
Shhh!

Woman *(OOV)*
But, Roger, just because Dr Prentis isn't qualified, it doesn't make him a murderer.

Bishop
See, Henry?

Man *(OOV)*
But Otto Klein saw him in Maidenhead the afternoon Paula Winters was murdered.

Archdeacon
What did I say?

Woman *(OOV)*
He could have been mistaken.

Man *(OOV)*
Otto Klein mistaken? I think we should call on Mr Otto Klein.

Sound of car driving off and hurry music.

Archdeacon
Now we shall see, Bishop!

Bishop
We certainly shall, Henry.

Noise of car stopping, car doors opening and closing, footsteps.

Bishop
Ah, there's the antique shop.

Noote
They are wasting their time going to see Otto Klein. Why don't they go and see the insurance agent?

Bishop
The lock-keeper is the chap they want. *(Shop door bell.)* Ah, here he is. Now, quiet everyone.

Archdeacon
I didn't speak.

Bishop
Shut up, Henry! Sh!

Otto Klein *(OOV)*
You are interested in this pair of duelling pistols? Exquisite workmanship, is it not?

Man *(OOV)*
Yes, a friend told me he had seen them here. *(Significantly)* last week.

Otto Klein *(OOV)*
Ach, I have many peoples here who admire them.

Man *(OOV)*
You might remember my friend, his name is *(significantly)* Dr Prentis.

Otto Klein *(OOV) his voice shaken*
Dr Prentis?

Dean *calling off*
My lord, my lord!

Bishop
What was that?

Noote
The Dean, my lord. He's coming downstairs.

Bishop
What on earth does he want? Turn the sound down, Noote.

Noote goes to set and turns down the sound.

Dean *entering*
Good news, my lord! The light is capable of realignment.

Bishop
Really? That is good news. Well, I expect you will send someone round in the morning, will you?

Dean
Certainly not. I cannot allow you to have another disturbed night. The adjustment is a simple one, if you will lend me a stepladder, I will do it at once.

Bishop
Ah, there we can't help you I'm afraid—

Noote *interrupting*
Yes we can, my lord. There's one under the stairs.

Dean
Then if someone would show me.

Bishop
But, really, Dean, there's no need to do it now.

Dean
I insist.

Bishop
Oh, very well. Noote, get the stepladder.

Noote
Me, my lord? Why me?

Bishop *pointedly*
Because you've been so helpful telling everybody where it is.

Noote *realising*
Oh. It is just through here, Dean. *(Goes to door and holds it open.)*

Dean *following*
Thank you, Noote. With the aid of a stepladder I can soon settle the problem. Through here, you say? *(Exits.)*

Noote *calling after him*
On the left, Dean. *(To **Bishop**.)* You will tell me what happens, won't you?

Bishop
Yes, yes.

Noote
Promise?

Bishop
Yes, yes. Hurry up!

Noote exits.

Bishop
Quick Henry, turn the sound up. We are missing what Otto Klein is saying.

*The **Archdeacon** turns up the sound.*

Woman *(OOV)*
Thank you, Mr Klein. That was all very interesting. Goodbye.

Door closing. Noise of street, car doors, car starts, car drives off.

Archdeacon
Oh, we've missed it!

Bishop *crossly*
Really!

Archdeacon
Where are they going now, Bishop?

Bishop
I've no idea. *(Suddenly)* Hullo, there's the river. They're stopping.

Sound of car pulling up on gravel. Doors slam. Birdsong.

Man *(OOV)*
We'll take a boat on the river, it'll be safer.

Woman *(OOV)*
Good idea. This place makes me uneasy.

Man *(OOV)*
This one will do.

Sound of people getting into a boat, splashing etc.

Bishop
Henry, look at that boatman watching them. He's going into his hut.

Sound of phone dialling.

Archdeacon
Who's he ringing, Bishop?

Bishop
I don't know, but I don't like the look of it!

The dialling changes to a phone ringing.

Archdeacon
Can you see who is answering it, Bishop?

Bishop
No, that could be anyone's back. *(Hopefully)* I expect it's the lock-keeper. Ah! Here we are, back on the river.

Sound of river, boat being rowed.

Woman *(OOV)*
It is so peaceful here. I can hardly believe that this time last week Paula Winters was alive and well.

Man *(OOV)*
Don't upset yourself, Frances, we must talk.

Woman *(OOV)*
Of course, Roger. Let's go carefully over everything Otto Klein said.

Archdeacon *happily*
Oh good, now we'll know.

Bishop
Henry, we're in luck! *(They lean forward expectantly.)*

Dean *off*
My lord, my lord—

Archdeacon
Oh, No! Don't switch it off, Bishop.

Bishop
I'll just turn down the sound. *(Rises, turns down sound and calls.)* What is it, Dean?

*The **Dean** appears in the doorway.*

Dean
May we bring the stepladder through here into the garden, my lord?

Bishop
Can't you take it out through the back door?

Dean
I suggested that, but Noote insists it will be quicker to bring it through here.

Bishop *grimly*
Does he? Very well, but please hurry.

Dean
Thank you, my lord. *(Calling off.)* All right, Noote?

Noote *(OOV)*
Yes, Dean.

Dean *entering and holding door*
Careful round the corner, Noote.

***Noote** enters carrying stepladder. He hurries to the television and looks at the screen.*

Noote
What's happening? What's happening? What's happening?

Bishop *pointedly*
You will be as quick as possible, won't you Noote?

Noote
Oh, yes, my lord.

Noote goes reluctantly towards the French windows, still looking at the screen. Exits, tripping as he goes. The Dean stands looking at the screen. The Bishop and Archdeacon exchange a look.

Bishop
Do you want something, Dean?

Dean
No, no. Is that the Thames?

Bishop
Yes it is.

Dean
I thought it was.

Bishop
Well, don't let us hold you up.

Dean
Which part of the river is it?

Bishop
Maidenhead.

Dean
I thought I recognised it. I had an aunt who lived there.

Archdeacon
You must tell us about her— another time.

Bishop
Forgive us, Dean, but this is getting rather exciting— isn't it, Henry?

Archdeacon
Yes, Bishop— it was.

Dean
Of course, of course. What is the title of the work?

Bishop
"The Affair at Cookham Lock".

Dean
I believe I know it.

Archdeacon
I suppose you had an aunt who lived there, too?

Dean
No, Archdeacon, I know the book.

Bishop
I thought you didn't like thrillers, Dean?

Dean
I don't, but when I was on holiday last summer it was the only book in the hotel, so I was obliged to read it.

Bishop
Did you enjoy it?

Dean
No. I thought it a trivial work. *(Exits.)*

Archdeacon
Quick, Bishop, turn up the sound.

*The **Bishop** turns up the sound. Rowing and river sounds, birdsong etc.*

Man *(OOV)*
Well I think that covers everything Otto Klein told us.

Archdeacon
We've missed it again.

Man *(OOV)*
We'd better get back, Frances, we are getting near the weir.

Woman *(OOV)*
Roger, what's that power boat doing?

Man *(OOV)*
What power boat?

Woman*(OOV)*
That big blue one coming this way.

Noise of power boat approaching.

Man *(OOV)*
Great Scott! It's coming right for us!

Woman *(OOV)*
We shall be pushed over the weir!

Noise of weir and power boat.

Man *(OOV)*
Hold on, Frances, hold on!

Sound of weir. Woman screams. Power boat roaring close.

Bishop *excited*
Who's driving it?

Archdeacon
I can't see.

Sound of power boat engine roaring.

Bishop
We shall in a moment, it's turning round.

Noote *entering hurriedly*
My lord, my lord.

*Bishop and **Archdeacon**, startled, turn towards him.*

Bishop
What's the matter?

Noote
What's happening?

Noise of power boat and weir subsides, replaced by gentle river sounds.

Bishop
Noote— really! Did you see who it was, Henry?

Archdeacon
No, Noote startled me.

Bishop
And now it's gone. Really, Noote!

Noote
I'm sorry, my lord. I wanted to know what was happening.

Bishop
Well, we can't tell you now.

Noote
But you must, you promised.

Archdeacon
We did, Bishop.

Bishop *relenting*
Oh, very well. Where were you up to?

Noote
They were just seeing Otto Klein in the antique shop.

Bishop
Ah, yes, of course.

Noote
Well, what did he say?

Bishop
We don't know.

Archdeacon
We missed that bit.

Noote
Oh dear, well, what happened then?

Bishop
They began to discuss everything Otto Klein had said.

Noote
Oh, splendid! So what was it?

Bishop
We don't know.

Archdeacon
We missed that bit too.

Noote
Oh dear, so what happened then?

Bishop
They drove down to the river and went for a row.

Noote *eagerly*
Yes?

Archdeacon
And the boatman saw them and made a phone call.

Noote
Who to?

Bishop
We don't know.

Archdeacon
We couldn't see who it was.

Noote
So what happened then?

Bishop
They began to discuss everything Otto Klein had said.

Noote
Really? So what had he said?

Bishop
We don't know.

Archdeacon
We missed that bit as well.

Noote
Well, it strikes me you just haven't been paying attention.

Bishop
Noote! That is most uncalled for. There is no need to be rude.

Noote
I'm sorry, my lord.

Bishop
I should hope you are.

Noote *politely*
May I ask what is happening now?

Bishop *rudely*
If you will sit down and shut up, we'll find out!

Archdeacon
They've gone over the weir.

Splashing noises.

Noote
Oh, look, there they are in the rushes.

*The **Dean** enters unobserved and stands behind them.*

Man *(OOV)*
Come on, we must get out of these wet things.

Woman *(OOV)*
But where?

Man *(OOV)*
Look, there's the lock-keeper's cottage. Come on.

Bishop *excitedly*
Ah! Now we are getting somewhere!

Dean
Why do you say that, my lord?

Bishop *surprised*
Oh, Dean. Well, because I believe the lock-keeper did it.

Dean *smoothly*
Really? What an interesting theory.

*The **Bishop** reacts and, rising, turns down the set.*

Bishop *tetchily*
Dean— what do you want?

Dean
It is most frustrating.

Archdeacon
It certainly is.

Dean
After all, the spotlight is not amenable to adjustment.

Archdeacon
Does that mean you'll be going, Dean?

Dean
I fear so, Archdeacon. There is nothing more I can do.

Bishop *brightening*
Never mind. Let me show you out.

Dean
It is regrettable that there is not a more convenient branch on the mulberry tree. It is only a matter of a few inches.

Bishop *cheerfully, putting his arm round **Dean** and leading him to the door*
Oh, don't worry about it, Dean. You've done your best, no man can do more. I'm sure you are anxious to get home.

Dean *troubled*
If only there something else I could fix it to.

Noote
What about the wall?

Dean *stopping and turning*
The wall?

Noote
Yes, the wall of the Palace.

The **Bishop** and **Archdeacon** *react.*

Archdeacon
No good, I'm afraid!

Bishop
No, out of the question.

Dean *thoughtfully*
I wonder.

Noote
I'm sure it would work. *(Goes to windows.)* You could put it just up here. The angle is the same and it could not possibly shine into your bedroom, my lord.

Bishop
Nonsense, Noote, you don't know what you are talking about.

Dean *going to window*
I think your chaplain has got something, my lord.

Bishop *grimly*
If he hasn't now he soon will have!

Noote *modestly*
It's just an idea.

Bishop *angrily*
Yes! And a deeply stupid one! Dean we mustn't waste any more of your time.

Dean *cheerfully*
It won't, my lord. It's a straightforward job and won't take a moment. I'll go and get my tool bag.

Dean exits to hall.

Bishop
Really, Noote, of all the idiotic ideas. The last thing we want is the Dean fiddling about outside the French windows. Don't you want to see this final episode?

Noote *contritely*
Yes, my lord. It just suddenly struck me.

Bishop

It's a pity it didn't strike you a bit harder. Goodness knows what we are missing, they were just going to see the lock-keeper.

Dean *entering cheerfully with tool bag*

Here we are!

Bishop

Dean, you don't mind if we go on watching the television, do you?

Dean

Please do, my lord. I would not dream of interrupting you.

Bishop

That is so kind.

Dean

Not at all. If someone will just help me with the ladder. *(Exits to garden.)*

Bishop

Go on, Noote, go and help him.

Noote

But I helped him before.

Bishop *firmly and loudly*

And you will help him again and again and AGAIN!

Noote

Oh, yes my lord— yes— of course. *(Exits hurriedly to garden.)*

Bishop

Quick, Henry, turn the sound up.

Archdeacon

Bishop— look!

Bishop

What? What's that?

Archdeacon

The lock-keeper's wife.

Bishop

You see what I mean? She's tall, isn't she?

Archdeacon *appreciatively*
Yes, Bishop. A fine figure of a woman!

Bishop
Well, if you ask me, she did it, Henry…

Archdeacon
Sh! Sh!

Country Woman *(OOV)*
Motor boat? What motor boat?

Man *(OOV)*
A big blue one.

Country Woman *(OOV)*
Blue? Ah, that that one there belongs to Mr Peters, the insurance agent.

Man *(OOV)*
Mr Peters?

Country Woman *(OOV)*
Yer, funny sort of bloke. Have you noticed his eyes?

Man *(OOV)*
What about them?

Country woman *(OOV)*
They're too close together.

Bishop and Archdeacon exchange a glance.

Noote enters.

Noote
What's happening? What's happening? What's happening?

The Dean is seen through the French windows setting up the stepladder.

Bishop
Sit down and be quiet!

Noote sits.

Noote *whispering*
Where are they, Archdeacon?

Archdeacon *whispering across the* **Bishop**
At the lock cottage.

Bishop *crossly*
For goodness' sake stop whispering, Henry!

Man *(OOV)*
Thank you, you've been very kind.

Country Woman *(OOV)*
That's all right, sir. Goodbye.

Man *(OOV)*
Goodbye.

Sound of footsteps followed by sinister music.

Bishop
I don't like the way she's standing there.

Archdeacon
Really? I'm enjoying it.

Bishop
There's more to that woman than meets the eye!

Archdeacon *warmly*
Yes, indeed!

The **Dean** *climbs stepladder holding the lamp.*

Distorted sound.

Archdeacon
Hey, what's happening?

Noote
The picture's gone.

Bishop
Oh, this is too much. I'll give it a knock.

Archdeacon
Is that wise, Bishop?

Bishop
Yes, yes. I know what I'm doing; I understand it's idiosyncrasies.

*Bishop rises, goes to set and hits it with a scientific flourish. At the same time, through the window, the **Dean** is seen descending the stepladder.*

Sound becomes normal.

Bishop
There you are!

Noote
Oh, well done, my lord.

Bishop *proudly*
You see! It's just knowing exactly where to hit it. Now *(sitting)*, can you see who it is?

Noote
No, he's gone into the cottage.

*Through the window the **Dean**, electric drill in hand, prepares to climb stepladder.*

Bishop
Hullo, the door is opening, now we'll see.

*The **Dean** climbs the steps.*

Distorted sound.

All *frustrated*
Oh!

Archdeacon
Quick, Bishop!

Bishop *rising*
Don't panic! *(Goes to set and hits it.)*

Archdeacon
It hasn't worked.

The **Bishop** *hits the television again.*

Noote
It's no good!

Bishop
But it always works.

*The **Bishop** lifts hand to strike the set as the **Dean** comes down stepladder.*

Sound becomes normal.

Bishop *puzzled*
It must be a delayed action.

Noote
No, my lord, it's the Dean.

Bishop
The Dean? What are you talking about?

Noote
When he goes up the steps, look.

*They turn to see the **Dean**, with the bracket, screwdriver and a mouthful of screws, climbing the stepladder.*

*Sound distort. **Noote** points to set. **Bishop** and **Archdeacon** nod.*

Bishop
Dean, Dean!

*The **Dean** climbs down the stepladder and enters.*

Dean *removing screw from his mouth*
What is it?

Bishop
You're interfering with the television.

Noote
Every time you go up the stepladder, it goes wrong.

Dean
I find that hard to believe.

Bishop *sharply*
I can't help that, Dean. It's true!

Dean *slowly*
Let me get this straight. You are suggesting that each time I go up the steps, I interfere with your television picture?

All
Yes, yes!

Dean *calmly*
But that is impossible.

Bishop *indignantly*
What do you mean?

Dean
Simply that I'm not on the steps now.

Bishop
But the picture isn't distorted now!

Dean
Indeed it is, my lord.

The clerics turn back towards the screen.

Announcer *(OOV)*
We are sorry for this break in transmission. Normal service will be resumed as soon as possible. In the meantime, some music.

The clerics react.

To the sound of cheerful music, mix to:

Scene 4
Studio / Exterior / Night

Outside the French windows.

*From the study comes the unbroken sound of cheerful music. The spotlight is in position, the **Dean** is at the top of the stepladder, the **Bishop** stands gloomily beside it, holding the electric drill.*

Dean *at top of stepladder*
There, my lord, your little problem is solved. *(Descends.)*

Bishop *unenthusiastically*
Thank you, Dean.

Dean *calling towards garden*
Noote, have you found the cable?

Noote *(OOV)*
Coming, Dean.

Bishop *calling into the study*
Any sign of it starting, Henry?

Archdeacon
No, Bishop, it's still the picture of the swan.

Bishop *crossly*
Fancy this happening in the middle of the last episode. I've a good mind to withhold my licence payment.

Dean
If you want to know what happens, you only have to ask, my lord.

Bishop *coldly*
Thank you, Dean. I prefer to wait.

Noote enters, he looks dishevelled and is unwinding the end of the cable.

Noote *out of breath*
Here we are, Dean.

Dean
Splendid.

Noote
I thought it wasn't going to be long enough, but then I found it was wound all round the rhododendrons, so I've straightened it out to make it reach. *(He brings cable to within a foot of the Dean.)* Here, Dean.

The Dean takes cable and holds the end towards the wall. It is clearly too short.

Noote
Oh dear.

Bishop
Really, Noote, you might have checked that before making bright suggestions about putting it here!

Dean
It looks as though I shall have to use your power supply, my lord.

Bishop *indignantly*
My power supply? Certainly not? What an idea!

Dean
May I remind you that all this trouble I'm taking is in your interest, my lord?

Bishop
And may I remind you, Dean, that if you had engaged a proper firm as I suggested, it would not have been necessary.

Cheerful music ceases.

Archdeacon *(OOV)*
Quick, it's starting!

Bishop
What? *(Realises.)* Here, Dean. *(Thrusts drill under the **Dean**'s arm.)*

Announcer *(OOV)*
And now we rejoin our thriller serial, "The Affair at Cookham Lock".

Dean
But what about the power?

Bishop
Oh, do what you like. *(Exits hurriedly to the study.)*

*On **Dean**'s reaction, mix to:*

Scene 5
Studio / Interior / Night

The study.

*The **Archdeacon** sits in front of the set on the sofa. The **Bishop** and **Noote** hurry in from the garden and sit with him.*

Dean *entering*
My lord—

Bishop
What is it now?

Dean
May I plug into this socket?

Bishop
Yes, yes, but do be quick about it.

Archdeacon
Sh!

Woman *(OOV)*
Roger, this means the murderer can only be one person.

Dean *discreetly*
My lord—

Bishop
What is it now?

Dean
May I switch on?

Bishop
What? Oh, yes, yes— do what you like, Dean.

Archdeacon and **Noote**
Sh!

Woman *(OOV)*
To think we've suspected so many people, and yet all the time it was…

Blackout. Sound cuts off.

Bishop, **Archdeacon**, **Noote** *and* **Dean** *together:*

Bishop
What on earth?

Archdeacon
Here, I say!

Noote
What's happening?

Dean
Dear me.

Bishop *(beside himself)*
Dean, what have you done?

Dean
I appear inadvertently to have fused the lights.

Archdeacon
Oh, no!

Noote
Oh, how could you?

Dean
If you will show me where the fuse box is?

Bishop
Oh, no. I'm not having you touch my fuse box!

Dean
Don't you wish to see the rest of the performance?

Bishop
Yes, and that's why I'm not letting you near my fuse box!

Noote
But we've got to get someone to mend it?

Bishop
And we will! A qualified electrician. Ring Mr James. Tell him it's an emergency!

Noote
Right, my lord.

Noote rises and picks way in the dark to telephone.

Bishop
Let's hope he's in. We must know how it ends.

Dean
I can always help you there, my lord.

Bishop
Thank you, Dean. You've helped us quite enough for one evening!

Noote *into phone*
Hullo, Mr James? This is the Bishop's chaplain speaking, how are you? Oh, good, and Mrs James? Splendid. And little Andrew, got over his whooping cough, has he?

Bishop
Get on with it!

Noote *to* **Bishop**
I'm sorry. *(Into phone)* I mean, I'm glad— I'm not sorry he's better. There was something else, Mr James. Yes, well we've had a fuse. Could you come round? It's an emergency. Oh, that is kind. Yes, right. We'll look forward to seeing you. *(Replaces phone.)* He's coming round, my lord.

Bishop
Thank goodness for that.

Noote
Yes, he'll be here in quarter of an hour.

Bishop
Can't he come any quicker?

Noote
No, he says he's watching the serial and he must know how it ends.

Bishop
I've never known such selfishness! What about us?

Dean
Well, if you won't allow me to tell you.

Bishop
There's only one thing I'll allow you to do, Dean— and that's give me your tool bag. I'm going to mend this fuse.

Noote
But do you know how to, my lord?

Bishop
I intend to find out. Where's that bag?

*The **Bishop, Noote** and the **Dean** feel round in the dark for the bag.
Suddenly the lights come on.*

Bishop
Ah, some light, that's better!

Dean
I'm sure I put it here.

Noote *helpfully*
Perhaps you left it in the garden.

Dean
No, I brought it in and put it down here just before the lights fused.

Bishop *realising*
The lights!

Noote
They've come on!

Dean
But where's my tool bag?

Archdeacon *entering with tool bag*
Here, Dean. I borrowed it to mend the fuse.

Bishop *delighted*
Henry, old friend!

Noote
Oh, Archdeacon.

Archdeacon *looking at screen*
Isn't it on?

Bishop
It's got to warm up. Don't worry, we shall see enough to find out who did it.

Dean
I fear not, my lord. The time. *(Indicates his watch.)*

Bishop
Time? *(Looks at his watch)* Oh, no!

Noote
We've missed it! We've missed it! We've missed the end!

Bishop
This is too much.

Dean
Fortunately, my offer is still open.

Bishop
Is it? Well, let me just tell you Dean what I think of your offer—

Archdeacon
Bishop!

Bishop
What, Henry?

Archdeacon
Well, we must know, Bishop.

Noote
Yes, we must, my lord.

Bishop *with bad grace*
What? Oh well, I suppose. All right, Dean, please tell us what happens.

Dean
With pleasure, my lord. May I sit down?

Bishop
Oh, yes, of course.

The **Dean** *sits and makes himself comfortable.*

Dean
Well, now. You recall that Mrs Winters was found dead on her houseboat.

Noote *protesting*
But that was the first episode.

Bishop
You don't need to go back that far!

Dean
As you wish. You are aware perhaps that Paula Winters was murdered with a duelling pistol?

Bishop, Archdeacon *and* **Noote** *together*
Yes!

Dean
A highly improbable event, if you will pardon my saying so.

Noote
Oh, do you think so?

Dean
Certainly. No duelling pistol would fire after that lapse of time.

Bishop *raging*
Never mind that, get on with it!

Dean
There's no need to be impatient, my lord.

Bishop
Who did it? Who did it?

Dean
Well if that is all you want to know—

Bishop
It is, it is!

Archdeacon
Bishop—

Bishop
Henry, don't you start!

Archdeacon
But it's still on!

They swing round to look at screen.

Sound of a fast car, exciting music etc.

Bishop *mystified, looking at his watch*
But how on earth?

Noote
But of course, the break in transmission. They are running over time!

Dean
Well, as I was saying—

All
Sh!

Dean
Don't you want me to tell you who did it?

Bishop *going to door*
No, Dean, we don't. Please take your tool bag and go.

Dean
But you specifically asked me to tell you.

Bishop
Please do as I say.

Dean
Very well. *(Goes to door.)* I will return in the morning with the extra cable.

Bishop
Yes, yes, good night.

*Pushes the **Dean** out and shuts door and hurries back to his seat.*

Archdeacon *and* **Noote** *together*
Sh!

They crane towards the screen.

Woman *(OOV)*
Poor Mrs Winters. I can't stop thinking about her.

Man *(OOV)*
Well at least her murderer is safely behind bars.

Woman *(OOV)*
Oh, Roger, I'm so glad it's over.

Man *(OOV)*
So am I, Frances.

Woman *(OOV)*
What will you do now?

Man *(OOV)*
I've always wanted to see the pyramids.

Woman *(OOV wistfully)*
Then you'll be leaving Cookham?

Man *(OOV)*
Yes, but only if you'll come with me, Frances.

Woman *(OOV)*
Oh, Roger!

Man *(OOV)*
Oh, Frances!

Music swells up. The clerics look dismayed.

Archdeacon
Oh, Bishop!

Noote
Oh, my lord. What shall we do?

Bishop
Do Noote? There's only one thing to do. *(Rises, goes to phone and dials.)* Dean? I'm sorry to trouble you, but would you be kind enough to answer a question?

*Credits roll over the **Bishop** speaking and the expectant faces of the **Archdeacon** and **Noote**.*

The Bishop Gives a Shove

Edwin:

Founded by Henry VIII in order to give him the divorce the Pope had refused, the Church of England has always been closely tied to government. This means that the appointment of archbishops, bishops and deans is in the hands of the Prime Minister. So when a vacancy for a dean or bishop occurs, the canons pray to the Almighty to give them a new one and receive a letter from 10 Downing Street informing them who it will be. One might think this a practical and very English solution; especially with a two-party system that ensures a political balance among voters is reflected in Church appointments.

Alas, it can also mean that a bishop and his dean, who, for the good of the cathedral and diocese need to work closely together, are often totally incompatible. This problem of incompatibility is aggravated by the fact that bishops and deans are appointed for life, so when a new bishop arrives at his cathedral and finds the dean antipathetic, he knows that it is a situation from which only death or translation[1] will rescue him.

The Bishop Gives a Shove is based on the idea that at St Ogg's the situation has reached stalemate, and the Bishop is desperate for a solution.

Frank Muir had given us a contact at Church House to whom we could talk and ask for information. When I rang him to ask how a bishop could get rid of his dean, the question fascinated him. He explained that the Prime Minister has an Ecclesiastical Appointments Secretary, with an office in 10 Downing Street, whose job it is to keep him abreast of Church affairs. He added that in 1957, during the Cold War, when Khrushchev and Bulganin came to London to see Prime Minister Macmillan, at a particularly delicate moment in talks that were designed to try to improve British–Soviet relations the ever-vigilant Russians asked for a room where these matters could be discussed in total security.

Number 10, it seems, is short on space and the officials had difficulty finding a room free until they looked into the office of the Ecclesiastical Appointments Secretary and, finding he was absent, ushered in the Russians. But the Ecclesiastical Appointments Secretary was not absent. He had enjoyed his customary excellent lunch at the Athenaeum and was having a quiet nap in

---

1. Bishops are not moved but 'translated'.

his private lavatory. On waking, however, he was terrified by hearing Russian spoken. Had he been discovered, the whole course of history might have changed.

Pauline:

Part of *The Bishop Gives a Shove* takes place inside Number 10, and I am struck by how different things are now from when this episode was written. Today it is impossible to reach the street, let alone the house, protected as it is by huge gates and police with guns and dogs; but then, when Edward Heath (who was famous for being a remarkably good pianist) was Prime Minister, you could walk straight up to the front door of Number 10 and have your photograph taken with the friendly policeman who stood by the railings.

Whether he would have let you knock on the door and ask to see someone without an appointment, however, is another matter. But this is the gentle world of *All Gas and Gaiters*, where a certain rearranging of reality is allowed, so if you want to pop up to London and see the Prime Minister's Ecclesiastical Appointments Secretary without telling him you are coming there is nothing to prevent you from doing so – particularly, of course, if you happen to be the Bishop of St Ogg's.

The Bishop Gives a Shove

Series Four
First transmitted on BBC One, 15 April 1970

Scene 1
Studio / Interior / Day

The study.

*The **Bishop**, the **Archdeacon** and **Noote** are opening the mail with enthusiasm.*

Bishop
How much money is in that one, Henry?

Archdeacon
Two pounds fifteen, Bishop.

Bishop
Who's that one from, Noote?

Noote
The Vicar of Ketsby, my lord.

Bishop
And how many pools coupons has he sold?

Noote
Ninety. There's a postal order for four pounds ten.

Bishop
My word! That's excellent! Ketsby's a small parish. *(Opening envelope.)* Now, what have we here? Ah, the Rector of Oxcombe— a cheque and a letter!

Noote
What's it say?

Bishop *protesting good humouredly*
I can't read them all out, Noote. Though this one is rather nice. *(Reads)* "Congratulations on your brilliant new fund-raising scheme, my lord. Anyone can see it was your idea." *(Beaming with pleasure)* How nice of him!

Archdeacon
But, Bishop—

Bishop
What's the matter, Henry?

Archdeacon *protesting*
It was *my* idea.

Bishop
Henry, it doesn't matter who's idea it was. I've told you before.

Archdeacon
Yes, Bishop. I know you've told me.

Bishop *tartly*
Really, Henry, this desire for acclamation is most unbecoming in a man of your years. Now, please note that the Rector of Oxcombe has sold two hundred and fifty of our football pools coupons and sent us a cheque for twelve pounds five shillings, which makes the total we have received— Noote?

Noote *counting*
Six, nine, four, three— carry seven that's divided by twelve, nought plus five carry two—

Bishop
Get on with it!

Noote
Er— forty-nine pounds, nineteen shillings.

Bishop
How splendid. Fifty pounds!

Noote
No, my lord; forty-nine pounds nineteen shillings.

Bishop
Don't quibble, Noote— it's fifty pounds— less ten pounds prize money— that's forty pounds we've raised for the Old People's Home. At this rate we should be able to complete it by Christmas.

Noote
Oh, my lord, wouldn't it be wonderful if we could?

Sound of doorbell.

Bishop
Go and see who that is, will you, Noote?

Noote
Right my lord.

Noote exits to hall.

Bishop
Fifty pounds! What do you think of that, Henry? Not bad for the first week?

Archdeacon
No, Bishop. *(Pointedly)* I always thought it was a good idea.

Bishop
It certainly is— and such fun! I'm really looking forward to the football results on Saturday.

Archdeacon *warmly*
Me too! I'm on a winning streak.

Bishop
My dear Henry, you sound like a regular gambler.

*Enter **Noote**.*

Noote
My lord, it's the Dean.

Bishop
The Dean? Oh dear.

Noote
Shall I show him in?

Bishop *heavily*
Yes, Noote, I suppose you'd better.

*Exit **Noote**.*

Bishop
What do you think he wants, Henry?

Archdeacon *pointedly*
Perhaps he's come to congratulate me on my pools idea.

Noote *entering followed by the* **Dean**
The Dean, my lord.

Dean
Good morning, my lord— Archdeacon.

Bishop *cheerfully*
Morning, Dean.

Archdeacon *cheerfully*
Good morning, Dean.

Bishop
What can we do for you?

Dean
I have come about this, my lord. *(He holds a paper.)*

Bishop *delighted*
One of our coupons! Dean, how nice of you to buy it!

Dean
I did not buy it. It was sold to my wife. I thought I should bring it to you at once, my lord.

Bishop
Oh, Dean, I'm afraid you're a bit early—

Archdeacon
We shan't know the results till tomorrow.

Dean
I am not interested in the results.

Bishop *roguishly*
You're not? Not even if you wife were to win ten pounds?

Dean *sharply*
I can assure you I should not be interested were my wife to win ten, twenty, or thirty pounds.

Archdeacon *surprised*
Why? Have you come into money?

Dean
Certainly not! My lord, will you please be good enough to tell me whose idea this is?

Bishop
Whose idea? Well, Dean—

Archdeacon
Er, Bishop—

Bishop
Does it really matter whose idea it was?

Dean
It does to me, my lord.

Archdeacon *proudly*
Mine, Dean, mine. It was my idea.

Dean
Indeed. I thought it might have been yours, my lord.

Archdeacon *firmly*
No, Dean. It was definitely mine.

Noote *loyally*
Yes, Dean. The Archdeacon thought of it all by himself. You see he got this letter from Liverpool— didn't you, Archdeacon?

Archdeacon
Yes, asking me to join the Happy Circle.

Noote
And he thought— why not make our own Happy Circle— here, in St Ogg's?

Dean
I see. Then, Archdeacon, I must tell you I strongly disapprove.

Archdeacon *prepared for a compliment*
Oh, thank you. That is— *(Realising.)* Oh— do you?

Dean
Yes, I consider football pools a most pernicious and insidious evil and I demand you to cease operations forthwith.

Bishop
Cease operations?

Noote
Forthwith?

Archdeacon
Does that mean stop?

Dean
Certainly it means stop. I am amazed that you ever thought fit to start. Are you not aware that gambling is the new English vice?

Archdeacon *interested*
Really? What was the old one?

Bishop
But, Dean this isn't gambling, is it Henry?

Archdeacon
Isn't it, Bishop?

Dean
Certainly it is gambling, my lord. It is as much gambling as the turf at Newmarket or the baccarat tables of Monte Carlo.

Bishop *outraged*
What? People giving a shilling towards an old people's home with the hope they may win a small cash prize?

Dean
"He that maketh haste to be rich shall not be innocent", my lord. Proverbs, chapter twenty, verse twenty-eight.

Bishop
"Cast me not off in the time of my old age; forsake me not when my strength faileth", Dean. Psalm seventy-one, verse nine!

Dean
"Would you buy the poor for silver and the needy for a pair of shoes", my lord? Amos, chapter eight, verse six.

Bishop
"I was a father to the poor; and the cause which I knew not, I searched out", Job, twenty-nine, verse fifteen.

They pause.

Archdeacon *suddenly, loudly*
"Look not upon the wine when it is red."

Bishop
What's that got to do with it, Henry?

Archdeacon
Nothing, Bishop. It just came to me.

Dean
I see no point in continuing this discussion, my lord. I insist that every penny of this money is returned to the donors.

Bishop *outraged*
Every penny? But there's fifty pounds here.

Noote
No, my lord; forty-nine pounds nineteen shillings.

Bishop
What about the old people's home?

Archdeacon
They need the money.

Noote
Yes, Dean. They need five hundred pounds to finish the building.

Dean *loftily*
It is better the building remain unfinished than be built with tainted money. Good morning, my Lord, Archdeacon. *(Exits.)*

There is a pause.

Noote *suddenly*
Well, I call that a bit thick! You won't send the money back? Will you, my lord?

Archdeacon
I should think not, indeed!

Noote *relieved*
Good, then I'll just collect up these cheques and postal orders and take them to the bank.

Bishop *sitting down heavily*
No, Noote. Leave them.

Noote
Leave them? But, my lord—

Archdeacon
Aren't you going to fight, Bishop?

Bishop *wearily*
No, Henry, I'm afraid not.

Noote *concerned*
Oh dear. Aren't you feeling well, my lord? I said you should not have stopped taking your pills.

Bishop
It has nothing to do with my pills, Noote. It is simply that I have spent ten years fighting the Dean— and I can't go on.

Archdeacon
But you can't let him win, Bishop.

Bishop *gloomily*
Why not? He always has. When I think how excited I was at the prospect of coming here: the day I received the letter from the Prime Minister's Appointments Secretary— it came as a complete surprise.

Noote
Did it, my lord?

Bishop
Yes. Apparently my dear old Bishop had heard St Ogg's was coming vacant and he had made a point of going himself to Downing Street to recommend me.

Noote *surprised*
Whatever made him do that?

Bishop *coldly*
Presumably he thought I would make a good bishop.

Noote
Oh, I didn't think of that.

Bishop
I remember being fitted for my gaiters. The tailor was such a nice man. He was the first person to call me "My lord". Then, the day I came down here— you met me at the station, Henry—

Archdeacon
I remember, Bishop.

Bishop
You'd arranged a little party in my honour.

Archdeacon
That's right, a sherry party.

Bishop *gloomily*
It was there that I first met the Dean.

Noote *surprised*
You asked the Dean to a sherry party, Archdeacon?

Archdeacon
No. He called to complain about the noise.

Bishop
And he's been complaining ever since. Do you remember when I wanted to introduce those nice new cassocks for the choir?

Noote
He said there was plenty of wear left in the old ones.

Bishop
He did. And the time I suggested we put seats in the Close?

Noote
He said it would only encourage people to sit down.

Bishop
Typical of the man!

Archdeacon
And what about the time he stopped me showing my slides at the verger's party?

Bishop
Yes, Henry— I can't say I altogether blame him for that. Still, be that as it may, I've had enough.

Archdeacon
You're throwing in the towel, Bishop?

Bishop
I'm afraid so, Henry. From now on I shall just sit and wait for him to leave.

Noote
But he'll never leave, my lord.

Archdeacon
He likes it here.

Bishop
I know he does, but he might leave— if he was offered something better.

Noote
Better? You mean a bishopric, my lord?

Bishop
Oh, if only the Prime Minister would give him a bishopric!

Archdeacon
Then why not recommend him?

Noote
What a splendid idea! Why don't you, my lord?

Bishop
Don't be ridiculous— besides, there isn't a bishopric vacant.

Noote
What about Chelsea?

Bishop
Chelsea? There isn't a diocese of Chelsea.

Noote
But there is, my lord. They've just created it.

Bishop
Have they? I know there's been talk of a new diocese in London—

Noote
It's in the *Church Times* this week.

Bishop
Really?

Noote *going to desk and fetching the paper*
Here it is. *(Reads.)* "The usual consultations are taking place prior to the appointment of the first Bishop of Chelsea. It is understood the Prime Minister is having some difficulty in finding a suitable man for this key position where great administrative ability is so necessary." You see, my lord?

Bishop
Yes, but I can't go to Downing Street and recommend the Dean.

Noote
I don't see why not, my lord. He's a very good administrator.

Bishop
Is he?

Noote
Well, he's efficient.

Archdeacon
He's certainly that.

Bishop
Efficient? Yes, I suppose I could say he's efficient, couldn't I?

Noote
Oh, why don't you, my lord?

Archdeacon
Yes. Let's go now. I'd enjoy a trip to London.

Bishop
Would you, Henry? Well, I'm afraid you can't come.

Archdeacon
Why not, Bishop?

Bishop
Because all these cheques and postal orders have got to be sent back!

Archdeacon *indignantly*
But why should I have to do it?

Bishop
Because my dear Henry— as you keep telling us, it was your idea. Come on, Noote, we must hurry.

Scene 2
Exterior / Day

The front door of No. 10 Downing Street. Sound of street noise. A **police constable** *stands in the foreground.*

The **Bishop** *and* **Noote** *enter.*

Bishop
Good morning, Constable.

Constable
Good morning, sir.

Bishop *at door*
Well, Noote, here we are! Ring the bell.

Noote *overwhelmed*
Just think, my lord, we are at the nerve centre of the nation: the hub of British political life, the great bastion...

Bishop *interrupting*
Never mind all that, ring the bell!

Noote *reverentially*
The bell? *That* bell, my lord? You want me to ring *that* bell?

Bishop
Is there another?

Noote
No, no. But think of all the thousands and thousands of great and famous people who have rung it over the past two hundred years— of all their hopes and fears— as they waited here, on this spot where we are waiting—

Bishop
And shall continue to wait if you don't hurry up and ring the bell, Noote!

Noote
Oh, yes, I'm so sorry, my lord. (*Pushes bell-push.*)

A pause

Bishop
Better ring again.

Noote *pushes bell-push. There is another pause.*

Noote
Do you think they're out?

The door is opened by a **workman** *wearing overalls and a cap.*

Workman
Did you ring?

Noote
Oh, good afternoon. Yes, in fact I did.

Workman
It's out of order.

Bishop
We have come to see the Prime Minister's Ecclesiastical Appointments Secretary.

Workman
Well, I suppose you'd better come in.

Noote
Oh, thank you. After you, my lord.

Exeunt **Bishop** *and* **Noote** *through front door.*

Scene 3
Studio / Interior / Day

The entrance hall of No. 10 Downing Street.

Bishop
Where do we go?

Workman

Blowed if I know. I'll tell the chap you're here. *(Exits.)*

Noote

Do you think he's Mr Heath's butler?

Bishop

Butler, Noote? In dungarees and a cap? Have you ever seen a butler dressed like that?

Noote

No, my lord, but I thought Mr Heath might be trying to make the Trade Unionists feel more at home.

*The **Butler** enters.*

Butler

Good afternoon, Gentlemen.

Bishop

Good afternoon. Are you the Ecclesiastical Appointments Secretary?

Butler

No, my lord. I am the butler.

Noote

Then who was the gentleman who opened the door?

Butler

The electrician. He is mending the bell. *(To the **Bishop**)* Is Mr Dobson expecting you, my lord?

Bishop

No, I'm afraid it wasn't possible to make an appointment. We came on an impulse.

Noote

Yes, you see we suddenly decided to get rid of the Dean.

Bishop *quickly*

My chaplain means we suddenly decided to see Mr Dobson on an important matter.

Butler
I'm sorry, my lord, Mr Dobson has an appointment with the Prime Minister in ten minutes.

Noote
Is it about Chelsea?

Butler *formally*
I couldn't say, sir.

Noote *confidentially*
They're having great difficulty, you know— finding a suitable man.

Butler *coldly*
Indeed, sir. Mr Dobson is extremely busy. Perhaps you will call again, my lord?

Noote
But we've come all this way!

Butler
I'm sorry, sir, but without an appointment—

Bishop *authoratively*
You will please tell Mr Dobson that the Bishop of St Ogg's wishes to see him on a matter of importance.

Butler *impressed*
Oh, very well, my lord. Perhaps you will wait in the morning room, through here.

*Exit the **Butler** followed by the **Bishop** and **Noote**.*

Scene 4
Studio / Interior / Day

The morning room.

*The **Butler** ushers the **Bishop** and **Noote** into the room.*

Butler
If you would care to sit down, my lord, I will tell Mr Dobson you are here.

Bishop
Thank you. *(He sits.)*

*Exit the **Butler** closing the door.*

Noote
Isn't it a nice room?

Bishop
Yes, very pleasant. Just the right shade of blue.

Sound of a piano in a room above being strummed.

Noote *excitedly*
My lord, my lord, do you hear?

Bishop
Hear what?

Noote
The piano. Mr Heath is playing the piano! Listen— *(Sound of a scale being played and repeated a couple of times.)* Hasn't he got a lovely touch?

Bishop
I don't know about his touch, but I don't think much of his repertoire.

*The **Butler** enters.*

Butler
Mr Dobson will be with you in a moment, my lord. He asked me to apologise for keeping you waiting.

Bishop
Thank you. That is quite all right.

Noote *politely*
Yes, we're enjoying the recital.

Butler *sympathetically*
Oh, I'm sorry, I'm sorry about that, sir. I'm afraid we all have to suffer when he does this.

Bishop
I suppose, under the circumstances, it is rather difficult to object.

Butler
It's completely hopeless, my lord. It's not even as if he's a reasonable man.

Noote
Isn't he?

Butler
Not a bit. I tried remonstrating with him once.

Bishop
And what happened?

Butler
He spent the rest of the morning banging away at the same note to get his own back.

Bishop
Really? You amaze me.

Butler
It's a fact, my lord. He's a very petty man— and in my opinion he is tone deaf.

Noote
But surely Mr Heath is an accomplished musician?

Butler
Mr Heath is, sir, but I'm talking about the piano tuner. Ah, here is Mr Dobson now.

*Enter **Mr Dobson**, a distinguished-looking senior civil servant.*

Dobson
Thank you, William.

Butler
Thank you, sir. *(Exits closing the door.)*

Dobson
Good morning, Bishop. I don't think we've met. I haven't managed to get round all the smaller— *(Correcting himself)* That is, quite all the dioceses yet.

Bishop *determined not to take offence*
Of course, of course. I quite understand. My chaplain.

Dobson *looking at his watch*
How do you do? Is that really the time? Well, Bishop— what can I do for you?

Bishop
Well, Mr Dobson, we've come to see you about our Dean.

Dobson *losing interest*
Oh, have you?

Noote
Dr Pugh-Critchley, Dr Lionel Pugh-Critchley D.D.

Dobson
What's he done?

Bishop
Done?

Dobson
To make you come and complain.

Bishop *taken aback*
Complain? What makes you think we want to complain?

Dobson
Well, don't you? Most bishops do.

Noote
Do they? Do they really?

Dobson
Gracious yes, I've had a couple in this morning.

Bishop
Bless my soul!

Dobson
But it's no good, you know; there's nothing I can do to help. He's a Crown appointment like yourself— and unless he's done something— heresy, adultery, set fire to the Cathedral— you haven't a leg to stand on. In fact you want to watch out he doesn't get you for "malicious, frivolous and ill-conceived complaint". If he did, you'd be for the high jump. Well, I must go and see the PM. So nice meeting you, Bishop! *(Turns to go.)*

Bishop
One moment, Mr Dobson—

Dobson
What is it?

Bishop
We haven't come to complain—

Dobson
You haven't ?

Bishop
Certainly not. I should not like you to think I don't get on with my Dean. Should I, Noote?

Noote *earnestly*
Oh, no. The Bishop would not like you to think that.

Dobson *very surprised*
Really? Well, well, well. *(Warmly)* I must congratulate you, my lord. You are the first bishop I've ever met who gets on with his Dean. I can hardly believe it.

Bishop
Oh, we get on— famously— don't we, Noote?

Noote
Oh, yes, my lord. "Two souls with but a single thought; two hearts that beat as one."

Bishop
Yes— well, I don't know that I'd put it quite like that. But if I tell you I've come here today especially to recommend him for the new bishopric of Chelsea.

Noote *confidentially*
We understand you are having some difficulty finding a suitable man.

Dobson
We certainly are. But why do you think Pugh-Critchley would be suitable?

Noote
Oh, well— er—

Bishop
That is easily answered, isn't it, Noote?

Noote
Is it, my lord?

Bishop
Yes, of course. You see, Mr Dobson, he's efficient.

Dobson
Is he?

Noote *earnestly*
Oh, yes, he really is, Mr Dobson. He is efficient.

Dobson
Efficient. I see.

Bishop *forcefully*
Yes, efficient.

Dobson
I see. Tell me, what are his politics?

Bishop
Politics?

Dobson
Yes. Is he by any chance a socialist?

Noote
A socialist? The Dean? Of course he's not a socialist. What a suggestion!

Bishop
One moment, Noote. Mr Dobson, why do you ask?

Dobson
Because we try to keep a balance in these matters. The PM, in spite of his own convictions, believes it is a mistake to make too many appointments of the same political persuasion.

Bishop
I see. *(Thoughtfully)* Well, between ourselves, I happen to know that— in spite of what my chaplain obviously believes, the Dean is a socialist.

Noote *amazed*
What? Is he, my lord?

Bishop
Yes, does that surprise you?

Noote
It certainly does.

Bishop
Of course he's very discreet about it. That is another of his talents, Mr Dobson. Not only is he efficient, he is discreet. Isn't he, Noote?

Noote
He certainly is. I'd never have guessed he was a socialist— Why, I remember at the last election—

Bishop *interrupting*
You see, Mr Dobson, how totally unaware my chaplain is of the Dean's political sympathies. It explains, of course, why we work together in such harmony— even though— I must confess my own political loyalties lie elsewhere—

Dobson
It certainly does. He sounds just the man we are looking for.

Bishop *triumphantly*
I knew it! And I'm sure you won't regret it!

Dobson *interrupting*
And it's such a pity—

Bishop
A pity?

Dobson
His being a socialist, you see. The PM is determined to have a Conservative for Chelsea.

Bishop *dismayed*
A Conservative? But I thought you said he liked to keep a balance.

Dobson
Precisely. The last appointment he made was a socialist.

Bishop
But surely, you wouldn't refuse the perfect man for a trivial reason like that?

Dobson
I'm afraid the PM's mind is made up. Still, there is one consolation.

Bishop
What's that?

Dobson
You won't be losing your Dean, will you?

*On the **Bishop**'s reaction mix to:*

Scene 5
Studio / Interior / Day

The hall of the Palace.

*The front door opens. Enter the **Bishop** and **Noote**.*

Bishop *wearily*
What a wasted journey! Hang my hat up, will you? *(Hands hat to **Noote**.)*

Noote
Of course, my lord. *(**Noote** hangs hat on hat stand.)*

Bishop
Let's go into the study. *(Goes to study door.)*

Scene 6
Studio / Interior / Day

The study.

*The **Bishop** enters followed by **Noote**. The **Archdeacon** sits at the desk.*

Archdeacon *looking up*
Afternoon, Bishop.

Bishop
Henry? What are you doing here?

Archdeacon
I've just finished packing up the pools to send them back. *(Eagerly)* Have you got rid of the Dean?

Bishop *gloomily*
No, Henry. I'm afraid not.

Archdeacon
Too bad!

Noote
Isn't it, Archdeacon— and all because he's a socialist.

Archdeacon *surprised*
The Dean!

Noote
I know, I was surprised, but apparently he's very discreet about it— isn't he, my lord?

Bishop
Oh, shut up, Noote! Yes, Henry, complete failure of mission I'm afraid.

Archdeacon
At least you had a trip to London.

Bishop *bitterly*
Some trip! The club was closed for decorating, we put up for the night in a frightful hotel, then Noote dragged me to see the most incomprehensible film. What was it called— *The Flower People of San Francisco*?

Noote
I thought it was about horticulture.

Bishop
Get me a sherry, will you, Noote?

Noote
Right my lord.

Bishop
It took you a long time to pack up these coupons, Henry.

Archdeacon *cheerfully*
There were a lot of them, Bishop. I chucked it in at eleven last night and started again this morning.

Bishop *sympathetically*
Poor old Henry! What a frightful job. Did it get you down?

Archdeacon
Oh, no, Bishop. I managed to keep my spirits up.

Noote
My lord—

Bishop
What is it Noote?

Noote
The decanter seems to be empty.

Bishop
Empty? It can't be, I filled it yesterday. Who can have drunk it? *(Realising)* Henry!

Archdeacon
I got so dry, Bishop, all that licking.

Bishop
That's nice, I must say. Come home after the time we've had and not even a glass of sherry.

Archdeacon *contrite*
Sorry Bishop.

Bishop
I should hope you are.

Noote
Shall I go and post these coupons, my lord?

Bishop
Yes, you might as well, Noote. What a Saturday afternoon!

Noote
And to think we'd all have been waiting for the results now.

Bishop
Don't remind me, Noote, don't remind me!

Noote
Hullo, you've missed one, Archdeacon. This is addressed to you, my lord.

Archdeacon
Oh that, that arrived this morning.

Bishop
Let's have it.

Noote hands letter and the Bishop opens it.

Bishop
Another poor parish sending us their contribution to the Old People's Home, I suppose, which, thanks to the Dean, we must fling back in their faces. *(Looking at letter.)* Hullo, it's from Mr Dobson. *(He opens letter.)*

Noote *excited*
Perhaps he's changed his mind.

Bishop *reading*
No, Noote, he hasn't.

Noote
Oh, hasn't he? How disappointing!

Bishop
Not altogether.

Archdeacon
Why, Bishop?

Bishop
Because he has offered the Bishopric of Chelsea— to me.

Archdeacon
What?

Noote
He has? Why should he do that?

Bishop *reading*
"I was so impressed by the generous way you spoke of your Dean yesterday that I mentioned it to the PM. He agrees with me that, as good staff relations are bound to be of paramount importance in the creating of a new diocese, the Bishopric of Chelsea should be offered to you— particularly as your political sympathies suit the requirement."

Noote
Moses!

Archdeacon
What will you do, Bishop?

Bishop
I shall accept, Henry.

Archdeacon
You mean you'll leave us, Bishop?

Bishop
Not you, Henry. I shall need an archdeacon at Chelsea— I hope you'll come with me.

Archdeacon
Oh, thank you, Bishop— Archdeacon of Chelsea, eh?

Bishop
You should find it stimulating.

Archdeacon
I'm sure I shall, Bishop. The King's road; all those dolly shops!

Bishop
I didn't quite mean that, Henry. Though I must confess there is a certain attraction at the thought of living within delivery distance of Harrods.

Archdeacon
Yes, and Fortnum & Mason's.

Bishop
Then there's the theatre— I always love the theatre.

Archdeacon
And the nightclubs, Bishop. I've never been to a discotheque. My word we'll have some fun!

Bishop
Do you know, I rather think we shall, Henry.

Noote
Er, my lord—

Bishop
Yes, Noote, what is it?

Noote *forlornly*
I suppose you won't need a chaplain at Chelsea.

Bishop
But of course! Don't worry, Noote. I expect I'll take you as well.

Noote *fervently*
Oh, thank you, my lord— thank you, thank you, thank you!

Bishop
"A threefold cord is not easily broken", is it, Henry?

Archdeacon
It is not, Bishop.

Noote
Oh, no, my lord. *(Suddenly thoughtful)* "Ecclesiastes, chapter four, verse twelve".

Bishop
But I'll tell you who I am leaving behind…

*The **Dean** puts his head round the door.*

Dean
May I come in?

Bishop
Oh, Dean. Of course!

Dean
The door was open.

Archdeacon
Afternoon, Dean.

Dean
Good afternoon, Archdeacon. *(Seeing the pile of envelopes)* Ah, I see you have taken my advice, my lord.

Bishop
What advice?

Dean
You have abandoned this pools nonsense. I see you are sending the money

back. Excellent, you have been very wise.

Bishop *coldly*
Perhaps you will be kind enough to tell us to what we owe the pleasure of this visit on a Saturday afternoon?

Dean
Of course, of course. I have received a letter.

Archdeacon *with surprise*
Whoever from?

Dean
Downing Street, Archdeacon. The Prime Minister's Appointments Secretary.

Bishop
Really?

Noote
So you've heard the news, Dean?

Dean
News?

Noote
About Chelsea.

Dean *puzzled*
Yes, but is it known generally?

Bishop
Not generally, but I have naturally told the Archdeacon here and my chaplain.

Dean
I was not aware that even you knew, my lord.

Bishop
Surely, Dean, you didn't imagine Downing Street would inform you of such a thing without first telling me?

Dean
I suppose not, my lord.

Noote
What do you think of it?

Dean

Frankly, it has come as a surprise

Bishop

But a pleasant one— eh, Dean?

Dean *earnestly*

Oh, certainly, my lord, certainly.

Bishop

Well that's frank anyway!

Dean

I'm sorry if I appear to be pleased at the prospect of leaving you, my lord.

Bishop

You mean of me leaving you.

Dean

No, my lord. It is I who am leaving you. It is, after all, I who am going to Chelsea.

Archdeacon

You Dean?

Bishop

But you can't be!

Noote

No, Dean, not possibly— not with your politics!

Dean

Politics? What have my politics to do with it?

Noote *confidentially*

Well, you know— *(Hums the red flag.)*

Dean *mystified*

I beg your pardon?

Noote

It's just that I happen to know that, for Chelsea, Mr Heath wants a Conservative bishop.

Dean
Bishop? I am not going to be the Bishop.

Bishop
I should think not, indeed!

Dean
I am going to be the Dean.

Noote
The Dean, Dean?

Bishop *appalled*
They've offered you the Deanery of Chelsea?

Dean
Yes, my lord. I must say I find it rather gratifying. I had not realised my work here had been so much appreciated. Well, well. I must go and write my letter of acceptance.

Bishop
No, Dean— you mustn't do that!

Dean
Mustn't I, my lord? Why not?

Bishop *floundering*
Because, because—

Noote
Because the Bishop is going to—

Bishop *quickly*
Going to miss you— that is, I shall miss you, Dean.

Dean *surprised*
Really, my lord?

Bishop
Oh, yes. We get on so well together, Dean.

Dean *very surprised*
We do, my lord?

Bishop
Of course we do. Why, we were only talking about it yesterday— weren't we Noote?

Noote
Yes, Dean, we were, as a matter of fact.

Bishop
What was that poem you quoted, Noote— "Two whatsits that something or other"?

Noote
"Two souls with but a single thought; two hearts that beat as one".

Bishop
Yes, that's it. That's what we were saying, Dean— about you and me.

Dean *impressed*
Really, my lord? You consider those lines a description of our relationship?

Bishop
But of course, Dean. Can you doubt it?

Dean *overwhelmed*
Well, well. I must admit I had not realised you felt so strongly. *(Recovering)* Still, I fear I must accept this offer, my lord. My wife has set her heart on it. She fancies a town life.

Bishop
Mrs Pugh-Critchley? What a mistake.

Dean
A mistake?

Bishop
Dear lady, she's every inch a country girl, isn't she, Henry?

Archdeacon
Yes Bishop, every inch.

Bishop *pleading*
Please reconsider, Dean, please do—

Dean
I'm sorry, my lord. I appreciate you do not want to lose me. However, my mind

is made up. I am going to write my letter of acceptance. Good afternoon, gentlemen.

*Exit the **Dean**.*

Bishop *exploding*
Of all the bad luck! What on earth does Dobson think he's doing? Fancy landing me with him as Dean again!

Noote
Never mind. Perhaps he'll be different when he gets to Chelsea, my lord.

Bishop
Different? A leopard doesn't change its spots, Noote, especially a miserable leopard like him. Oh, is there no escape?

Archdeacon
Yes, Bishop.

Bishop
What, Henry?

Archdeacon
Don't accept.

Bishop
What do you mean, don't accept?

Noote
Of course! If you don't accept, my lord— the Dean will go to Chelsea and we shall all be here at St Ogg's.

Bishop
But of course! Henry, how splendid— Noote I've done it. I've actually done it: I've got rid of the Dean!

Archdeacon
Bravo, Bishop!

Noote
Congratulations, my lord!

Bishop
Quick Noote— my pen.

Noote
Here, my lord. *(Hands pen.)*

Bishop
Henry, paper—

Archdeacon
Here, Bishop. *(Hands paper.)*

Bishop *sitting to write*
Thank you. Now then— "My dear Dobson, it is with regret—"

Noote
How about "deep regret" my lord?

Bishop
Splendid! "Deep regret"…

Archdeacon
No, Bishop,

Bishop
No, Henry?

Archdeacon
"Deepest", Bishop— deepest regret.

*On the **Bishop** writing, fade down and fade up on his finishing addressing the envelope.*

Bishop
10 Downing Street, SW1. There, Noote, go and post it, will you?

Noote
With pleasure, my lord— and I'll post these pools envelopes at the same time.

Bishop
But there's no need now.

Archdeacon
No, not now the Dean is going!

Bishop
In fact we might as well start opening them again, Henry.

Archdeacon
Good idea, Bishop. Get the evening paper, Noote, so we can see the results!

Bishop
I wonder who will win.

Archdeacon
Me, Bishop. I shall win!

Bishop
You think so?

Archdeacon
Certain of it; I'm on a winning streak.

Noote *with letter*
Right, I'll be off then. *(Exits to hall.)*

Scene 7
Studio / Interior / Day

The hall.

Noote enters from study and goes to the front door and opens it, revealing the Dean. He carries a letter.

Dean
Ah, Noote. I was about to ring the bell. Is the Bishop in?

Noote
Yes Dean. He's in the study. I'm just popping out to the pillar box.

Dean
Then perhaps you will post this for me?

Noote *taking letter and reading the address*
"Downing Street"— With pleasure, Dean! *(Exits.)*

The Dean exits to study.

Scene 8
Studio / Interior / Day

The study.

The **Bishop** *and* **Archdeacon** *are opening the pools envelopes.*

Dean *entering*
My lord, Archdeacon.

Bishop
Hullo, Dean, back again?

Archdeacon
Written your letter, Dean?

Dean
Indeed I have, Archdeacon— but what are you doing there?

Bishop *casually*
Undoing the coupons, Dean.

Archdeacon
For our Happy Circle.

Dean *a flicker of annoyance*
I thought you agreed not to persist in this folly.

Archdeacon
We've changed our minds.

Bishop
You can hardly object, Dean, now you are leaving—

Dean
I am not leaving, my lord.

Bishop
Not leaving?

Archdeacon
But you've written your letter—

Dean
Yes, refusing.

Bishop *startled*
Refusing?

Dean
I have refused the Deanery of Chelsea.

Bishop *aghast*
What? But why?

Dean
It was something you said, my lord.

Bishop *horrified*
Something I said?

Dean
Or rather, something your chaplain said.

Bishop
That's more like it!

Dean
How did it go? "Two souls with but a single thought"?

Bishop
Oh, that? You don't want to pay any attention to that, Dean. It's only poetry.

Dean
Nevertheless, it made me reflect. Frankly, my lord, I had not realised you looked on our relationship in quite that way.

Bishop
Oh, don't give it another thought.

Archdeacon
No, don't let it stand in your way!

Dean
I can't help it, it has, Archdeacon. I went home and told Grace.

Bishop
What did she say?

Dean
She was surprised.

Bishop
I bet she was!

Dean
At first she would not agree, but we talked it over. I quoted to her from Ecclesiasticus, chapter nine, verse ten— "Forsake not an old friend, for the new is not comparable to him."

Bishop
I disagree! That's nonsense, isn't it, Henry?

Archdeacon
Complete rubbish!

Bishop *urgently*
Dean, I beg you not to do anything rash. At least sleep on it—

Dean
Too late, my lord. The die is cast, your chaplain is at this moment posting my letter of refusal.

Enter **Noote** *carrying a newspaper.*

Noote *cheerfully*
Hullo, Dean, still here?

Dean
Have you posted my letter?

Noote
Rather, Dean!

Bishop *anxiously*
What about mine, Noote? Did you post it?

Noote *cheerfully*
Oh, yes, my lord. No worries on that score! Here's the evening paper, Archdeacon. You can check the football results. *(Hands paper.)*

Archdeacon *taking it*
Oh, thank you.

Dean
Well, I just wanted you to know my decision, my lord. I must get back to Grace. All this excitement has brought on one of her heads. By the way, now that

I am staying, I trust we shall hear no more of this deplorable football pool nonsense?

Bishop
Now, look, Dean, if I want to run a football pool in aid of a worthy cause, I'm not going to let anyone—

Dean *interrupting him and holding up his hand*
If I can make a sacrifice for friendship— I'm sure you can.

Bishop *after a struggle*
Oh, very well, Dean. You win. I'll send them back.

Dean *smiling warmly*
Thank you, my lord. Remember, "Two hearts that beat as one"! Good evening, gentlemen.

*Exit the **Dean**.*

Noote *mystified*
What did he mean by that?

Bishop
Simply that he's staying, Noote.

Noote
Staying? Moses, but whatever for?

Bishop
Chiefly, it seems, Noote, on account of your idiotic poem.

Noote
Oh, I'm sorry, my lord.

Bishop
Sorry, so you jolly well should be! Thanks to you, not only have we lost the chance of going to Chelsea but we are stuck back here with the Dean, we've got to pack up and send back all these coupons, and the old people are going to have to go without their home.

Archdeacon *suddenly*
No they're not, Bishop

Bishop *startled*
What Henry?

Archdeacon *holding up newspaper*
I've won the pools— you know, the Happy Circle!

Bishop *sympathetically*
Henry, dear old friend, I'm afraid today has been too much for you. You obviously have not grasped the full horror of the situation; there is no Happy Circle.

Noote
The Dean has stopped it, Archdeacon.

Archdeacon *beaming*
Not this Happy Circle— the one in Liverpool.

Bishop
You mean you did the real pools, Henry?

Archdeacon
Yes, Bishop

Noote
And you've won, Archdeacon?

Archdeacon
Look, eight draws. I told you I was on a winning streak!

*The **Archdeacon** holds up the newspaper and all three crowd round it as the credits roll.*

———

EPILOGUE

1 June 2014

The telephone rings.

Pauline: Hullo?

Edwin: *Bonjour.*

Pauline: Oh, it's you. Did you get the latest version?

Edwin: Yes. Is that it, then? Have we said everything?

Pauline: Shouldn't think so, there's probably masses we've left out. For instance how Michael Mills became a fan of the show — after initially wanting to end it when he first took over from Frank Muir. And what about Robin Nash, who directed some of the last series? He did us proud.

Edwin: So did the set designers. I was remembering the first episode, when we arrived for the dress rehearsal; the extraordinary experience of walking on the set of the Palace and seeing something we had imagined realised in every detail. It gave one the feeling of having waved a magic wand.

Pauline: And what about the music? We were so lucky having Stanley Myers to do it. It was so clever the way he arranged Bach's Toccata in D Minor as the signature tune.

Edwin: We haven't said that we chose the name St Ogg's because my aunt had a friend called Teddy Ogg, who grew dahlias, and we liked his name so much we decided to canonise him.

Pauline: People thought we'd taken it from *The Mill on the Floss.*

Edwin: It could have been in our minds, we both knew the book.

Pauline: Didn't we get a letter saying there really is a St Ogg's ?

Edwin: Yes, and do you remember— No, on second thoughts, I think we've done enough remembering. I've got an exhibition in December that needs some work.

Pauline: December? I've got one in August!

Edwin: Still, it's been interesting working together after nearly fifty years.

Pauline: And unexpected.

Edwin: What do you think people will make of the book?
Pauline: No idea. I must go and prime some canvases.
Edwin: Okay. Keep in touch.

Replaces telephone.

———————

Returning to work written fifty years ago has not been easy, and would have been impossible without the considerable help and encouragement we have had from our families and friends. Our thanks to them all, and in particular to Peter Leek, Anna Christoforou, Shelley Bennett, Christopher Tremayne, Julia Walte and our publisher, Patrick Durand-Peyroles.

Pursued By Bishops
The memoirs of Edwin Apps

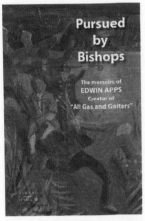

"During the 1950s and '60s, Edwin Apps was a familiar face in repertory theatre, before he became known on British television. His account of playing in rep through-out Britain makes this book an excellent record of the time before the spread of TV, when local theatres flourished. Apps's memory is exceptional – his descriptions flow, and one blinks with surprise at the famous people he met, and who were part of his working life."

The Church Times, 19th July, 2013.

Actor, writer and painter, together with Pauline Devaney, Edwin Apps created *All Gas and Gaiters*, the comedy series about the Church of England, which at its peak attracted audiences of more than 10 million viewers and was the third most watched programme on BBC television, paving the way for many of the UK's most popular TV sitcoms.

Today a successful painter in the West of France, Edwin Apps was born into an eccentric family of East Kent hop farmers and auctioneers with a dark secret. Though neither the son of a clergyman nor an orphan, in 1940 he was sent to the clergy orphan school in Canterbury ("stuck in a time warp circa 1900"), but was soon evacuated with the school to a luxury hotel on the Cornish coast, where he learnt Latin in the cocktail bar and trained wild falcons. At seventeen, he joined a weekly repertory company in the north of England.

First coming to prominence as Mr Halliforth in *Whacko* with Jimmy Edwards, he subsequently appeared in almost all the well-known TV comedy shows of that time, including *The World of Wooster*, *Harry Worth*, *Steptoe & Son* and *Benny Hill*, as well as series such as *Danger Man* and *The Avengers*.

Bishops and other species of clergy have loomed large in Edwin Apps's life. And comedy, too. Such as his gallant rescue of Dorothy L. Sayers from a bomb crater during the Canterbury Festival and his experiences as a reluctant National Serviceman. Learning to act, the horrors of theatrical landladies, getting to know Compton Mackenzie, the pitfalls of live television comedy with Jimmy Edwards and with Harry Worth, friendship with Frank Muir and Glenda Jackson… are all part of the highly entertaining narrative, supplemented by a wealth of photos and contemporary letters.

ISBN : 978-2-915723-94-6
Size : 6x9' – 152 x 229 mm
Pages : 412 with B&W Photos

Printed and bound in EU
by bookpress.eu

2015